DOUBLE JEOPARDY

DOUBLE JEOPARDY

Bill James

Severn House Large Print
London & New York

This first large print edition published in Great Britain 2005 by
SEVERN HOUSE LARGE PRINT BOOKS LTD of
9-15 High Street, Sutton, Surrey, SM1 1DF.
First world regular print edition published 2002 by
Severn House Publishers, London and New York.
This first large print edition published in the USA 2005 by
SEVERN HOUSE PUBLISHERS INC., of
595 Madison Avenue, New York, NY 10022.

British Library Cataloguing in Publication Data

James, Bill, 1929 -
    Double jeopardy. - Large print ed.
    1. Discrimination in criminal justice administration - Great Britain -
        Fiction
    2. Murder - Investigation - Great Britain - Fiction
    3. Detective and mystery stories - Fiction
    4. Large type books
    I. Title
    823.9'14 [F]

    ISBN-10: 0-7278-7446-2

Printed and bound in Great Britain by
MPG Books Ltd, Bodmin, Cornwall.

One

Lately, whenever terror took hold on Kerry Lake it was never from fear for her own life but for Vic Othen's. She had a detailed vision of how his death would come. This was, of course, entirely make-believe, a guess vision, but one which turned up so regularly in her head that it had created for itself the sinews of the real: at these times she saw three downward knife blows in the back of his neck, nothing lower than that, the knife a six-inch-by-two blade, its handle blue plastic or possibly purple, death not instantaneous even after the third strike, but less than eleven minutes life left, and none of these minutes with complete consciousness or even close to it. No wry Vic-brand jokes, just blood from his mouth, lips too slack to get around a witticism.

As a matter of fact, the vision was giving her its filthy private pictures now. It did not specify the colour of the hand holding the blue or purple plastic. The wounds were graphic, though: very neatly grouped and not gaping but fine, as if the blade had been impeccably sharp and elegantly managed. Where did people learn such skills? How could they practise? After all, necks were not just available for the asking. Or maybe wounds appeared like that only in visions. Visions could falsify. Oh, come on, come on, visions were *utterly* bogus, weren't they? Visions edited. Visions could give the colour of a knife handle, or at least options, but nothing of the colour of the hand holding it. Possibly this was a politically correct vision.

Rubbish, rubbish, rubbish. Visions were only sick nonsense, weren't they, for heaven's sake? Kerry longed to escape hers. All right, Pharaoh had his dream in Genesis about the fat cows and the thin ones, and it turned out exact as a forecast of good times, bad times. But that was only if you believed everything you read.

Of course, there were absolutely no *actual* neck wounds on Vic Othen, not yet anyway. From where she sat at present she could watch him and listen to him, though he was not talking to Kerry, nor looking at her, definitely not. The back and side of his neck, which were all she could see, actually appeared pretty good, the skin smooth and taut like the skin of someone much younger, say thirty-four or even thirty-three. Most of his body was like that, not just the visible bits. It used to irritate her. He had been around all those extra years, and getting shot at and

6

clobbered in the job, yet his skin was as good as hers. She would console herself by thinking of all the ciggie soot that must coat him inside.

He was tense now – of course he was tense, and angry, perhaps – but you would not pick any of that up from the angle of his neck and head or the way he sat. Kerry could tell he was seriously anxious from a slight, almost unnoticeable tinniness in his voice; but noticeable to her because she loved his voice as it usually was, comfortable and comforting, thick, deep, warm – perhaps thanks to the blurring of his larynx by tobacco smoke. There had to be *some* gains from all that mouth burn. She used to go to him to be comfortable, and now and then, when things grew jagged, to be comforted.

But all that was very pre bloody Julie. Kerry looked about the crowded Inquiry chamber. Vic's bloody Julie was definitely not here. Didn't she know the danger Vic was in – not from neck wounds, from other kinds of danger this afternoon, less visible kinds, but grave? Almost certainly she did not. It would probably seem an ordinary day to her: Vic had gone to work, as usual.

7

Two

Kerry thought the tone sounded amiable, almost off-hand ... and devastating. It was lawyerspeak: 'Detective Constable Othen, do you know a businessman called Philip David Pethor, often referred to simply as P.D.?'

'Yes.'

'He is the brother, is he not, of Peter Vincent Pethor, known familiarly as Scout?'

'Yes.'

' "Scout" Pethor, with a man called Matthew Gain, was charged with the murder of Angela Sabat, was he not? Both were acquitted.'

'Yes.'

'The Pethors are twin brothers, I think? Not identical twins, but twins.'

'Yes.'

'And, in the way of twins, probably very close, would you not say?'

'I don't know. It's possible.'

'Very well, Detective Constable. But you'd agree that P.D. Pethor would have been very worried when his brother was so charged?'

'Yes.'

'Thank you. Would you tell the Inquiry what is your relationship with P.D. Pethor?'

'Relationship?'

Oh, God, wrong friends, wrong right friends, Vic.

Snottily, obligingly, dangerously, Geddage, the Inquiry lawyer, said: 'Shall I rephrase? How did you come to know Mr Pethor, Detective Constable?'

'In the course of my work I have had occasion to speak to him from time to time.'

Oh, God, the pomp. Did Vic really hope this nothing answer could build a wall against more questions? Geddage knew about walls, how to chip at them, finally flatten them. Kerry sensed – was certain – that, sooner or later in this Inquiry, Geddage would accuse Vic of a cover-up. The Inquiry had protection from the libel laws. Geddage could allege what he liked. And at the right time, as he saw it, Geddage would like to allege that Vic deliberately concealed some prime evidence from his investigation into the race killing of Angela Sabat. The suggestion would probably be that Victor did it because of a secret, improper link with P.D. Pethor, and to protect dear Scout. Of course it would be.

Why hadn't Vic talked to Kerry in advance? She could have warned him this would be the line. But he must have known that for himself, surely? If Kerry could see it, Vic could, and clearer, most likely. *In the course of my work I have had occasion* ... Was this dud answer something he'd rehearsed with the newly installed Julie? What the hell did she understand of such things? So, why was he living with her? So, why wasn't she with him here, now, as support? How could anyone be called Julie at her age?

The lawyer said: ' "In the course of your work" ... Yes. So the Inquiry may be clear, would you say what your work is?'

'I'm a detective officer. I investigate crimes.'

'I think we would all understand that. Which kind of crimes?'

'Various.'

'Serious?'

'Some.'

'You are a very experienced detective, are you not?'

'I have been a police officer for thirty-three years, a detective for twenty-six.'

They were figures, that was all. He spoke them as such, no flourish, no swank. Was it worth swanking about? Vic would sense that some people here, including lawyer Geddage, might doubt it. What went wrong, Vic?

'I think I am right in saying that after thirty years a police officer may retire on full pension, and may even be encouraged to retire,' Geddage asked.

'Yes.'

'But you decided to continue and have, presumably, been asked to continue?'

'Yes.'

'This would suggest that you are not only experienced ˙ but successful and highly valued. You would be trusted to deal with major crimes.'

'Some.'

'Are you being modest, Detective Constable?'

'I still *am* a Detective Constable – the lowest rank. I'm fifty-two.'

She loathed it whenever he spoke his age, that rotten exactitude. It never troubled Kerry to tell friends she liked older men. But at times *fifty-two* in words could seem older than older.

Geddage said: 'Nevertheless, you have been allowed to continue beyond normal retirement age because you can offer special skills, special knowledge based on your years of experience in the job.'

'I think people have grown used to me around the place.'

'If you please,' Geddage said. 'When you spoke – perhaps continue to speak – to P.D. Pethor in, as you say, the course of your work, what would be, as you termed it, the *occasion*?'

'Various.'

'Various crimes? You have kindly explained that your work is to investigate crimes, some of them major. Would you on *occasion* be speaking to P.D. Pethor about major crimes?'

'These would be confidential matters.'

'Obviously, neither I nor the Inquiry members wish to infringe upon sensitive conversations related to a police investigation, but do you agree, in view of what you have told the Inquiry earlier, that it is reasonable for us to infer that you spoke – speak – to him about one of the crimes you were – are – looking into?'

'I don't think I can answer on what you might or might not infer.' Vic's voice picked up suddenly, turned into a fine defensive snarl. He hated bullshit terms like *infer*, used to mock Kerry for employing them sometimes – 'The Oxon touch,' as he would say then.

The chairman backed him: 'Detective Constable Othen is surely correct, Mr Geddage. One wonders whether that is an admissible question, even for a judicial Inquiry. Our rules may be more relaxed than a court's, yes, but there are still proprieties.'

'I'm sorry, Chairman. You are, of course, right and I withdraw the question. Detective Constable Othen, how often did you have conversations with P.D. Pethor in the course of your work?'

'I couldn't say exactly.'

'But two or three times? Ten? Twenty? A hundred?'

'I couldn't say exactly.'

'More than two or three?'

'Probably.'

'More than ten?'

'Perhaps ten.'

Wrong friends; wrong right friends, Vic. Kerry's vision of neck and knives began a replay. These catastrophic spells of dread would not last more than three or four minutes, maybe even less, and certainly not the eleven her imagination scripted for Vic's death. But such rough interludes did her big damage, always produced the same disgusting symptoms. Her mind would be spattered all over the place and unuseable except to stoke more breakdown. Perspiration came in a quantity that demanded the longer word – *sweat* was too terse and for brows only. This perspiration soaked, but everywhere. Christ, now, in her spectator's pew at the Inquiry, her *elbows* were wet. She had shakes in her arms and a choking shortage of spit. Throat and chest pains clobbered her. Her bladder boiled.

Strange: a year ago, when she and Vic were seeing each other, making love to each other as often as they could find time and a spot, she had not felt like this, no matter what risks he was helping himself to at work. Vic was never short of risk. Perhaps she had felt without realising she felt it that her association with him put a kind of guardian aura around

13

Vic: he would be all right because she needed him to be all right, and therefore assumed he *would* be all right. This certainty chimed with the barmy grandeur of her ego, she would admit that.

Now, the distance between them seemed to bring hellishly disabling fret. Mad? Did she think he could not run his job safely without her influence? He had run it safely and with at least street-level distinction for years – decades – before she badgered her way into his life. Yes, but anxiety tore at her all the same. And guilt. She felt as if she had abandoned him. Perhaps she had. These days she was very certificatedly married, wasn't she? And not to Vic.

Naturally not to Vic. Vic was with Julie. He had never really been a husband prospect, and for more reasons than his lowly money and his age and the eternal ciggie. In fact, none of those, nor all of them combined, would have ruled him out for Kerry as a groom, would they? Would they? So what *had*? Perhaps he ruled himself out, didn't want it, conveyed this to her without ever actually saying it, the ungrateful idiot.

Geddage said: 'I'm interested, Detective Constable. You have conducted ten interviews with P.D. Pethor, seeking information about crimes in your locality?'

'Perhaps ten.'

'Over what period?'

14

'I couldn't be sure.'

'But perhaps you would have a general idea, as with the number. Would it be a year, two years, less than a year, more than two years?'

'Perhaps a year.'

'Perhaps. We'll settle for that then, shall we? "Perhaps" is a recurrent motif.'

'Perhaps.'

'Would you regard ten interviews with P.D. Pethor over a year as a lot, quite a lot, average, few?'

'I can't think of any standard by which I'd judge that.'

'These would be interviews about not one crime but various?'

'Various.'

'Is P.D. Pethor well informed about crimes in your locality? He hears things, does he? Rumour, "the buzz", as I believe it is known.'

'I talk to many people during investigations.'

'Do you talk to many of them as often as ten times in a year?'

'Some.'

'If you please. Where would these meetings with P.D. Pethor take place?'

'Various locations.'

'At the police station?'

'No.'

'At his home or place of work?'

'No.'

'What kind of locations then, Detective Constable?'

'The places where I met Mr Pethor would be private locations,' Vic said.

'Secret locations?'

'These would be private locations,' Vic replied.

'Why would they need to be private, Detective Constable?'

'Some of these matters were sensitive.'

'Couldn't sensitive matters have been discussed behind closed doors at the police station or at P.D. Pethor's home or office?'

'Perhaps.'

'But you or he chose otherwise?'

'We agreed the locations.'

Oh, of course, of course. Vic would see where it was all going. Absurd and arrogant to think she could have enlightened him. He would have known before he took the stand where the lawyer would want to take it. And Vic would also have known he would be on his own, no backing from on high. It was what happened when you had wrong friends as informants: grasses, touts, narks – whatever you wanted to call them. You might just get away with having wrong friends as long as the wrong friends produced what was required, and as long as you kept them out of sight and unheard by all but yourself. Then they might be the right wrong friends, indispensable friends. Vic had used all his flair and experience to keep P.D. out of sight. Now, though, the Inquiry was going to hear about Vic's skilled efforts, and this obviously meant they had not worked. Vic was alone. Except, that is, for Kerry. She had taken a day's leave to bring him some backing: silent, appalled, useless backing.

And why hadn't Julie come down to the Inquiry to bring him silent, appalled, useless backing, too? Kerry still couldn't see her. Yes, there had been big home changes for Vic as well as Kerry. He was shacked up – happily? Kerry did want him happy, didn't she? – did she? It would be juvenile to wish someone you'd loved miserable because he was with another woman, wouldn't it? – would it? Anyway, he was shacked up with this lady who was about as old as himself, apparently, or even older. But that might be all right. Kerry had read that quite a lot of women in their forties and even fifties could remember what it should be about. As for Vic, he looked as he had almost always looked, beautifully clothed and shod, slick silver hair with matching roots, ditto moustache, everything in order, at ease: the smug, lung-charred, destructible, destructive chancer.

Geddage said: 'The Inquiry has heard from a witness who saw you and Mr Pethor talking in a parked vehicle at night in Amery Close, a quiet cul-de-sac. Was that one of your agreed locations?'

'Yes.'

'Was another in woodland on Thale Hill in the north of the city?'

'Yes.'

'These are out-of-the-way spots?'

'Yes.'

'I will not use the word *infer* again. But it would appear that one objective in choosing such places was secrecy. Is that correct?'

'Confidentiality.'

'If you please. You did not wish to be seen together, is that what you are saying?'

'Confidentiality can be very important in detective work.'

'These meetings were for the exchange of information, were they not?'

'They were confidential.'

Occasionally at home – no, more often than that – Kerry would say: 'You're going to be nastily dead, Vic, and not from smoking. Wrong friends.'

No reply would come, although she might speak the words slowly at normal tone twice. 'You're going to be nastily dead, Vic, and not from smoking. Wrong friends.' She would be alone when she made these pronounce-ments, alone among abundant discount potatoes. Such potatoes were big in Kerry's marriage. Her husband had a boardroom job in catering, and knew where to buy them very cut-price by the sack. There was far more to Mark than cheap potatoes, but he did believe in smart purchasing. They were stored in the garage and Kerry would go there sometimes to think about her career and/or Vic, and, if it was about Vic, perhaps talk to him like that. She could sit on a full sack. Sometimes, when she was deep into one of those rough moments because of the knife pictures in her head, Kerry's arms would shake, her saliva disappear and her brain put the shutters up. She would speak aloud to herself and the potatoes to prove she could still do something with her mouth despite the foul dehydration. 'You're going to be nastily dead, Vic, and not from smoking. Wrong friends.'

She might weep a little. It would prove there was still some juice in her. No torrential weeping, though. She liked it when tears dropped on to a sack, making wet circles: visible, countable items anticipating grief. They soon dried and became undetectable. The weeping was another reason she came to the garage. To sob in the house about Vic would have seemed a betrayal of Mark and the marriage property. But the garage was outside, not really part of the homestead: hard to think of treachery sited amid bulk potatoes. Although the potatoes were so personal to Mark, she did not feel shameless about sitting on them while thinking of Vic, talking to Vic, with her legs slightly open for balance. The terror and sadness brought on by this recurrent savage fantasy of Vic's death were bound to skew her thinking briefly. Just the same, she believed she had things deep-down right about him and what might happen. Any day, any night. A black girl had been murdered, apparently only because she was black. No convictions followed. There might be people who would want revenge for that death if they thought a detective had made convictions impossible. And even when the worst of the fright spell had passed she would still hear in memory the warning to Vic, and it still made sense. 'Wrong friends.'

Of course, she could have offered the same sort of wrong-friend warning to almost any detective who would ever get anywhere. They all had at least a few cherished wrong friends. Kerry had a few wrong friends herself. But, yes, wrong friends were sometimes the *right* friends to have in this work and, as a matter of fact, took a hell of a lot of finding and hanging on to, and paying and protecting – often, protecting from one's colleagues.

But bugger it, no. No. Wrong could never be right, not even in police work. Could it? She should have told Vic that, and told him as his superior in rank. Shouldn't she? Did Julie worry like this? Did she exude so much sweat sometimes when thinking about knife wounds that her deodorant surrendered?

God, in Kerry's garage sessions it could be so damn dank, the mixed odour of underarm and dirt and potatoes by the hundredweight in a small place. No, live-in Julie would stay as cool and non-twitch as fridged mousse most probably. Fucking old igloo.

Geddage said: 'I do not ask about the content of the meetings with P.D. Pethor. But they were for the exchange of information, were they not?'

'They were confidential.'

'If you please. I wish to come back to a term you questioned when I used it at the beginning of this examination. It is *relationship*. What was – perhaps still is – the relationship between yourself and P.D. Pethor?'

'Relationship?'

'Was P.D. Pethor used by you on a regular basis as an informant?'

Of course, Vic would have in mind a basic precept for lawyers on cross-examination: ask no question to which you do not know the answer. Someone, or more than one person, had supplied a lot of insights on Vic's meetings with Pethor: number, place, period. Vic would see that he had to answer with something like the truth. Amery Close, Thale Hill, and wherever and whenever else – they had him charted.

'I would ask Mr Pethor certain questions,'

he replied.

'About certain crimes?'

'Various crimes.'

'And he would reply? Obviously he would reply or you would not have continued to meet him, would you, Detective Constable?'

'Mr Pethor and I would have conversations.'

'There is a properly regulated system for dealing with people who help the police as informants, is there not?'

'Yes.'

'An informant has to be officially registered, is that not so?'

'Yes.'

'The officer who deals with him is known as his handler, isn't he? And above the handler is a controller, and then the registrar of informants, who holds the full list?'

'Yes.'

'Was – is – P.D. Pethor so registered?'

'No.'

'You see this man ten times in a year for information about crimes, yet he is not formally treated as an informant? Why?'

'He is not designated an official informant.'

'Did you – do you – regard yourself as his handler?'

'Handler is a term used in relation to registered informants. Mr Pethor is *not* an official informant. I went to visit him on occasions to ask him questions about certain matters, that's all. I was not, am not, his handler, because he is not a registered informant.'

'Was he, is he, an *un*registered informant?'

'All official informants have to be registered.'

'If you please – but what I'm asking you, Detective Constable, is whether P.D. Pethor was, is, an *un*official informant and consequently *un*registered.'

'I don't believe there is such a category as unofficial informant.'

'Isn't it a fact that some experienced detectives wish to keep their informants private to themselves?'

'A registered informant belongs to the whole police force, not to any one officer.'

'I know this is what the rules say, and it is admirable that they should say so. But take the case of an experienced detective such as yourself, a detective who has carefully built an arrangement with an informant – would he really be willing to regard that informant and what he discloses as the property, not of himself, personally, but of all detectives?'

'That's the regulation.'

'Do you like it?'

'That is the regulation.'

'Is it not a fact that, despite the regulations, some experienced detectives fail to register their informants because, in a competitive career, they want the material provided by their informants to be private to them? And,

perhaps for their own interests, some informants would prefer not to be registered but to
work secretly with one trusted, experienced
detective?'

'I believe the rules governing the use of
informants were established for the benefit of
all parties.'

Plonk, plonk. Piety, Vic. But was there
anything else you might have said? Kerry
couldn't think of how to better it. So, Vic
summoned sanctimoniousness and invited
destruction. Didn't his new woman realise
what was happening here? Kerry had been
told her name and had often tried to forget it
to prove it could not rate, but it would not
disappear. Julie Crane. Always that first
name enraged Kerry. It was not just young, it
was flip. Pre-police, Kerry had had three
undergraduate friends at Oxford called Julie.
They were twenty, at the most twenty-one.
That age was about right for a Julie. This
Julie Crane longed to hitch-hike back a
generation or two. She had picked her name
out of the *Eternal Youth* sachet. Her real name
was probably Margaret or Sandra or Isobel,
something *Festival of Britain*. She was not in
the police and so would never understand
the stupid, worthwhile dangers that Vic stuck
himself into, despite age. She thought going
to work was just going to work. Of course, he
would not tell her anything major. He had
not told Kerry, either, when they were seeing

each other, but she did not need him to tell her, because she had her own ways of knowing, and, failing that, her own ways of intuiting.

Although Kerry had never met Julie Crane, she despised her out and out for not being more anxious about Vic. What kind of affair could it be, for God's sake, where one partner was indifferent to the hazards facing the other? On the other hand Kerry would have loathed it if she thought Julie Crane suffered more anxiety over Vic than she did. To feel anxious about him gave Kerry a kind of ownership still, didn't it, regardless – a sort of hold? His connection with Julie Crane must be something slight and short-term convenient, mustn't it? Perhaps there had been time during Julie Crane's earlier cohabs to learn how to iron shirts nicely. At her age she must have stacked up a real collection of relationships and a flair for drudgery. Vic was a hell of a dandy and would do anything for a nicely laundered shirt.

Geddage said: 'I am sure that, as you say, Detective Constable, the regulations about informants were shaped to guarantee integrity on both sides of the transaction. Money can be involved in these dealings with informants, can't it?'

'It is permissible to reward an informant for outstanding help.'

'The regulations would ensure that these

sums were drawn from a police fund and duly accounted for and administered, wouldn't they?'

'Yes.'

'Yes, where the informant was officially registered. But what if an informant is *not* so registered? How would he be rewarded then? There can be no drawing on the official police fund for informants, can there? Because this informant is *not* official.'

'I would not know. I've never come across that kind of situation.'

'In such a situation might a detective become bound to an informant not by money payments but through other kinds of favours?'

'I don't think I understand you,' Vic replied.

No, *don't* understand him, Vic. But, of course, you do. Oh, Vic, dear Vic, wrong friends, wrong friends.

'Detective Constable Othen, this Inquiry was called to look at the way the police investigation into the murder of Angela Sabat was conducted, an investigation which might have been at fault in several very serious respects. Now, I have to suggest to you that your relationship with the brother – *twin* brother – of "Scout" Pethor might have had some bearing on the way the police investigation of the Angela Sabat racist killing was conducted, might have curtailed it,

26

undermined it, deprived it of evidence.'

And this was where Kelly's knife visions came from. Vic had got rid of important evidence in the Sabat case, had he, because he owed a favour or two to P.D. Pethor? Had he? Oh, did you, Vic? And if Vic did, would it make him very liable to a cleansing attack by people who thought someone should be done for the girl's death?

Geddage said: '*Did* your relationship with P.D. Pethor have a bearing on the investigation?'

'Relationship?' Vic replied.

Three

It unnerved her, this Inquiry. God, the innocuous *ordinariness* of the City Hall room, with its workaday, light-coloured modern furniture – no mahogany, no panelling, auraless.

What was it, anyway – an *Inquiry*? Why was it? Of course, she knew in general what the term, with its capital letter, meant, and she knew all sorts of outfits organised *Inquiries* when things had fucked up majestically and some sort of apportion-the-blame show was needed. After all, she was an Oxford graduate bright enough for fast-track promotion. But she had never actually sat in on an *Inquiry* or thought about its machinery and structure, its lungs and liver, examined its special ways. Through police work, she had naturally become used to courts, but this was not a court: besides no mahogany and no panelling there were no wigs or robes, no prisoner at the bar. Auraless. This was an *Inquiry* into what had happened in a court, or what had not happened. What had happened was acquittals. What had *not* happened was convictions. The Inquiry wanted to know why. Was Vic why? Generally, a *not guilty* verdict in a British court, or almost any advanced country's court, was the absolute final word. Heard of O.J. Simpson? But not the same here. How so?

No, not a court, but *like* a court. All that vicious politeness from the lawyer would have suited a court – the *if you pleases*, and *would you not says?* and his sneeringly precise use of Vic's title, 'Detective Constable Othen.' Nobody was in the dock here, although Vic might be wondering about that. Kerry wondered about it, and the wondering took away more of her strength, flattened her morale further.

At an Inquiry everything was public, on show, open. But, in the trial of Scout Pethor and his friend Matthew Gain for the murder of Angela Sabat, there had been several long

28

closed sessions – one of them nearly two days – just the judge and the briefs doing all their professional law bit together, no jury, no press, no spectators. Perhaps these breaks in proceedings should have given the warning that convictions would be tricky. And so, the acquittals. Then, not long afterwards, the Inquiry.

A panel of three sat, picked by the Home Secretary, its chair an only slightly fading Q.C. named Bert Nipp. He refused to be called Bertram or Albert or Egbert, or whatever it was, probably because he thought 'Bert' made him sound *of the populace* and not some loaded ninny from Middle Temple. He *was* from the Middle Temple, and so far forward in his career he ought to be loaded, and would be more so on the pay for this job. Ninny? She thought he had done well to stand up for Vic. Perhaps he would turn out all right.

Kerry did not know much about the two who sat with Bert Q.C. – a middle-aged woman civil servant, of zooming rank, obviously, and the other man a retired town clerk, and therefore another lawyer. They all asked questions now and then and made notes. Kerry could not work out how they would merge their impressions finally and make a report. What was the procedure if they disagreed? Did Bert Q.C. have the big final say-so then? Was he entitled to drag the others into unity? Might there be a minority report, a minority of one? Kerry understood how a court functioned: a judge to direct, a jury to decide. She could trust that. In a court...

In a court ... She had been at the edge of the Angela Sabat case and was present for some of the trial. The rest of it she knew thoroughly enough from press reports, from one conversation with Vic, and from general informed gossip around headquarters, the kind police stations specialise in. A court could give you the feel, the sounds, the griefs and terrors of a crime. In the words of witnesses you might see this black, American girl, Angela Sabat, leave the bus at Pord Corner and get taunted by the two white men as soon as her feet hit the road. They had apparently been waiting for the same bus but suddenly seemed to decide instead to follow her across Bale Street and up towards Lakin Street, shouting, hooting, laughing, baying, until she started to run and they ran, too. Yes, the court trial made it all so damn painstakingly vivid, and so agonising – you could hear the running footsteps, breathe the street muck in the air, watch the spit bubbles around the hate words when the men yelled.

By comparison, the Inquiry seemed far off from the events it was inquiring about. Although the questions were often tough or slimy or tough *and* slimy and brought absolutely authentic bad moments, they did not recreate those bad, bad, bad moments between Bale Street and Lakin Street, and did not aim to. The Inquiry's job was different: to come up with a finding, not on who killed Angela Sabat, but on whether the police attempts to find who killed Angela Sabat were at the least a mess and possibly a cover-up. Vic and a few other officers had been invited to help with the second of these propositions. It was an invitation they had to accept.

'Detective Constable Othen, we know from the court proceedings that it was you who discovered Angela Sabat's body.'

'Yes.'

'This was on ground between Bale Street and Lakin Street which at the time was being developed as a housing estate, since completed.'

'Yes.'

'The body was not in the open, not obvious? It would not have been obvious even in daylight, but certainly not when you made the discovery at just after three a.m.'

'No, not obvious.'

'So that the Inquiry may be clear about this sequence I am going to read from the transcript of evidence you gave to the trial court. "I approached one of the partially completed houses. No doors had been fitted and I was able to enter. I had a flashlight with me. In a

31

downstairs room I discovered the body of the woman I now know to be Angela Sabat. She was fully clothed and lying on her back. Her arms were stretched back in a V on either side of her head. I went closer and took her wrist to see if there was a pulse. I could not detect one. I could see injuries to her head and neck. There was blood on the white blouse, which is now an exhibit. I concluded that she was dead. I reported the discovery to the police control room by hand radio and then examined the room, using the flashlight. After about a quarter of an hour other officers arrived and then the doctor. He made an examination and declared the woman dead." ' The lawyer paused for a few seconds, as though expecting applause for the verve of his reading. Then he said: 'Detective Constable Othen, this remains an accurate account of events on that night?'

'Yes.'

'Now, you were, of course, asked at the trial why you were on the building site at that hour and apparently conducting a search. May I read your reply from the transcript?'

'I know my reply. I said I was acting on information received.'

' "I was acting on information received." ' Geddage would not ditch the chance to do an encore. 'You were asked to elaborate on this reply.'

'Yes.'

'You declined?'

'Yes.'

'Why?'

'Confidentiality.'

'Detective Constable Othen, the phrase, "acting on information received" is a police formula, is it not?'

'Formula?'

'A technique.'

'Technique?'

'An evasion technique.'

'Evasion?'

'An answer, but no answer.'

'I was acting on information received,' Vic said.

'It is a formula answer designed to conceal more than it discloses, is it not?'

'It is accurate.'

'Nobody doubts its accuracy, Detective Constable Othen. What is in question is its adequacy, its fulness. Do you see that?'

Kerry knew how she would like him to answer. Give them some ego, Vic. Give them some poison. *I was there and searching because that is me – me, the Detective Constable Othen you keep so fucking smarmily naming in your* de-haut-en-bas, *cut-price Marshall Hall style. Detective Constable Othen hears things early, does he not? Often he acts on what he hears before colleagues have a hint of it, does he not? This is how it is if one has been a detective in the same city for nearly thirty years and has acted reasonably straight, or as straight as a detective can if he means to survive for nearly thirty years. Detective Constable Othen knows people, all sorts of people, and they owe him, some of them, and because they owe him they tell him things, do they not? And so, information is received, is it not? But Detective Constable Othen does not tell poncy rattletraps like you whom such information is received from or how, because it is part of the deal that he does not, and, if he did, there would be no more information received and no more inspired searches of building sites, no solo discoveries of dead girls.*

'I was acting on information received,' Vic told Geddage, a touch of real amiability, even sweetness in his voice, a sort of love-bird cooing. Kerry had heard it before when Vic loathed someone. He had never used it on her, not even at the break-up.

'If you please.'

Yes, I do *please, you divine forensic crud.*

'Did this information received lead you directly to the right house?'

'This was confidential information.'

'But it is not confidential now, surely, Detective Constable Othen. It is known to us all that the body of Angela Sabat lay there.'

There was no question. There was no answer.

'Very well,' Geddage said.

It did not mean *very well,* of course. It was a code for Bert and the other two tribunes. It meant, *Very well, stew in your own fucking silence, Detective Constable Othen.* It meant, *Very well, we will all notice that you dodge out of some replies, and we deduce what we ought to deduce about such tactics.*

'Could you tell the Inquiry how you approached first the building site and then the actual house? Did you, for instance, come to the site along Bale Street and going towards Lakin Street?'

'Yes.'

Apparently, Inquiries did not go in for visual aids. At the trial there had been a large, multi-tinted display plan of the area where Angela Sabat arrived by bus and began to walk and then run. Kerry had done geography at A-level and was good at maps. Her memory still held the street plan and she could visualise the 31 bus pulling up at the glassless shelter near Pord Corner, with Angela Sabat on the conductor's platform, ready to alight. She wore a dark, calf-length skirt, the white blouse, black beret, black zip-up leather jacket. Her office gear. At the trial it came out that straight after work she had gone with three girlfriends to the cinema for a showing of *Rebecca* in the Olivier season, and then caught the bus to near Lakin Street, where she was required to do some research on provincial city nightlife. She had come to Britain on a journalism training scholarship, and this was one of her assignments. Six people were waiting for the bus, including Scout Pethor and his friend, Matthew Gain. Then came the change of mind by these two when they saw Angela Sabat.

The prosecution at the trial had shown with a pointer on the street map the progress of the three, Angela Sabat ahead, the men following. Kerry could visualise it now, that pointer moving from Pord Square. And beyond the pointer and the map she could imagine the actuality, imagine it again: the girl crossing Pord Square, walking naturally at first, though aware of the men yelling behind her, then quickening probably as she entered Bale Street. There would be fewer people about here and she must have felt more exposed, though who could say whether she'd have been given any help or protection, no matter how many other people were around? Bale Street was narrow, not very long, mostly small shops, a couple of cafés, small office buildings, all of them closed at this time of night, a bit of the old, unredeveloped town. The witness sightings dried up about three quarters of the way up Bale Street. A woman motorist going in the opposite direction saw Angela Sabat look back towards two men and then start to run. The driver had her window half down and heard what she described at the trial as shouting from the men, but she could not distinguish words. She said the shouting did

36

not strike her as 'friendly'. One of the men also began to run or trot, then the other. She was troubled enough to drive around the one-way system and come back via Lakin Street into Bale Street, but by then the three had disappeared.

In the top left hand corner of the map at the trial was a mauve-shaded area representing the building site where town houses and flats were under construction. The property where Vic found Angela Sabat was coloured blue. The pointer had followed a supposed route along Bale Street, then across it at the top and into the construction area to the blue circle, but in fact nobody could tell the court how Angela Sabat reached that spot. Had she done what the pointer did? Why would she run to a building site in the dark? Panic? Did she think it would be easier to hide there than in a narrow, straight street? Had she run somewhere else and been brought to the uncompleted house? Scout Pethor and his friend claimed at the trial that she had run fast up Bale Street and into Lakin Street, leaving them so far behind that they lost her and did not see her again. She must have met someone else, perhaps more than one. Lakin Street was a busy main thoroughfare with cruising taxis, a couple of cinemas, four or five pubs, four or five restaurants. It would have been reasonably easy to get out of sight. The two men did not deny they had followed her from the bus stop and did not deny they had been shouting at her, but they claimed it was cheerful banter, not abuse or threats. Was she alive or dead when first at the house? The doctors could not say as a certainty.

'Detective Constable Othen, you told the trial that you searched six houses before you found Angela Sabat.'

'Yes.'

'That is true, is it?'

'Yes.'

Was it, Vic? Was the tip really so vague? Would you have regarded it as a likely if it couldn't place things more exactly than that? Would you have bothered to quit the fascinating Julie's bed to investigate?

'The house where you found Angela Sabat's body was not in a position that anyone entering the estate from Bale Street would go to first, was it?'

'There were a lot of options. That house might have been one of them.'

'If you please. You told the court that you had been informed an incident had taken place in the Bale Street, Lakin Street vicinity.'

'Yes.'

'Nothing more detailed than that?'

'No.'

'You did not know, then, that you were looking for a young woman?'

'An incident.'

'Would report of "an incident" automatically prompt you to search the houses?'

'I could see no evidence of an incident in Bale Street or the square.'

'So you assume there might be a girl's body in one of the houses?'

'I had been informed an incident had taken place in the Bale Street, Lakin Street vicinity. The building site is in that vicinity.'

'I have to suggest, Detective Constable Othen, that you had been told what you were looking for and where to look.'

No question again. Again no answer needed.

'Only someone who had been a party to the murder, or who knew someone who had been a party to the murder very well, would be able to give such precise guidance, is that not so?'

'If the guidance had been precise.'

'Do you understand that people are mystified as to how you so efficiently focused this search, located the body and were not detected by the site watchman?'

Because I am Detective Constable Vic Othen. I know how to search, I know how to avoid watchmen. 'Neither was the murderer, or murderers, detected by the watchman. Perhaps he was in another part of the site.'

'But it is *your* activities we are interested in now, Detective Constable Othen.'

'I was acting on information received.'

Four

When the Inquiry was suspended at the end of the day, she waited for Vic in the hall, standing next to a noticeboard full of municipal announcements about park concerts and the permanent closure of an underground lavatory, but naming alternative facilities less than a mile and a half distant, with short-cut routes. Hanging around like this was a risk – to her pride, that is, and her happiness. Vic could do a lot for her happiness, and against.

He might not want to see her, not here. She would understand this: not forgive it, but understand it. Although they bumped into each other of course at headquarters now and then and spoke, that was inevitable, meaningless, easy to keep casual: the past stayed where it maybe ought to stay, in the past. Yes, maybe it ought to, but she couldn't keep it there. The past had a life if you'd let it, and she found she longed to let it. This would not be one of those accidental meetings. Now, she hoped to ambush him, looking for deep talk, at least that. Perhaps he would walk past, eager to get back after the stresses of the day to consolation from stay-at-home, age-compatible fucking Julie. Yes, fucking Julie. He might not fancy close conversation with someone who had scarpered to someone else for a life mate, and someone who had just watched Vic rough-housed for hours and used as a beak sharpener, that traditional, demeaning, cop-in-the-witness-box function. Possibly Julie had it right in staying away. For her, he could still seem unhumiliated and impeccable. To Julie his head would continue to look grey-sleek and jaunty, not like something worn out and dubious, just rolled off the chopping block.

If Vic were with anyone when he emerged, Kerry would abandon it. The Police Federation should be looking after him and might have a representative at the Inquiry. Things between her and Vic had never been public, although some people suspected. Officially, she had been Mark's cohabiting girl even then. And there was nothing at all between Vic and her now, was there, to give Kerry a right to corner him, except that possibly dying, flimsy past? Was there?

What did she want to say to Vic, anyway? Not much more than that she believed in him, or at least half-believed in him, and that she had never heard more gifted blank answers when testifying, even from much higher ranks, and hoped he could do it again tomorrow and all the other tomorrows if they

41

took that long with him. The lawyer had left his teeth in Vic's flesh and would need to reclaim them eventually or how could he smile at Inns of Court functions? Today, she was Madam Love on ice, and Madam Lust on ice, but also Madam Therapy and Madam Esprit de Cop Corps. All worthwhile roles.

When he appeared, Vic was alone. She thought he looked as good as she had ever seen him. That lawyer could not reduce Vic Othen any more than the imagined wounds in his neck could. He was upright, nimble, eyes lively, a cigarette in one hand ready to be lit and consumed in three or four vast, healing drags as soon as he was outside the no-smoking precincts. She liked this. It was Vic as Vic. His grey suit seemed perfect. You would never guess he had sat in it for hours today while Geddage clawed. Perhaps Geddage wondered how Vic dressed like that on a detective constable's money. Perhaps Geddage would ask how, tomorrow or the day after – not ask direct, of course, but ask in a way Bert Nipp and the others must spot and be interested in. Geddage earned mightily for asking others how they earned what they earned and hinting that they did not earn it right, not the way he did. Seeing Kerry, Vic grinned and waved the cigarette hand. She liked that, too. It was his favoured hand, the one he smoked with, and – wonders! – he had devoted it to her. He came over. 'Did you learn anything, you know-all?' he said. 'Kerry, I was glad you came.'

'Why?'

'Because I—'

'I can't do it every day. I had time off.'

'And gave it to me.'

'Do you want to go somewhere?' she said.

'Somewhere?'

'Prick. Don't try that stalling game on me.'

'Prick?'

'Try *that* on me. But not your Dumbo technique from the Inquiry.'

'Technique?'

'The Coronet?' she said. 'Not in the room with the holy pictures, but the one where the cat sleeps.'

'Take both cars?'

'Naturally. We go to different homes afterwards, don't we?' she said.

'We have so chosen.'

'Right.'

'Is it? Of course it is,' he said.

'Yes, of course it is. But do you want to go somewhere?'

'The Coronet. Where the cat sleeps,' he replied.

Would *he* have proposed it, if she hadn't – asked her that question, Did she want to go somewhere? She hoped he would not have. It was *her* design, *her* impulse, this trip to the Coronet Hotel. She needed to show him her need, and she needed to show him her need was sharper than anything he himself would ever manage or imagine under that neat old thatch, because she was the one where real love dwelt, and where it grew, regardless of his age-driven treachery with that venerable cow, Julie. And regardless of Kerry's own twenty-something-driven and lifestyle-driven treachery with Mark. She was on accelerated promotion and already a rank ahead of Vic, so her feelings were bound to be more distinguished, weren't they? She had a plan. She wanted to hold Vic's nuts gently in a cupped hand for a while so he might know he could be had by the balls – but pleasantly, not as when that lawyer had him by the balls today, in the cause of truth, justice and career.

Vic, of course, would know this already. Just the same, as she drove to the Coronet, she practised the nest shape with one hand off the wheel. If people had looked down on her in the car from a bus they might have guessed by the configuration of palm and fingers what she was thinking of and felt heartened. That would be her to Vic, and the best in the way of comforting she could offer. Then there would be him to her. Mainly, she wished to get fucked alight by him some-where more relaxed than in a car or spinney and she wished it to happen after at least nineteen minutes of good messing about, to include, obviously, mutual going down, plus some intelligent biting in the chest, arms and buttocks regions. And then at least seven minutes for the actual act, although she might be able to settle for six, and if that cat was in the room and started humping its back and hissing because of the humping, terrific: it brought extra crackle into things. The rotten greenness and blackness of its eyes said, *Evil is everywhere outside, Kerry, so make the most of pinched Coronet moments with your knees up.* Visualising this scene, her own eyes grew hot and misty, and, with the one hand still off the wheel, she found driving a challenge. This was the kind of sparkle that could get into her desires through concentrating on some part of a man she fancied in circumstances when she could not have him: for example, Vic and that so far well-preserved neck at the Inquiry. His voice had been tinny, yes, but his voice she did not require.

At the reception desk there was already some mild and loving contact. His hand travelled very lightly back and forth a couple of times across the denim covering her behind, as a dragonfly might skim a pool. This was probably as much as she could expect at this point. With his other hand, Vic was counting out cash in advance for Mrs Coronet, a cigarette held in his mouth for now. Very briefly, Kerry fondled him, too, when his lower body was shielded by the desk. It would have seemed prim and thin-blooded not to, and was irresistible in any case. She tried to keep the fingering mild, not full-out celebratory, despite the long time since she had last touched him. He had to be able to count out the money properly without a twitch or gasp, while talking with sense to Mrs Coronet about the continuing problems in the Balkans. She came from that area and dropped great tears on Vic's tenners as they spoke of the aftermath chaos, the way Kerry's tears would fall on potato sacks. This was how life operated: there were big, general, often tragic themes, but also the personal urgencies brought on by, say, separation, then reunion. These could push the mightier topics out of sight for at least a while. Vic thought the religious pictures in parts of the hotel might be Greek Orthodox, and had said one day that Mrs Coronet's deep unconcern about the cat being in guests' rooms was possibly to do with her Slavic expansiveness, though Kerry consider-ed this bullshit.

When Mrs Coronet turned to find their key on the rack, Kerry whispered very close to his ear, 'I want to yell out about your monstrous, implacable, magnificent desires.'

'I'm a police officer, for God's sake.'

The Inquiry could put an end to that. She did not say this, did not want him annihi-lated. She found it difficult to think of Vic as being other than a police officer. *Was* there a Vic as just Vic?

Mrs Coronet led them to the room. She continued weeping quietly. It *was* the cat room. Grand. Kerry hated icons – religious icons, anyway – and even pictures of religious icons, as in the other room they were sometimes given. The artwork always seemed to crowd her there and the pale, holy colours made her want to pee. In *their* room, the cat slept on a straight-backed chair, not the bed this time, and opened only one of its filthy, unafraid eyes when they came in, then slept again. She liked this. It was as though the cat's indifference set a lovely tone of peacefulness. Cat on chair asleep – it said order, normality. Cat on bed asleep would have been different: an aggressor and coloniser again, like a slice of Balkan history. Kerry felt a grand leisureliness as Mrs Coronet shut the door on them. All that groping through clothes – fierce, yes, but juvenile: rather like under-the-desk Form 4, or was it Form 3 – a distraction from schoolwork – but she would have hated to be in a single-sex class.

She and Vic were not even standing close now. He was at the side of the window looking out on to the street through the net curtain. They would be close when it was right to be close, but now it was nice to be in the same room at ease, and, of course, with a bed available – the most promising item, no question, but not the whole thing.

The room had a kettle, tea bags, sugar and sweetener packets and dried milk. She could mock up domesticity. Kerry loved that, the mocking up aspect. She did not think she had ever wanted real domesticity with Vic. Would she have married Mark if so, even if Mark did have a golden future? And Vic was getting *his* domesticity with equi-age Julie. Kerry filled the kettle at the washbasin and set it to boil. She arranged two cups and saucers on the bedside table. For, say, half an hour these vessels would have as much to do with their intimacy as the one she had made with her hand earlier. She knew his milk and sugar likings from that other time. This was wonderful familiarity. When the steam began to push out from the spout, thinly at first, she felt the frail jet somehow brought additional solidarity: as though they had a hearth to set themselves around.

'Geddage is saying that because you had some sort of relationship with one twin you protected the other who was accused of a race murder? Am I reading things right, Vic?'

'Like that.'

'Protected how?'

'There were faults in the investigation. Things that might have been found were not found.'

'He thinks you're responsible? How? I mean, how at ... Well, how...?'

'Don't worry about tact, Kerry. You can mention my rank. How at my rock-bottom level could I influence an investigation that much?'

She poured the tea.

'He sees me as a symptom of something. If he can suggest I messed up one small bit of evidence he might be able to go on and show there was a general conspiracy to mess up evidence and scupper the prosecution case. I'm a lowly way in. Victor minorum.'

'I know you wouldn't do anything like that.'

'Of course you do.' He sipped and nodded. 'P.D. *was* a grass for you?'

Vic crossed the room and sat on the bed. Kerry stayed standing. She did not want to push the cat from the chair and its serenity. For the moment, its serenity plus the homely odour of the tea were important to her. 'I'd speak to him about certain crimes,' Vic replied.

'Now, don't muck me about with get-lost answers. I told you, I'm not the Inquiry. He was a grass for you? So, you have obligations?'

'That's what Geddage says.'

'Obligations, Vic?'

'You know how they are, Kerry, people like Geddage and maybe Bert Nipp – the slightest contact between a cop and someone with a record and a dirty business set-up, and it's, Let's get this guy for corruption. He's handling it sweetly.' He eyed her. 'You're not offering just a sympathy fuck, are you?'

'I feel *some* sympathy. There'll be elements of sympathy.'

'That seems to be OK,' he said. 'How will they show, the *elements*?'

'Probably I'll hold you more tightly, lovingly, unbreakably, with arms and legs when you're in me.'

'That's all right then,' he replied. 'I can do with that sort of sympathy.'

'And I expect I'll dig my nails into your shoulders and back and jam a finger or two up your arse.'

'Well, you always do that,' he said.

'Of course. I need some way to get inside you. It's mutuality. But this time it will be done especially sympathetically.'

'I'll watch out for the difference.'

'Did you talk to Pethor too much? Wrong friends?'

'You know how it is, Kerry.'

'No.'

'You will when you've been around a bit longer.'

'Can you hold him off, Vic?'

'Geddage? I wouldn't think so. No. He's committed.'

'Why? Has he got it right?'

Vic said: 'He's on his high horse and he's used to riding a high horse – wins prizes for it. Any day he'll be a QC. At least. He thinks he knows how things work. He might half know. Or only a little less. That makes him damn dangerous. This is normal lawyer's vanity and expert malice, plus a bit. He'll keep flailing about, to prove himself. He might hit something by accident.'

'What?'

'Oh, something that gets through to Bertie Nipp and the other two clunks.'

'But not true?'

'Not necessarily true,' Vic said. 'Just something they can notice and deduce from and stick in their report with a public-concern flourish. People like Bert Nipp crave flourishes.'

'But not true?'

'Not necessarily true.'

She took his cup and saucer and put them with hers in the washbasin. Enough conversation. Almost. 'You didn't undermine the investigation deliberately, did you, Vic?'

'How could I?'

'Did you?'

'We've been over that. At this rank, how could I?'

'You're smarter than your rank, Vic. More influential than your rank. More influential than *my* rank, and than most of them above both of us.'

'Now, I fear you grow idolatrous.'

'Yes, *I've* always been afraid of that, where you're concerned. Why I don't like the competing icons in the other room, maybe.'

No, she did not really fear it. This was another of her needs, to idolise him. It was only *religious* icons she disliked. Sometimes she felt ashamed of this tilt in herself towards adoration of Vic. Perhaps she had married Mark in an attempt to correct it, kill it. Evidently, this did not work. Although she and Vic could occasionally fall into what looked like absolutely ordinary living – kettle and teabag ordinariness – there had to be something else, of course, something that denied this comfortable plateau. It had to be something ungovernable and quaint, like the nonsensically intemperate worship of a man getting on a bit, silver hair, prissy grey moustache, dandyish, smoke-impregnated, in an inferior rank and belonging to another woman. This damn devotion to him could knock her off her perch.

Who wanted to be on a perch non-stop?

It really got up Kerry's nose that this idol would never undress her. She knew why, but the unspoken refusal still disappointed her. She loved to be got undressed. Not just to *get* undressed but to be *got* undressed. She did not want her things torn off her, not *necessarily*, as Vic might say, although she would not have minded. But she would have liked to see a real frenetic drive at getting to her, getting to her naked. She did not dismiss as nothing the stroking through her clothes, even though, obviously, this was remote and an approach only: pre-pre-foreplay. The trouble was, he had some delicacy, Vic, and always feared he might seem like a dirty old man, or *older* man, anyway, imposing himself on a young – youngish – woman. She had to do her own stripping as a sign of not just willingness but urgent enthusiasm. Well, of course she felt that. She had waylaid him, hadn't she? In any case, she was a bit more than gullible, seducible sixteen, wasn't she, a good bit more? *Give me something unbridled, Vic.* All right, he would later – no complaints on that. If only he would do some button fiddling, zip dragging, elastic tugging early – show high Vickish contempt for garments.

Decorously they began to get out of their clothes, but dropping them anywhere, as if they had servants. Of course, she could have laughed at herself soon afterwards if she had been capable of laughter. She must have been barmy to set that nineteen-minute requirement for the build up. Suddenly, she wanted him up her, and not just tonguing or biting or fingering. The need came a long time before nineteen minutes, she would guess, though she was not studying her watch much now. All that other stuff was grand and could definitely be a plus in some circum-stances, but when real priorities were assess-ed she wanted to get fucked, and getting fucked meant bye-bye to the cossetting,

53

whether head to toe or head to head and Gimme, gimme, gimme, Vic, stick me and keep me stuck, bang me and let the banging bang on. She could tell he knew she wanted it like that then, but the bastard went on playing, touching, mouthing, nibbling, dodging, kept his dick from her, or from where she wanted it now, so that she thought of back-jabbing her elbow ferociously into his face once or twice, maybe breaking a cheekbone or his nose, never mind the blood, as long as she could show this was serious and it was time to get definitive. Probably the build up had been more like four minutes, not nineteen, but she had not told him she wanted the nineteen, so why was he holding off, the coy creep? He could give a new sense to the term prickteaser. It was the prick that was teasing, not being teased.

'Shag me, Vic!' she bellowed at him. 'Get there. Scare the smugness from that cat.' The cat actually slept through things. Possibly it was used to this kind of scene and shouting, this cunt triumphalism.

Five

It was expensive, the hotel. They used to go there quite often before her marriage, but had never been bold enough to ask for a room at reduced rates, although they did not stay the night, of course. Vic paid in advance the full bed and breakfast charge and they would always leave after a few hours. She and Mark were already living together then and she had needed to get back at some credible time. And perhaps Vic needed to, now he was into cohabitation.

Tonight, Kerry was going with Mark to a Woody Allen season showing of *Zelig*, which would be on the screen in the WDL cinema complex at about nine fifteen. That meant leaving the Coronet no later than seven p.m. They would have had two-and-a-half hours, about average. Knowing the pattern by now, Mrs Coronet probably did a swift sheet change and let the room again. To Kerry, that made things seem a bit grubby. But, then, so would paying for a room by the hour, if it had been possible. Well, things *were* a bit grubby. Sex on the side was like that. All men had known it for aeons and learned how not to get upset. And some women: perhaps the number was on the up. She was in the number? Not altogether, yet. She could still get hit by guilt. She could still feel slaggy. But she was developing the power to shelve these self-reproaches, push them far back and out of the reckoning – nearly. She could nearly convince herself – another nearly – that if what she and Vic had was grubby it was only a *bit* grubby. There had to be more to it than that. Of course. Would she be going back to him like this otherwise, regardless of all the minus factors: age, moustache, ciggies, the smarty-boots image? Some women would have liked his coxcombery, felt it was their due, especially younger women: they'd see it as the old guy compensating for being old, as he should. Kerry half liked it half of the time and found it a joke some of the time. Not a sly or secret joke: she and Vic used to laugh about it now and then. Men of Vic's age had learned how to see themselves as a bit of a joke.

OK, so there were these minuses to Vic, but now possibly other graver defects, too. Crookedness? Corruption? Geddage, the wannabe QC, yearned to discover big socio-political themes in Vic. Through these big themes, the lawyer could express his big soul and plump up even more his big prospects. The tactics were, fix those deep failings on to

Vic, then, through him, on to the system.

But, no, never *those* massive dirty failings in Vic, surely. Oh, surely.

On the way home she was aware after a few miles of a car following her and staying very close, a tail which did not pretend to be anything but a tail. Although it was dark, she thought she could make out two men in this large Toyota. She did not recognise either: the one in the passenger seat, fair, possibly late twenties, the driver more like forty, also fair-haired but losing it, unhelpful looking. She was driving on a long bit of bypass road which had little traffic at night. It followed the foreshore: on her right were the docks, then a bulky, angular, steaming steelworks, rail sidings and some wasteland; and to the left, between the road and the sea, the smooth brown mountains of a cinder dump, followed by an itinerants' caravan village and more wasteland. It was not a piece of road she liked using alone in the dark, and she liked it less with the Toyota at her rear window. She considered dropping a word on her car phone to the control room. Premature? Nothing had happened except a bit of hoggish driving on a grim slab of otherwise empty road. It might be only a couple of loonies who got off on harassing women drivers: tossers. She must not slip into panic, yet. Must not be seen and heard to slip into panic, not ever. That would do the cause of fast-track Kerry and of women police generally no good in the control room. Fast track to frenzy.

And then something did happen. She had kept well in, offering the Toyota space to overtake: little harmless lady in little harmless car cowering compliantly away from male motorised toughies out on a blitz run. The Toyota had not bothered to get around, of course. Its game was different. Or had been. A bit like Ernest Borgnine dogging Spencer Tracy on that mountain road in *Bad Day At Black Rock*. Now, the Toyota suddenly accelerated, went ahead of Kerry and cut in at once, then slowed, making her slow, too. As the car passed, she had risked turning her head for a second to glance at the two men. She still did not know them. The one in the passenger seat signalled to her with his left hand, a couple of sort of stroking movements, two fingers extended. It meant pull over on to the patch of wasteland just beyond the caravans. She did not have an option, anyway, once the Toyota was ahead and had boxed her in. Perhaps she could have backed, pulled out and tried to race away. They would be ready for that. In any case, she felt some curiosity. And the man in the passenger seat – there was something to him, at least on the evidence of a very swift look with slag rail wagons as backing.

Both cars stopped on the rough grass. The

two men immediately left the Toyota and came quickly towards her Corsa, perhaps determined to ensure she had no time to phone. The passenger seat man would be about twenty-eight, maybe a bit younger. He was round-faced, but not childlike or goofy looking, his nose straight not podged. Slightly over six feet, he had a heavy build, possibly about to go to fat. He wore navy cord trousers, a navy, lightweight, nicely tailored jacket over a plain cerise T-shirt, and black, very formal-looking lace-up shoes. This ensemble had needed thought. The driver was possibly past forty, shorter, slimmer, in what might be a dark suit or coordinates, his shoes also pricey-looking black lace-ups. She had the idea the younger one was in charge, though did not know how she had decided this. Neither of them appeared to carry any weapon.

She drove with her doors locked. The two men seemed to assume she would and did not attempt to open the car at once. The younger one reached under his jacket and now she did expect to see a weapon of some kind – perhaps for breaking a window – as starters. But he brought out what looked like a small wallet, which he flipped open and held against the car window. There was a kind of flourish about the action, as if it were a joke she would immediately see, a piece of theatre she was familiar with. And, even in the darkness, she could make out a police warrant card, with a mugshot of him in the bottom right corner. She did not have time for the name but saw the word, Inspector. She unlocked the passenger door.

'Oh, no, I'd recognise every inspector around headquarters,' she said.

'No, not from headquarters. Would we be?' He laughed. 'Outlying stations, both of us. The sticks. Unfamiliar faces were needed for this.'

'This what?' she asked.

'Not that it worked.'

'What?'

'He spotted us. Of course he did. He sees everything, that one. We'd been warned he would.'

'Vic Othen?'

'I'm Groves. Did you see on the warrant card? This is Norman Shewring. Mind if we get in?'

'I'm due home,' she said.

'I should think so,' Shewring replied. The accent struck her as suprisingly refined and bordering on the languid. His face was beaky, cluttered, leering-bright, no class at all.

Groves pulled the passenger seat forward and let Shewring into the back. Then he climbed into the front with Kerry and shut the door. That gave her the other profile and she thought it all right, too.

She should have felt relieved. These were colleagues, or said they were. 'You've been tailing Vic?' she asked.

Shewring laughed this time, then leant forward so that he spoke between the two of them, still in that highfalutin tone, the content supremely unwholesome: 'When he came to the window in the Coronet and stared out at the Toyota – real *up yours* to us, like saying, I'm in here with a prime bird, thank you very much, nice and comfy, and you two, you can sit out there and grieve, you're not going to get even a whiff of it. I don't know Vic, but I like him for that, the neck, the serenity. I can believe all the tales I've heard about him and read in his dossier. Real exploits.'

She began to wonder if she had it wrong and Shewring was the boss here. He was building a tone, an insulting, la-di-da, destructive tone, but a tone.

'Follow him why?' Kerry asked.

'And follow *you*, obviously,' Shewring replied. He reached forward with his left hand and might have wanted to touch her shoulder. Kerry forced herself not to pull away. But he left the movement incomplete, never actually reached her. He withdrew his hand. 'Well, we transferred Vic over. When we knew he'd spotted us, another team had to take him, naturally, another car. We took *you* instead – a privilege. Did he mention us to you in the room? Well, he wouldn't, would he? He's a vintage gentleman and he wants a fully realised love session, so he's not going to say things about surveillance that will upset you, get you on edge, Kerry, is he? He's looking for delight and affirmation, not someone so tensed up you can't ... well, interact. And you'd be jumpy already, I should think – the blame aspect. Mark – a good man, after all, with unimaginable prospects and kindly nature. These impulses of yours, though! Inquiries, courts, they can turn people on, I've heard about it. Perhaps you had, too, Kerry. And now it hits you! Well, it's a humiliating lesson, isn't it, dear one? None of us is so different from anyone else. We are all vulnerable.'

'You're a new element for us, you see,' Groves said. 'We weren't looking for a trip to the Coronet.'

'Exactly what I meant by impulses,' Shewring said. 'We'd learned up on you, certainly, but we thought all that was closed. I'm sure it *was*. I don't think you pre-planned today's trip, Kerry. This is a conversation in the vestibule and suddenly the impact of the Inquiry, plus enchanting memories you two share – yes, suddenly all that brings you the compulsion to get back to the love nest and see if you can't recreate those splendid pre-Inquiry, pre-Angela Sabat other times. It was a grand womanly gesture, if one may say. I know he'll appreciate it. Any man would. And do we moralise, Tom Groves and I? Hardly! A woman may be overwhelmed by her desires, even though, on the face of it, those desires should be directed towards someone else, a husband or regular partner. A woman's desires, even allegedly "unfaithful" desires, are not to be pooh-poohed, oh, never to be pooh-poohed. Tom, would you pooh-pooh a woman's desires? Never! Tom and I are very much at one on this. I think of Madam Bovary or Meryl Streep in *The Bridges of Madison County*. Oh, absolutely – precedents. I can think of no reason why a woman detective shouldn't be various in her affections and nor can Tom, I'm sure.'

'Following Vic Othen to protect him, clearly,' Groves said.

'Don't you ever get afraid for him?' Shewring asked.

'For Vic?' she replied.

'Don't you ever visualise possible violence? He looks indestructible, sure – the swagger and neatness and sheer duration of him in the service. But he's into new terrain now, isn't he?'

'What new terrain?' she replied.

'I'd be surprised if you don't fret about him sometimes in these new conditions,' Shewring said. 'Your mind would stay with Vic, even if you weren't actually with him in ... well, the flesh.'

'What new conditions?'

'Imagining something terrible that might come to him,' Shewring replied. 'This is from another sort of self-blame. You feel you've abandoned him, I expect. So, the Coronet – as emotional recompense. It's what I said – grand, womanly.'

'You'll want to get back to Mark, I'm sure,' Groves said.

'Your timetabling must be difficult sometimes,' Shewring said. 'An Inquiry like this could make Vic a target for all sorts, that's the trouble.'

'We felt we should warn you,' Groves said.

'Obviously, you'd contemplate telling Vic about this baroque encounter with us, Kerry, but by and large we'd recommend you didn't.' Shewring puffed out his cheeks and turned his face puzzled for a second. 'I'm not sure why I say this. After all, he knows we're about – no question of that. Just the same, we'd prefer it's in confidence, at this stage. Best that it's in confidence all round, isn't it? I mean, you and your marriage and so on, however ... well ... *genuine* your feelings undoubtedly are, Kerry, for both men. Simultaneously.'

She started the Corsa's engine.

'What is it tonight, some nice social thing?' Shewring asked.

'You're not following him as protection at all, are you?' Kerry replied.

64

'He's got jeopardy, believe me,' Groves said.

'Why can't he be told, if you're only minders?' Kerry asked. 'Who ever gets protection without being notified?'

'Well, quite,' Shewring said. 'But we're given our orders. I think people hoped we could learn a bit, too.'

'And you have, haven't you?' Kerry said.

'Plus, Vic Othen might not like it – protection,' Groves said. 'He's quirky. He's independent, isn't he?'

'You tail him for all the standard reasons,' Kerry replied. *Fuck this lad's profile and good shoulders. He was as slippery as the one in the back.* 'You want to know who Vic's seeing. You want to know if he still associates with Pethor – P.D. Pethor, despite all the stink. You'd be pleased with that. You're getting together your own case against Vic, aren't you, so, when the Inquiry reports, he can be scapegoated for every detail of the Angela Sabat mess up?'

'Lord, there's plenty of those!' Shewring said.

'And I and the Coronet will be one of the items you can use against Vic, yes?' Kerry asked. 'That's if he decides he's not keen on acting scapegoat and some leverage is needed to compel him?'

'Oh, he's wily, nobody would deny that,' Shewring replied. 'Outstanding. In a way, I can see it's a distinction for you to be associated with him, despite his rank. What's rank but luck and favouritism? Vic is Mr Kudos. Was. Really best not to stay close to him now, Kerry.'

'You're trying to isolate him,' she said, 'forcing him into a spot where he can carry everything for everybody. No support.'

'We want Vic safe,' Groves said. 'For that, we need his movements reasonably predictable. Then we can always be ready to help. The love break-away with you today – inconvenient, dangerous. This girl, Angela Sabat – black, American, on a scholarship, hard-up widowed mother back in the States – this was bound to be a killing and a trial to reap the publicity. Still does, of course. All sorts might decide they have a mission to avenge her.'

'On Vic?'

'Obviously, Vic didn't kill her,' Groves replied, 'but...'

'Perhaps on Vic,' Shewring said. 'Perhaps on others. We worry about Vic at present. He's *worth* worrying about, isn't he? He's one of ours.'

'Yes, he is,' Kerry replied.

'Indeed,' Shewring said.

Groves opened the door and left the car, then tilted the seat forward for Shewring to get out. 'We felt a duty to speak this warning,' he said. He gestured towards the cinder heaps and steelworks. 'Un-ideal location. But

66

you wouldn't want us at your residence. This is not a chat we could do at headquarters. We don't go into headquarters, do we, in a doomed attempt to stay sort of secret?'

By the time she reached home, Mark had become nervous and was ready to leave for the cinema at once. 'Sorry,' she said, 'an interrogation session that went on and on before producing.' She loved the film. Mark was a Woody Allen fan and expert and had seen *Zelig* many times. He still laughed at it, though. Kerry felt wonderfully in harmony with him tonight. They held hands in the cinema like kids of a distant era. The film was about a character who changed personalities and even appearance according to the company he mixed with. In a Greek restaurant he turned into a Greek. It was exaggerated to make a comedy, of course, but Kerry knew we all behaved a bit like that, didn't we? Not much was constant. They had a restaurant supper afterwards. In bed eventually she told Mark she needed to sleep. He sympathised. Mark would never press. This always desolated her. She did not despise him for it – that would have been crazily out of proportion – but felt a grim, intelligent respect for his damn considerateness.

Six

Mrs Sabat said: 'Suddenly, you see, I found myself with some dollars again. A bad way to get them, but that's life, I guess. Or that's death, I guess. You know, Angela was on a journalistic project when she was killed? Oh, of course you know. Some sort of feature about new millennium nightlife in a big Brit provincial city. Well, perhaps what happened was part of new millennium nightlife in a big Brit provincial city. What do *you* think? Anyway, the company's insurance cover gets triggered for Angela, like for a reporter on a proper work assignment. So, there I am, sort of more or less OK for money all of a sudden, and I feel a debt to her, a debt two ways. Not riches, but OK. Why I'm here. This pay-out comes eventually and I think to myself, I'm going to take a trip, the way folk do when big unexpected cash turns up. But not what I'd call a *nothing* trip. Not just a trip for the sake of a trip, like the Orient Express crap. I decided this trip would be to where it all took place. In Detroit I felt a long, long way from her killing – an ocean and a bit from her killing. I wanted to see this town, that district, those streets, that house – maybe talk to some people – talk to police like this, but other people, too. I know London, worked there for a while, but not much about other English cities like this.'

'We understand, Mrs Sabat,' Harry Bell said. 'Kerry will look after you, show you everything.'

'That's kind.'

'If it's what you really want,' Bell said.

'You think it's morbid, might make things worse for me?'

'It's painful, Mrs Sabat.'

'Sure it's painful – but like I said, a debt, you know?'

'You said two debts, Mrs Sabat,' Kerry replied.

'Oh, yes. How I see it – Angela was crazy about journalism, writing, all that – crazy about it the way most journalists are. Not necessarily talented – just crazy about it. She never wanted to be anything else. Her father was the same. Got *him* killed, too, but it didn't stop her, did it? And far, far back, I was like it myself. Angela never had a chance! In the genes. Her father and I met on a reporting stint – as London correspondents, in fact. In Detroit they tell me I still slip into an English way of talking now and then. I have friends in London from those days. I've been in touch and a few said they'll make the trip and visit me while I'm over – a real reminder of those knockabout times.

'But knockabout times couldn't last. When the kids came I let it go. I didn't want to but had to. And now? I've been wondering, could I get back to it, maybe write something that would commemorate Angela in a way she'd appreciate, in a way she'd love? I thought one of those long, long aftermath pieces full of detail and atmosphere and prose for, say, the *New Yorker* magazine. Try for the best. The *New Yorker* likes considered examinations of big cases – big cases that seem to say something. Overtones, you know? This one might say something about the differences between here and the States, and the dirty samenesses.'

Bell said: 'If it's like that, maybe I'd better let one of our press people take you around.'

Mrs Sabat held up one hand: 'Press people, Superintendent Bell? Look, can we skip them? Your press people are fine, I'm sure, but I don't want spin, and that's what press people are trained to give. I remember it well. And I expect they're even better at it these days. Kerry will be fine – as long as Kerry doesn't mind.'

'Fine,' Kerry replied.

'Fine, then,' Bell said.

'The location, and then maybe a visit to the Inquiry,' Mrs Sabat said, 'just to get the flavour. They'll send me transcripts of the

70

actual words. I had them from the trial, too. I qualify for that, you see – free transcripts, being next-of-kin of a victim. It's generous. But I need to *see* the Inquiry, *breathe* it for a few hours. We don't have Inquiries like this in the States.'

'*We* don't have many like it,' Bell said.

'You resent it?'

'Kerry can take you there, no problem,' Bell replied. 'I'll make sure a couple of seats are kept.'

'I can understand it if you feel resentful,' Mrs Sabat said. 'You see these two guys get a *not guilty*, which must have been bad, bad, bad for you. And then this Inquiry, as if it was your fault they went free.'

'Kerry's very familiar with it all,' Bell said, 'And she won't give you – what did you call it? – spin?'

'Oh, come on, Superintendent, you've heard of spin.'

Early in the afternoon, Kerry walked with Mrs Sabat up Bale Street, the route Angela had taken towards the clubs and general provincial millennium night scene of Lakin Street. Mrs Sabat wanted to see things first in daylight. 'I'll come back on my own in the dark,' she said.

'I don't know about that.'

'For authenticity. Atmos. The sidewalk feels different under your shoes in the dark. Ever noticed that?'

Bollocks. Did they go in for whimsy in Detroit? Perhaps it was another hangover from her London days. 'Is that so?' Kerry replied. It struck her as supremely useless, this traipsing over old ground, whether by day or night. There had to be better things to do with insurance money. Mrs Sabat spoke as if she expected a mystical reunion with her daughter. In Mrs Sabat's subconscious was, perhaps, the gooey notion that she could offer protection to Angela, retrospective protection; imagined, belated protection. It irritated Kerry that this woman might fashion the case into a long slab of fancy journalism. All right, Mrs Sabat had real grief about her daughter. Kerry never doubted this. But to turn it into copy! That holy journalistic urge! Stuff it. Did she realise that a man's career might depend on this flash-back circus, and with it his self-esteem and peace of mind? And possibly even more of him than that.

'About here is where the woman motorist saw Angela, with the two men behind her, I think,' Mrs Sabat said. 'Am I correct, Kerry?'

Mrs Sabat knew the intricacies of the shambles better than Kerry, or at least the intricacies as they came out in court. The trial transcript must have fixed itself into her mind and imposed a shape there, like the frame of a tent. Now, she would have the

Inquiry transcript, too. 'Yes,' Kerry said, 'They were near the newsagent's. The men were twelve or fifteen metres behind, outside the Big Brekker café.'

Mrs Sabat crossed the pavement and went to stand near the newsagent's. She stared at the double front windows and the door. Then she put a hand on one of the window corner pillars, let her fingers grip it for a while, as if taking its essence and attempting to change this essence into the being of her daughter. Kerry was moved by it. She did not want to be, still thought it all flim-flam. Angela Sabat's remains were back in Detroit. This bit of shop masonry was shop masonry. It propped a shop that had helped tell the tale of Angela through the newspapers it sold, and would go on telling it: Inquiry, Report of Inquiry when it came, public and press and parliamentary chinwagging about the report of the Inquiry. But that was the only way this shop communicated anything about the case. Its brickwork had nothing to say to Mrs Sabat. Just the same, Kerry watched and felt enfolded in this visitor's grief.

Kerry said: 'The defence argued that the woman driver would surely have stopped or reported trouble on her car phone if Angela was in obvious danger. In the witness box the woman agreed.'

'Sure she did.'

Mrs Sabat was a surprise. Yes. They had all

heard of a widowed mother, less than well-off, living in the States, who had not been able or had not wanted to come over at the time of the girl's death, and Kerry had built a picture from that of someone tragic, dowdy, beaten, compliant. In a grey suit flecked with magenta, her blouse silk and glistening, hair expertly gamine, shoes Gucci class, she could have come direct from a finance house meeting or an editorial conference at the *New Yorker*. Her eyes were sad but also inquisitive and untrusting. Although her hand on the window pillar looked as if it had seen some hard work it was also long and elegant. 'And then the delay in finding Angela's body,' she said.

'Well, of course, nobody knew anything was wrong, Mrs Sabat. The woman motorist reported nothing because as far as she could tell there *was* nothing – nothing beyond a girl in the street and some noisy men behind her. And all gone, anyway, when she looked again. Most people wouldn't put themselves to even that much effort.'

'A *black* girl in the street and some noisy *white* men behind her,' Mrs Sabat said. 'But OK, that's hindsight. This was a caring, observant woman driver and I'm sure she would have reported it if there had been anything to report. Now, what did she say?' Mrs Sabat began to recite from memory: ' "I was worried, but I had seen no violence, heard no threats. It might have been boisterous but good-natured. I couldn't even be sure the men were concerned with the girl." ' Maybe one of Mrs Sabat's gifts as a reporter was total recall. She had fallen into a passable, flat, English accent, the Detroit rasp almost gone. It came back now. 'I was puzzled by that "concerned with".'

'I think the woman meant, whether they were even aware of Angela – were possibly just fooling among themselves.'

'Oh, right. No doubts about identification.'

'None. Not in Bale Street. The men admitted they were there,' Kerry replied.

'Just the problem of proving that this moment in Bale Street was not the last time they were close to Angela – the problem of placing them in Lakin Street and then at the uncompleted house.' She seemed to have stopped but after a second said: 'If it *was* those two.'

Kerry had the feeling Mrs Sabat tacked this sentence on because she thought Kerry was about to say it, out of automatic police deference to a *not guilty*. Kerry had not been going to say it. She felt no deference.

Mrs Sabat moved away from the newsagent's. Would she be telling the readers of her article about the texture of the shop front and the feel of the pavement through her shoes? Was that what the higher journalism went in for? She had not made any notes or spoken into a recorder. But perhaps the flavour of place came back unprompted if you possessed that kind of flair. And who was going to say you had it wrong, anyway?

Kill this fucking bitchiness, Lake. You're shepherding the mother of a dead girl, who's trying to reconcile herself to what happened, and entitled to do it how she likes. Kerry said: 'Do you think you'll be able to sell an article on this – an English incident and so long afterwards? All right, you say they like aftermath. This is very after, though.'

' "Incident".' Again for a moment that Anglicised accent, and reasonably close to Kerry's. A send-up? 'Yes, an incident. Do you remember, "Sex is an incident"? Harold Ross, first editor of the *New Yorker*, as a matter of fact, used to say that. Now, death is an *incident.*'

'I'm sorry, I meant—'

'From the magazine's point of view? I understand. No, you're right, I probably won't be able to sell it. I'll try. It will mean something to me, to have it written down. I can work out my reactions that way.'

'I do understand, Mrs Sabat. It was only that—'.

'Would it trouble you to think I'll be able to publish something about the case?'

'Trouble?'

'Make you anxious?'

'Why should it?' Kerry replied. Yes, the idea

made her anxious. Would there be another kick in the head for Vic, a transatlantic, fine-phrased kick on glossy paper?

'I expect you know people who were involved in the investigation? You might be close to one or two,' Mrs Sabat said.

'Some colleagues, naturally.'

The house where Vic found the body was completed now and occupied. So were the properties nearby, which Vic said he had tried first. They walked past them, Mrs Sabat trying to gaze into the death-site house through open front curtains. A grand piano, lid up, stood in the window bay, its dark timber aglow with price.

'No, we won't call on them,' Mrs Sabat said. 'These are people who've bought a place where a dead girl was found. I doubt they want to to be reminded of it. Perhaps already they see a ghost some nights. And now, a black woman at the door asking about Angela and the actual spot where she was found. Cruel.'

'What's that got to do with it, for God's sake – a *black* woman?' Kerry asked. 'In any case, one black, one white.'

'Could be spooky for them, though.'

'I could explain – being local, I mean, and a police officer.'

'Thanks, Kerry, but no. Wouldn't be right.'

They were big, double-garaged, porticoed houses, houses built to start reinvigorating, reclassifying, resurrecting the inner city. Mrs Sabat was probably right and people who could afford such a place would not care to keep looking at its grim history.

Well, fuck them. Why should they be insulated from all the horror of Angela Sabat's death? Suddenly, Kerry felt a compulsion to make up for the malice of her early attitude to Mrs Sabat. Or *some* of the malice, at any rate. Bits of it were spot-on. 'I think it *would* be right,' she said and walked up the wide path and knocked at the front door. It was solid, with two mortise locks and a Yale.

A voice box spoke, a woman: 'Yes?'

'Here's the mother of the girl found murdered in this house. She wants to get *in situ* for a few minutes,' Kerry said, bent over the box.

'Right. Reasonable.'

In a while a black woman of about thirty-five, wearing a green kimono and blue-and-white trainers opened the door. Mrs Sabat had hung back on the path. 'Come,' the woman said, holding the door wide. She took them into a wide lounge with polished floorboards. The grand piano occupied the window bay. A couple of red leather chesterfields stood facing each other in front of a tiled fireplace, the tiles demure and flowery, mock Edwardian or Victorian. Or even real Edwardian or Victorian. You could still buy fireplaces from demolished old properties.

The woman said: 'We believe the girl – your daughter, Mrs Sabat – was discovered here.' She pointed to an area on the handsome boards between the piano stool and one of the chesterfields. It was a small, respectful gesture, no theatricals.

'Does the knowledge disturb you?' Mrs Sabat asked.

'Yes, it disturbs us. Not all the time – we have other things to think about, especially my man. But some of the time.'

'Did you know about it before you bought the house?' Mrs Sabat replied.

'Oh, naturally. Everything else about the house we liked. It was that kind of decision – pluses and minuses. One plus was a minus. They took £5000 off for what they called "associations".'

Mrs Sabat went and stood near the place on the boards. 'Where was her head?'

'We think like this.' At once the woman lay down on the floor alongside the piano stool. Kerry thought she might have seen her, or a picture of her, before today, but could not recall where. 'Her hands and arms so,' the woman said. She stretched them above her head in a V. Again Kerry felt these were just the basics of a demonstration, no showiness.

'You've asked about it, then?' Mrs Sabat said.

'Oh, yes, it was best to know.'

'I think so,' Mrs Sabat replied.

'So much has been kept obscure. You think so, too, obviously, Mrs Sabat, or would you be here now? Are you police?' she asked Kerry.

'Kerry is giving me a tour.'

The woman sat up on the floor, then stood. She was tall, quite heavily made, her face long, thoughtful, combative. She brushed down the kimono.

Mrs Sabat pointed at the piano. 'You play? Or perhaps your husband?'

'No, it's something to put in the window, to state a lifestyle. Lie a lifestyle. You have to here. That sort of street. Same with the bloody chesterfields and this...' She gave a derisive tug at a sleeve of the kimono. 'The milkman expects to see you in such the-rich-at-leisure garb or he forgets you and doesn't deliver. My man's in jail at present – import, export, that kind of thing?'

'Would I know his name?' Kerry said.

'Maybe. I'll ask you what *you* asked *me*, Mrs Sabat – does it disturb you?'

'What?'

'That this place is owned by a crook and his lady.'

'Angela would laugh,' Mrs Sabat replied.

'They catch my partner for routine biggish business stuff – substance dealing, you know, really *normal* sort of major trading these days, yet they can't or they won't catch the ones who killed your daughter.'

'You mean because he's black?' Mrs Sabat said.

'Oh, he's not black.'

'You're Ferdy Nate's partner?' Kerry asked. 'He lives here?'

'Not at present. All right, I don't say he shouldn't be inside. He's large scale, yes, of course he is, and that's bound to mean risk. But Ferdy's not much good at building things between himself and truly influential folk. He could do with a twin brother who has special friends. I told him, see if he could get piano lessons while he's locked up, like some people do accountancy. If people heard "Für Élise" getting banged out on the keyboard they might think he was an *artiste* and we'd land more neighbourly invites.'

Seven

'Excuse me, Kerry, but are you fucking this guy?' Mrs Sabat asked. 'Or *were* you? You're married now, I know. That sort of thing does have a bearing sometimes.' Mrs Sabat whispered the question and follow-up, her mouth close to Kerry's ear. Close enough? It was during a slight pause in the Inquiry proceedings. Mrs Sabat said: 'I feel you're so tense

81

when Othen's answering – so sort of *involved*? Defensive for him. You like them older? Liked them? The feelings linger? Well, they do, don't they? OK, so there's marriage to someone else, but that might not wipe out everything. I can see he'd be attractive, the neatness of him, the arrogance and controlled snarl.'

Harry Bell had reserved very good seats for them. Kerry and Mrs Sabat were only about twenty metres from Vic and more or less directly in front of him this time, so that they were looking into his face as he tried to mess up this lawyer, in the style any targeted detective would, should. Kerry was not limited now to staring at the back of Vic's neck and imagining those three knife blows. And, of course, Vic's eyes would be on Kerry occasionally, alongside Mrs Sabat, and he could probably guess who she was and why Kerry had her in tow. Oh, God, would he regard it as treachery? She longed to stand up and yell she had been *ordered* to escort Mrs Sabat. In any case, why treachery? This was the mother of a murdered girl. She was due some sympathy, some help and hospitality, wasn't she?

This would probably be the last day of Vic's examination. Kerry wished Mrs Sabat had arrived on the patch twenty-four hours later. The Inquiry would still have been running then, and she could have made her visit for detail and 'atmos', but without any opportunity to get her intuition working so damned spot-on about Kerry and him. Was she that easy to read? The idea scared her. A cop should be able to manage inscrutability, especially a fast-track cop.

She had it wrong about Inquiries making no use of visual aids: the short break occurred as they brought in on a wheeled stand what looked like the same sketch of the area used at the trial. Kerry recognised the colours: the then partially built estate mauve, and the house where she and Mrs Sabat had yesterday watched Ferdy Nate's woman play act Angela on the floor, blue. Yes, Kerry must have seen a press picture or dossier picture at some time of Ferdy with the woman and had realised early on yesterday that she should have recognised her.

It troubled Kerry to see this plan produced now. Hadn't that area of questioning been covered already? Why return? She watched Vic's face, but Vic *could* manage inscrutability. He gazed at the plan, his face and body showing no movement. He was witness-box trained. He gave away only what he wanted to.

Geddage said: 'I would like to look in a little more detail than was covered in the trial at the period between your discovery of Angela Sabat's body and the arrival of your colleagues. Forgive me for reverting to it, but that interval did not perhaps seem as important then as now. The purpose of the trial was to decide whether the two men accused were guilty of the murder. Here, our purpose is wider.' He stared for a while at Vic, as if expecting him to agree and cry, 'Hear, hear,' or 'Well said.' Vic stared back and Geddage resumed: 'You have told us you found the body and that you sought a pulse. Unsuccessfully. What did you do then?'

'I searched the house.'

'Why?'

Vic sighed, letting Geddage and Bert Nipp and Bert Nipp's aides know he found the question idiotic. Kerry thought that before he actually answered his lips formed the word, Twat, the *a* very sharp. He said: 'I considered it possible that whoever had attacked Angela Sabat might still be there.'

'Why didn't you call an ambulance first?'

'I believed the girl to be dead.'

'But you could not be certain of that, could you? You are not a doctor. Did it never occur to you that medical attention given quickly might have saved Angela Sabat?'

'I believed her dead. My priority therefore became to find who might have killed her. Speed was vital.'

'You searched alone?'

'I *was* alone.'

'Wasn't that dangerous? Shouldn't you have waited for other officers?'

'It was important to search at once,' Vic said. 'If my arrival had surprised someone in the house – perhaps more than one – they might have hidden. I would give them no chance to disappear.'

'Wasn't it unlikely that the killer or killers would be still present?'

'It was a possibility. I did not know how long Angela Sabat had been there.'

'But it must have been a considerable time, surely – long enough for someone to telephone you about the "incident" in that district and for you presumably to get out of bed, dress and travel to the site, then search several other partially completed houses before you arrived at this one.' He touched the blue square with his finger. 'How long would have passed between the telephone call and your arrival, Detective Constable Othen?'

'The site is not very far from where I live. There is little traffic at that time.'

'How long? Half an hour? Twenty minutes?'

'Perhaps twenty minutes.'

'The assailant – assailants – would have had plenty of time to get clear, wouldn't you say?

'It is routine police procedure when there is evidence of a probable crime to search the immediate vicinity for suspects.' That was not a snarl – more the voice of a rule book automaton. Vic would never be that, though. He was stonewalling.

'Were you looking for anything other than suspects?' the lawyer said.

'Suspects.'

'What would you have done had you found a suspect, suspects?'

'Arrested him, her, them.'

'On your own?'

'I *was* alone.'

Kerry tried to keep her perspiration under control and the twitchings of her body, so Mrs Sabat would get no further indications – smell, sight, touch – that she fretted over Vic far beyond the range of colleague for colleague. More lover for lover. Of course, Kerry could see what the questioning was about. Of course, Vic would see what the questioning was about. Mrs Sabat might see. Geddage was suggesting that Vic had been sent there, by someone with improper power over him, to make sure nothing telltale had been left behind by the killer, killers, and, if anything had, to get rid of it. A detective with wrong friends could sometimes be asked, told, to vacuum clean a crime site for the sake of a wrong friend's friend, or possibly a wrong friend's kin or even twin. God, Vic, was it that? There had been hints at the trial. It was more than hints now. As Geddage had said, the purpose here was wider. Wider meant the stalking of Vic. Geddage wanted to establish that, for Vic, time on his own, unwatched, unsupervised would have been crucial. Even under the relaxed rules of an Inquiry, Geddage probably could not say this outright. He had no evidence, and such an accusation without proof would be outrageous. He would dance around the idea, almost get to it but not quite, so that Bert Nipp and his companions might sense what was being nearly said and imagine they had spotted it themselves. Geddage, this brilliant, evil turd, should have made it to QC years ago. *What he's saying – more or less saying – is not true – Vic, is it, is it?*

'Did you really expect to find anyone still there, Detective Constable Othen?'

'It was necessary to look.'

'If you please. Where did you look?'

'Ground floor, upper floor, garden – as it would be.'

'Upper floor? There was a staircase in this uncompleted building?'

'A ladder.'

'You actually risked going up a ladder alone in the dark in a construction completely strange to you when, in your view, there might have been a dangerous person, people, on the upper floor?'

'It was necessary to look. In police work it sometimes is.'

'And the search was unsuccessful.'

'I found nobody.'

'Did you find anything that might have been useful in investigating the murder?'

'Nothing.'

'No weapon, for instance, or something that could have been used as a weapon?'

'Nothing.'

'A brick, masonry, timber? There would be articles like this around a building site, I expect.'

'Yes, but none I could associate with the killing.'

'You did have this in mind, then?'

'What?'

'That an improvised weapon might be present.'

'Certainly. During the full, organised search of the site which began as soon as it was daylight nothing was found that showed evidence of having been used as a weapon.'

'I know that, Detective Constable Othen. What I am trying to discover is why this was so, you see.'

Yes, Vic would see. He stayed silent though. There had been no question. The lawyer said: 'During your search, might you have disturbed anything which could have been important to the investigation?'

'No.'

'But how can you be sure of that? You were on unknown ground and in the dark.'

'I had a flashlight. I was careful. It is routine police procedure to preserve the site of a crime intact until it has been thoroughly examined and perhaps photographed.' That frosty by-the-book tone again.

'How long did it take you – the search of the property where you had found Angela Sabat?'

'Perhaps five minutes.'

'What did you do next?'

'I reported what I had found to the control room.'

'We know that there was then a gap of approximately eleven minutes before your colleagues arrived. What did you do in that time?'

'I went to the girl again to see whether she had moved or shown any other evidence of life.' Vic glanced at Mrs Sabat for a half of half a second. Kerry read compassion in his face. Real? Oh, God, of course real. Vic said: 'She had not. I tried once more to find a pulse. I failed.'

'But you have told us that you believed Angela Sabat dead.'

'I wanted to be totally sure there was nothing I could do for her.

'But only after you had carried out your search of the property?'

'I knew at this late point there was nobody else in the building. I could therefore attend once more to the girl.'

'If you please.' Geddage was tall, slim-to-slight, pretty-featured, vigorous, sensitive-looking, endlessly alert. He was probably a grand asset to any social gathering. So, why didn't he fuck off to one of them? He said: 'And then, Detective Constable, from your evidence at the trial, we know you walked out of the building site into Bale Street. I don't think you were asked why you did this. Why did you?'

'I had searched the building site property. I wanted to see if there was anyone on Bale Street, perhaps having left the site by another exit. I also wished to indicate to the police vehicles which would arrive soon where they should go.'

'Don't police drivers know the area?'

'This was a building site only and not then on any street maps.'

'You saw nobody?'

'No.'

'Now, I think you waited here?' The lawyer pointed to the Bale Street entrance to the estate.

'Yes.'

'You didn't move along the street in either direction?'

'There was no need. I could see a good distance each way thanks to the street lights. There was nobody. If I was going to direct the police vehicles, it made sense to stay at that junction.'

'For seven or eight minutes?'

'Perhaps.'

Kerry picked up the suggestion that this had been wasted time, and Bert Nipp and colleagues would probably pick it up, too. The lawyer meant Vic might usefully have gone to the adjoining properties and done more than his swift search carried out when investigating 'the incident' on arrival. Geddage was raising the notion, without raising it, that Vic had gone into Bale Street to dispose of something, something he did not want to carry around longer than he had to, nor leave anywhere on the building site, which was sure to be toothcombed. There were probably refuse heaps outside shops and the Big Brekker café in Bale Street for night collection. Geddage wanted to know whether Vic had in fact walked along the street left or right and hidden something in one of the rubbish piles, then resumed his post before the back-up arrived. No weapon had ever been found.

'What's this guy saying – the lawyer?' Mrs Sabat whispered, again from close. Her breath was unintimidating.

'Who knows?' Kerry replied.

'You?' Mrs Sabat said. 'Othen?'

'So what kind of flavour did you get in there?' Kerry asked, as they crossed the vestibule on the way out at the end of the day. Vic's examination had finally closed.

'Look, do you meet him usually after an

Inquiry session?' Mrs Sabat replied. 'Am I in the way? You two like to sort of wind down together?'

Nothing like that today, Mrs Sabat. Vic has two tails, two *guardians*, probably outside waiting now. But Kerry did not say this. 'Did you feel there was something especially Brit about it, Mrs Sabat, something you might not get from transcripts? Not like a court, obviously – no dressing up. But the little rituals are there, aren't they and the famed English absence of passion?'

'I don't understand what your boss, Bell, is thinking. *Is* he thinking? He's crazy? He puts you – you! – puts you to look after me and take me to a joust like that where they're trying to knock over a lover boy of yours because he covered up for the killer, killers, of my daughter. You hump a man who was an accomplice post fact in the murder of Angela? Am I right? Does Bell believe this means we're made for each other, you and I? Now *that* might be especially Brit, I guess. You people adore irony.'

Eight

Well into the night, Kerry had a phone call at home from Harry Bell. He sounded madly troubled about Mrs Sabat and her safety. 'Thank God I could reach you, Kerry,' he said. 'Look, she's our responsibility, like anyone, but more.'

Although it was late, she and Mark were still awake. They had made gorgeously prolonged love earlier, and often following sex – even gloriously prolonged sex – he liked to talk for a while, a while sometimes being quite a while. It reversed the usual way of things, as Kerry understood them: traditionally the man wanted to go to sleep immediately afterwards, while the woman required a more gradual, chatty wind-down, with testimonials to her continuing beauty, pelvic spring and tightness. It was Kerry who would have liked instant sleep, if only to escape the spiky confusion she sometimes felt after making love to Mark. How could she move between two men like this, and take genuinely heartfelt, gasping pleasure from both? For a while, the problem had been at rest, of course, after the break between her and Vic, and her marriage, and Vic's filthy betrayals with Julie. Now, the break was broken you could say, and she didn't really know where she was.

Well, yes, she *did* know where she was – she was in bed with her husband. Nothing could be more right, and even righteous, could it? She did not despise this nor take it lightly. How *could* she take it lightly when the physical experience was everything the manuals and porn tales said a physical experience should be if two people were the right two? How could she take it lightly when Mark, on his back, relaxed and content now, talked so fucking interminably up at the ceiling, and with such method? People said Mark had a fine, analytical mind. She had come across a few of those at Oxford and thought it might be the place for them. Now, he was analysing their relationship, itemising with care the huge temperamental and taste differences between him and Kerry, but going on to prove that these differences ultimately demanded a wonderful, unique closeness, because without this overall, simplifying mutual magnetism they would have found each other not only unattractive but repellent.

'I wouldn't have been lying here with my legs strung up over your shoulders and everything, everything, on offer, if I found you unattractive or repellent,' she murmured from somewhere on the sweetly downhill link road to long-distance sleep.

'No, no, that's what I mean, Kerry, it's—'

The phone rang and she found herself half wanting to say, Thank God, and half ferociously resentful that here was another talk merchant mucking up slumber. She grabbed at the receiver, so perhaps the thankful half was the big half. Bell said *his* Thank God bit and then: 'The local nick had complaints about night noise at the house, Kerry.'

'The blue house?'

'This is piano playing,' Bell replied. 'They send a patrol and find Mrs Sabat there, hammering out tunes, the windows open. It was one a.m.'

' "Für Élise?" '

'What?'

'It's like an exorcism,' Kerry replied. Oh, Jesus, was that mystic flummery? She had another go at it. 'I think the piano playing is good for both of them. It gives the house a full role – as a house, you see, sir.'

'It does that, does it?'

'Is she still there?' Kerry said.

'It's a tricky one. This is two black women. You know that? We don't want overtones. Police oppressiveness. *Seeming* police oppressiveness.'

'No.'

'The other is apparently Ferdy Nate's lady.

He owns the place.'

'A kimono for the milkman?'

'What?'

'Is Mrs Sabat still there?'

'Our people didn't wish to seem to be leaning on them – in the present climate. These were complaints from white neighbours about the din. But the music was top-notch classics. Nobody disputes that. Not rap. More like a soirée. On the face of it quite ... well ... cultured? A late soirée.'

' "Für Élise"?'

'So, a request only – *Please tone it down, madam, and kindly close the windows.* The sergeant said Mrs Sabat is the lousiest pianist he's heard since his father died, but that's not important, is it? And, regardless, everyone could tell it had been good music until she got at it.'

'She's still there?'

'Could you slip around to the house, Kerry? She trusts you, doesn't she?'

'Does she?'

'I would obviously prefer she didn't walk back to her hotel alone from there. So late. In the present climate. That particular territory. Can you imagine the ... I mean, if she ... first the daughter, then ... Oh, God. It's the kind of thing Mrs Sabat might do, strolling solo in the dark. She's hunting actuality.'

'Yes.'

'She's not just a mother. She's a fucking

press writer. You know what they can be like for chasing the nitty-gritty. When it suits them.'

'Yes.'

'On the other hand, I don't want a uniformed patrol hanging about there, waiting to escort her, because it could look like heaviness against ethnics. Sorry about this. I suppose you're in bed. Conjugal.'

'Perhaps Mrs Sabat's going to stay the night there.'

'I wouldn't like that. I don't suppose she thinks much of us already. She's not going to hear anything sweet about the police from Lydia Nate. We ought to keep the contact to as little as we can. Please, get there.'

Kerry put the phone down, yawned a bit and lay back in the bed. 'I have to go out,' she said, not moving.

'Yes, I thought so. What's the blue house?'

She sensed her announcement would make Mark keen to have her again, and Kerry favoured this: anything that pushed the initiative hard on to him. She considered herself a true fan of the second or even third love session in a night. If she had to be awake, this was how the time should be used, not in theme talks. Subsequent acts always seemed to her more of an affirmation from a man. They could still be brilliantly passionate, but were adult, calculated, might tell of a future: she felt more *noticed* then. Mark would want to show now that although there were such differences between them, especially those created by what he once called her 'unbelievably quaint' job, the great, unifying influence of love would always impose its priorities.

Kerry worried a bit about Mrs Sabat, but much less than Harry Bell, and not enough to make her quit Mark at once. Bell had taken a battering over the first Sabat case and dreaded another. It was natural, but alarmist, surely. Mrs Sabat was not going to get killed tonight, was she? If she did not stay at the blue house she was unlikely to walk back to her hotel alone, but would probably call a taxi, call it by phone, so it would be a proper, safe cab, not a possible pirate. Also, in a way Kerry wanted to get back at Mrs Sabat for spotting so damn quickly and insolently that there was something between Kerry and Vic Othen. It would contradict that, wouldn't it, if she felt she could not leave Mark quite yet, even though Mrs Sabat was out there possibly unprotected and in danger? Well, sort of contradict it.

When Mark put his hand gently on her pubes she placed her own hand decisively on top of his and pressed down, getting his fingers involved, not just the useless blankness of a palm. He must not get any wrong ideas and imagine she was too concerned with the urgencies of her unbelievably quaint job to think of more love-making. With her other hand she took a confiding hold on the base of his dick and felt him start to harden. He turned towards her and put warm, ownership kisses on the side of her neck and then her cheek, ear and lips. It meant he had stopped chattering. Thank God for the great blood-stoked simplicities.

'Shag me, Mark,' she said.

'Forget the blue house.'

'Yes. Oh, yes.'

'You belong here.'

'Oh, yes. And you belong *there*,' she replied.

'Oh, yes. You belong only here, Kerry.'

'Oh, yes.'

'Nothing, nobody, can take you away.'

'Oh, no, never,' she said. It was about two thirty a.m. by the time she reached the blue house. There were lights on upstairs and down. No curtains were drawn and from the front garden path she could see the grand piano and the spot between it and a chesterfield where Vic had found Angela Sabat with her hands and arms above her head. The room seemed empty. The windows were closed. Kerry knocked on the door but nobody came. She knocked again and then began to grow anxious. Possibly after all it had been wrong to stay in bed getting herself re-gratified when a woman might be at risk on these streets. She knocked once more and tried the nearest windows in case they had not been closed properly after the ham-fisted recital. They had been. Still nobody came, and the windows did not yield. She might have to think about breaking in.

First, though, she turned and walked quickly up towards Bale Street and Lakin Street, hoping she might spot Mrs Sabat on her way back to her hotel. It was a stupid move. Hadn't she just driven half of Bale Street and seen nobody? And even if Mrs Sabat had left for her hotel, that would not explain why Ferdy's partner did not answer the door now. She might be unreachably asleep in there, but would all the lights be on? Although Kerry saw the illogicalities of her tactics, she still kept going. It was a kind of rerun of another script: Angela Sabat had been last seen alive in Bale Street, and Kerry longed to find Mrs Sabat alive there, too.

At the junction of the estate with the street she stood where Vic said he had positioned himself and stared left and right. After a few minutes a woman appeared, walking towards the estate entrance. Immediately, Kerry began to sprint to meet her. Soon, she saw it was Lydia Nate, wearing a belted overcoat which touched the ground, possibly a man's, and totally covering the kimono if she still had it on. 'I took her back to her hotel,' she said. 'Christine wouldn't stay the night. The house was still a sadness for her, even though we tried to party. But I've asked her to move in here for a while – save herself some money and perhaps make the memories more manageable.'

'Why didn't you drive?'

'She wanted to walk, because her daughter was walking.'

'But it's not safe for you to be on your own like this.'

'Oh, fuck off, kid,' she replied. 'Do you think anyone is going to try it on with Ferdy Nate's woman, even if he *is* locked up? Ferd has friends, can still reach out. You people don't know how to look after things, so some of us have learned to look after ourselves. That's a situation worldwide. No need to feel it's you especially.'

Balance. Ruthlessness. The overview, as it was called. Adult qualities. In the early part of her detective career, Kerry had worked with child informants. Kids possessed all kinds of strengths, including, quite often, brilliant freshness of mind and incredible persistence. Balance, ruthlessness and over-views they tended not to be hot at, though. Kerry had some readjusting to do.

Nine

Harry Bell called a meeting. Kerry was first there. She always thought that for a police superintendent and head of CID Bell looked remarkably sweet-natured. It was one of his big pluses. People talked to Harry. Even crooks talked to him, quarter trusted him, or possibly more – a third. They knew the genial appearance was not Harry's total, could not be anybody's total, except a halfwit's. But some of them would still talk to him when they'd talk to nobody else. This was a face you could never imagine being a party to torture or killing, a traditional face that in its younger times might have fitted into a Sunday school or charity walks. It was the kind of face most people wanted in a police officer, and the kind of face they liked to imagine nearly all police officers had before things got modern. Big-chinned, big-voiced, inclined to a lot of blinking, the adult Harry might have been taken for a middling successful, pre-Blair style trade union secretary; or a very senior hospital porter famed for considerateness, even to the old. Like Vic, he was slim and silver-haired but perhaps a little younger than Vic, and his skin less battle-fatigued. He did not smoke.

Yet Kerry could never have thought of Bell as a lover, could never even think of him as sexual, and this was not only because he looked so damn wholesome or gaga. To her, he was a man in a top job, nothing else. It baffled Kerry, this difference in her attitudes to him and Vic. Where was the aphrodisiac of power that people talked about? After all, Vic had negligible power. She had more herself. Bell had plenty and could use it very craftily despite his apparent mildness. The sweet-natured look was not *only* a look, but it certainly did not say everything about Harry. He would not be where he was if it did. When threatened, he knew how to turn devious, and savage, should it have to go that far: usually, he could be devious enough to do without the savagery. He was threatened now. In the Angela Sabat case Harry had presided over what could be regarded as a catastrophe and *was* regarded as a catas-trophe by most people who took any notice, though not by Scout Pethor, Matty Gain and their lawyers, loved ones and friends, or by busy race warriors – who might include their lawyers, loved ones and friends.

Bell said: 'Mrs Sabat has been on the phone, Kerry. She's keen to go to the Inquiry again. She's heard that our two innocents,

Pethor and Gain, will probably start their performances there tomorrow.'

'That could be sensitive.'

Bell puffed out his cheeks and made a helpless, lippy sound as he blew the air forward. He was blinking. 'Sensitive. Yes, that's the word. We have to cater for a potential riot outside, even inside, when they appear. This dead, foreign girl has acquired a lot of friends. She has acquired symbolism. It grows. Just the same, we have to guard those two cruds, Kerry. Pethor's brother will probably put some extra people down there to look after his prized twin in case we happen to go unintentionally slack on it. So, all-out street war is possible, with us taking most of the shit as a peacekeeping force. P.D. Pethor always manages to look after his prized twin.'

'Always?' Kerry said.

'So far.'

'*Something* has looked after Scout Pethor. So far,' Kerry said.

She saw Bell replay these words to himself. They meant nothing, except that nobody could say more than 'so far' about anything. But, behind the benignness, Bell eternally listened out for the unspoken. At his level, much was unspoken. Bell slipped a muted question to her, so offhand and mild it hardly sounded like a question: 'You know something?'

'Only that it's only *so far.*'

'Kerry, if you know something – think you know something – you must say. These are men cleared by the court. We have a duty to protect them, like any other citizen.' He made that last gasp sound again.

'We could warn Mrs Sabat there might be violence at the Inquiry,' Kerry replied.

'I *have.* A mistake. It's the kind of thing she wants to see, isn't it? Colour. Yes, colour. Race scene. Brit scene. She has the grief but also the need for hot copy. This prevails. If you know any journalists you'll understand.'

'I'd—'

'She says she didn't see you last night. If she'd mentioned this to you then you might have been able to talk her out of it. She listens to you.'

'Does she?'

'So, didn't you get over to the blue house after I'd asked you?'

'Of course. But she'd already gone.'

'Did you leave as soon as I asked? That was vital.'

She stared at him, at those bland, family-man, know-all features. 'My God, Harry, you mean you think this woman might try something against Pethor and Gain?'

'This woman? This woman is a mother as well as a journalist. Mothers can be rough, and this mother is from Detroit. Also, I don't know what allies and sympathisers she might have collected here and who might want to give her some heavy help, do I? She's seems to be getting close to Ferdy Nate's Lydia, doesn't she? Piano interludes. Ferdy can whistle up some very rough people, even from where he is. Did you leave for the blue house as soon as I asked?'

'Immediately.'

He did more blinking. 'Or were you and hubbie about the task of reaffirming devotion to each other, despite everything? That's lovely. A priority? I thought you sounded a bit breathless.'

'Get your fucking little prong out of my private life, Mr Bell. I left at once.' These days, if they strayed, you could talk to them like that, whatever their rank. It was the new political climate. Its sun shone even into a police station. About this kind of topic you could lie and lie and lie to the sod and he had to swallow it, or possibly land himself in front of a sexual harassment tribunal.

'I want this today to be a three-way meeting,' Bell replied with homely warmth, as if it were a longed-for reunion. 'I've got Vic Othen coming up here in a few minutes.'

'Oh?'

'This embarrasses you?' Bell asked.

Only because her entire life mission had defined itself lately as the salvation of Vic Othen from those who might stab him in the neck, or turn him into a sacrifice for the

106

greater good of the organisation. Harry Bell might be one who would like to turn Vic into a sacrifice for the greater good of the organisation and shift the full Sabat case blame his way.

'Embarrass me, sir?' she replied. 'Why?'

'I need to find from prime sources how the Inquiry has gone so far,' Bell said. 'Especially from Vic. He's central. I get transcripts, of course – after a week. But I want to know how he *felt* things went. The impression he made on the panel. People can believe in Vic, even three like those. I must have a view on all that stuff right away.'

This might mean: *Prepare to drop him.* Superintendents could get a Queen's Police Medal for Scapegoating Skills. Or it might mean: *Prepare to set Vic up as hero.* Superintendents could get a Queen's Police Medal for Projecting Successes of the Troops. 'You could have gone to the Inquiry, sir,' Kerry said. 'Vic would have liked the support.'

'He's never been interested in support.'

'Are you retaliating then?'

'He's got so much trouble.'

'You didn't want to be associated with it? Enough of your own?'

'Vic – *so* much trouble, Kerry. I don't know how it could happen to someone of his experience. I feel a true, immovable debt to officers like Vic. The years.' His big voice shrank and grew tentative, like a sergeant major sucking up to the commandant. 'Look, I know you two are ... or certainly *were* ... I know Vic and you— Look, I'm really fond of Vic.' She thought he might have rehearsed the inarticulateness. He said: 'I'd do whatever I could. I hope that can be regarded as built-in.'

He paused, maybe for a response. Bell was sitting at his measly, old, gimcrack deal desk. A desk should speak of authority, status. In a private company's office, Bell's desk would have spoken of bankruptcy. Kerry, in a measly, old, gimcrack moquette armchair was opposite him. She gazed at Bell and did some blinking.

Eventually, he said: 'I must keep upbeat. I'm not going to say anything about these anxieties to Vic now.'

'Why not, sir?'

'Vic's always tended to act on his own judgement, *only* on his own judgement. It's a strength, can be. I've known it to be a strength, no question. I hope I'm not somebody who believes everything can be done by – by formal, conventional means.' He waited a bit again.

Kerry also waited.

'Regrettably, damn regrettably, Kerry, there are also times when Vic's individualistic methods can be a terrible weakness. He makes himself liable to attack. I don't mean only judicial attack. Actual. Very actual.'

Kerry suddenly had her standard fantasised glimpse of Vic's neck and the three knife wounds. Inside her, she heard a voice. It could be any race. *That's for making a black girl's murder unsolvable, you bought and sold lout.* 'There's a buzz around? Why you've put minders on him?' she asked.

'Yet, I wouldn't want to talk to him one-to-one about his methods now, Kerry,' Bell replied.

'Why?'

'Would it be fair to either of us? He'd fear I might misrepresent any comments he makes.'

'What would *you* fear?'

'Oh, likewise. But I've asked you to be here, too, Kerry. Moderator. You'll judge. And one thing Vic can't allege is that you're pre-disposed against him.' The big voice grew bigger, good-humoured, hearty. 'Well, hardly. In the circumstances, I mean. The Coronet.'

'Get your fucking little prong out of my private life, Mr Bell.'

Bell lowered his head, a sort of apology. Then expansiveness, generosity, humanity came clustered and enlivening to him, like bottles on an air hostess's trolley. He said: 'I do understand the impulse, believe me: this lad – well, maturish for a lad, perhaps – but this lad, having had a fierce time in the Inquiry, you feel a very womanly – even very wonderful and selfless – a very *womanly* wish to restore him, as it were – reclaim him, in a sense. I see it as like those VAD nurses at the front in the Great War when some of them would quite voluntarily fuck selected soldiers because the boys were suffering such a hellish time and probably did not have a future. Yes, quite voluntarily, despite the standards of the day.'

'Who hasn't got a future?' Kerry replied. 'What happened to it, is happening to it?'

'And yet I can't see it as entirely a private-life matter, Kerry. Not Vic. There is the other way of looking at things when two police officers are concerned, wouldn't you say – their ... well ... romance having a possible bearing on a deeply controversial case?'

'It wasn't selfless,' she replied, 'not like the Great War. I wanted him. I'd never fucked someone who'd starred in a public Inquiry. Are you saying Vic and I might have some kind of ... some kind of dark pact over the Angela Sabat killing?'

Harry gave this some mull. 'Re-wanted him. Always, women have had a brilliantly noble fascination with the dick that might be forever gone tomorrow, through war death, career death, jail. Whereas the dick which is there for keeps, reliable, constant – say like Mark's – not the same, is it, Kerry? It should be, and even better, but somehow no. Oh, it's an eternal tale. Why, here's Vic now. Just the three of us, Vic. Come in. Sit, do.'

Vic chose a straight-backed chair near the wall and to the side of Bell's desk.

Bell said: 'I've been explaining to Kerry that everything I hear about you at the Inquiry tells me nobody could have looked after our position better.'

'Position?' Vic said.

Bell laughed, a huge, two-stage laugh – the first all surprise and extreme delight, the second very confirmatory: 'That affronted repetition! You're playing your technique on *us* now, are you? Bravo! *"Position?"* There's never been a brickier brick wall.' Gravity got a hold on him again. 'Yet, what we have to try and guess, Vic, is whether Bertie Nipp will admire as much as Kerry and I do this Get-fucking-lost way of dealing with lawyer Geddage or ... Well, Bertie's a lawyer, too, isn't he? Same fucking Inn of fucking Court as fucking Geddage? I don't know. Perhaps I should. Do they do feasts together up there, exchange smart puns and chortle collegiately, pick nits out of each other's wigs? Does Bertie note in his big, mock-independent mind that this officer, Victor Othen, is showing contempt to a legal colleague and therefore to the entire holy forensic contraption, as represented by Magna Carta and the Rest Home for Herniated QCs? Do we, in consequence, get backlash treatment in the report?'

'Does Vic, you mean?' Kerry said.

Bell held his arms wide. He was in shirt-sleeves and, posed like this, looked massive and forever spruce and reliable. 'I hope I see any criticism of Vic as encompassing us all,' he said. 'That is surely the nature of our service.'

Kerry blinked.

'No transcripts yet, so only the press cuttings,' Bell said. He brought a scrapbook from the drawer of his desk and opened it. He read a headline: *'Detective quizzed about missing minutes.'* He read it again and pretended to spit. 'Vic, what I want you to realise is that all of us – I mean, not just Kerry and me, but *all* of us to the highest level, the very highest level – and I'm referring to people beyond this police force, oh certainly – all of us are sure there was no calculated disturbance of evidence or concealment of evidence by you, or deliberate delay in reporting the girl's death on behalf of some favoured contact.'

'I'm glad, sir,' Vic replied.

Bell put the open scrapbook on to his desk and leaned forward, apparently to read some of the paragraphs under the headline. He said: 'Predictably, uninspiringly, this Inquiry returns to topics already exhaustively dealt with at the trial. Vic, how did Nipp seem to take your answers?' Bell struck the scrapbook a small blow with his knuckles. It was to signify disregard for the headline and comradeship with Vic. 'Look, I don't expect you to read Nipp's mind – but from your observation. I'd trust your observation. Have done, often, and never been disappointed.'

'What is it, sir – the Chief or higher, wants an early indication of how hard the report is going to bash us?' Vic asked. 'Bash *me.*' He looked all right, sounded all right. He was in a grey, double-breasted suit Kerry much liked and a dark blue tie with a white shirt. He could have been the manager of a damn good shop, a London, Bond Street shop selling crystal; or a Conservative Party agent when they used to win.

'Even with someone as gnarled as Bertie Nipp, the eyes can occasionally show where sympathies are,' Bell replied. 'Or the angle a subject sits at.' Another vast comradely laugh: 'Oh, God, am I trying to give Vic Othen interrogation tips?'

'The politics will be frogmarching him one way and only one way,' Vic replied.

'Yes, the politics,' Bell said. 'But Bertie has been active a hell of a time and he's sure to have heard of impartiality now and then, if only by accident.'

'The politics will be frogmarching him one way and only one way,' Vic replied.

'Yes, the politics,' Bell said. 'I've gone over the timings you gave at the trial for your actions on that night, really gone over them in person, in situ, and – more than once –

stopwatched them, and I cannot see anything preposterous in your version whatsoever.'

'I'm glad, sir.'

Bell struck the newspaper cutting another knuckles blow. *'Missing minutes.* What do they mean? There are no missing minutes. You've accounted for them.'

'What are the tails for?' Vic replied.

'Kerry spoke to you?'

'Kerry? How does she come into it?'

'Did you tell him, Kerry?' Bell asked.

'I don't need to be told. I saw them,' Vic said. 'Of course I saw them. I'm not going to do a runner, am I? The pension and leaving gift.'

'Not tails,' Bell replied. 'This is temporary protection.'

'Your idea, sir? Higher?' Vic asked.

'They're afraid you could be a vengeance target – because you're supposed to have covered up,' Kerry said. 'It's mad. Isn't it?'

'Which is mad,' Vic asked, 'the protection or the idea I covered up?'

'Both,' Kerry replied.

'Kerry's altogether with you, Vic. Well, as you know,' Bell said.

'They stopped me,' Kerry said.

'When?' Vic asked.

'After the Coronet.'

It took him a moment to consider that. 'Right,' he said.

'There's no significance in the fact it was

after the Coronet,' Bell said. 'That was unscheduled. Naturally it was unscheduled, even for you two, I should think. A happy love impulse.'

'Right,' Vic replied.

'What makes the divorce courts go round.' Bell stood and strolled to a corner of the room where he was as far as he could be from both of them. Kerry watched him. When he began to speak he was looking away, but did turn after a while and stared at somewhere between them. He had on the trousers of an old suit – bulky, navy, workaday, offering no definition of the arse.

'Kerry and I have been discussing it and on balance I do agree with her that we have no interest in matters between you such as the Coronet. None. I can, of course, see a hazard if the Inquiry report eventually comes out unfavourably to you personally, Vic, and the press starts a dig and comes up with you having it off with another detective involved to some degree in the case and who's married to a notable young businessman of the town. If it's still going on then, of course. We're talking months. Or even if your relationship is finished again by then – I mean, if the Coronet was just a one-off – I mean a one-off in this second phase of the affair – even if it's over again by then, reporters could still sniff it out of your past, Vic. I don't know whether that would do the force any good, in the circumstances. Or yourself. Or Kerry – Kerry with a possible big career on the line, and that fine marriage.'

He leaned against a glistening new filing cabinet, all wrong for the ramshackle room. Did he want to seem casual when what he was saying and what he was leading to could only be brutal?

'As I see it,' Bell stated, 'Kerry's very reasonable husband, Mr Mark Tabor, might be able to overlook, or at least come to terms with, the straying of his wife if that straying has been thoughtfully managed, not shoved under his nose. And I'd say, for instance, that a quick bang in the Coronet would normally have come very nicely into that thoughtful category. But, suddenly, because of the case and the overlap the Coronet gets known about to others. Namely, to four detectives doing protection duties on Vic and then to myself, whom they report to. Obviously, this is, thank God, a very discreet and discrete group of people. Am I going to blurt such compromising insights around the building, for instance? And, of course, I've spoken to the four lads, stressed the confidentiality aspect. And I can assure you they gave me guarantees. Oh, yes. The fact that you were observed at the Coronet by these two parties of surveillance officers is by no means the equivalent of a general public disclosure.

Obviously.

'But what we have to cater for is that, when the Inquiry report hits the newsstands, there might indeed follow general public disclosure about the ... well, *controversial* behaviour – is that fair, because I do want to be that? – the controversial behaviour of two detectives concerned, in varying degrees, with the Sabat murder. This Coronet business illustrates in a comparatively containable manner how the sexual side and the police side can become enmeshed. It does offer a warning about the future.'

Kerry said: 'What the fuck do you want, sir?'

'Want?' Bell did a comic eye roll and had another splendid laugh. 'Now, damn it, *I'm* using Vic's slow-it, brick-wall ploy. I don't feel I *want* anything, except, I hope, to see ahead and try to make things as comfortable as they can be made for Vic and you if things turn evil. As they might.'

Vic said: 'What the fuck do you want, sir?'

Bell stood straight in his corner and put his face in his hands for a second. It was modesty, it was tentativeness, it was determination to say what could not be said. Then he exposed his eternally temperate face. 'All of it – absolutely all of it – could be disposed of, couldn't it, Vic, couldn't it, Kerry, if the Inquiry were given the name of whoever told you on the night, Vic, about the 'incident' in the Bale Street area? As I see it. All right, you've finished your appearances at the Inquiry, but it would be the simplest matter to arrange for you to give a supplementary statement. An Inquiry's rules are so flexible they almost amount to no rules. You could certainly be accommodated, Vic. I've seen no transcripts of your examination but I'm sure that what Geddage wanted to know above all was the identity of your informant.'

'Of course,' Kerry said.

'He can go fuck himself,' Vic said.

'He can go fuck himself,' Kerry said.

'I respect your professionalism, Vic, naturally,' Bell replied. 'The loyalty to one of your voices.' He came and sat at his desk again, perhaps because he wanted a closer, more intimate appeal to Vic: 'But isn't there now at least an argument in favour of—'

'He can go fuck himself,' Vic said.

'You've more or less told him that, as I understand things, in the way you've answered at the Inquiry,' Bell replied.

'Right,' Vic said. 'I don't disclose sources.'

'I've said I repect your professionalism,' Bell replied, nodding, 'But in a sense it is *not* proper professionalism, is it, Vic? Neither you nor any other detective is entitled to private sources. An informant does not belong to you, personally. Sorry to go pedantic on you, but an informant belongs to the force. He, she, should be registered. I, at least, should know about your informants. Now, of course, I'm aware that these regulations are frequently ignored by experienced detectives who—'

'I don't disclose sources,' Vic said.

'So, *I* can go fuck myself?' Bell replied.

Ten

Mrs Sabat screamed – yes, a real scream – but the words precise and every consonant fierce: 'So, why didn't you fuck her, strip her, rape her first? You just kill her, no reason, no reason except she's black. Wasn't she good enough for you?' Christine Sabat said fuck as if her mouth had been custom-made to get all its corners and poetry.

Silence in the street, except for this and the sound of footsteps, a lot of footsteps, on their way to the Inquiry, where truth would be invited once again to strip off and show itself all round and in full. And might, or might not, who knew? Well, two people knew.

'No, you mustn't say that,' Kerry told Mrs Sabat and tried to pull her back.

'Why?'

'For God's sake – you're her Mother.' Kerry's voice gave it the big, big M.

'Was. Why didn't they? They cockless, then?' These words were said at normal voice, just a piece of womanly chat. Now, Mrs Sabat broke away from Kerry and pushed to the front of the crowd again and screamed once more: 'Why didn't you, you two? Are you cockless or something?'

'You can't say that. They're innocent. The court decided.'

'Hey, innocents, holy innocents,' Mrs Sabat called, 'you just killed for nothing? Whim not quim? That make you innocent? Face, tits, ass, legs – none of it counts, none of it gets to you?' She began to weep and her voice stayed loud but seemed to grow hollow, like an echo or 'Abandon ship' megaphoned on the boat deck. 'She was lovely, she was fuckable. But all you want to do is kill it because it's black, it's black, it's black, yes? God, the simplifying insolence.'

Kerry liked the British pronunciation *arse* better. It sounded cruder, jollier, more lewd. But neither of them was anywhere right for Christine Sabat to yell in a grey-brick official street about her murdered daughter. It was some kind of despair, some kind of madness.

Kerry wanted to tug at her arm again and turn her to face this way, but too late, probably. There were cameras here and Christine Sabat ought to give them the fairly anonymous back of her head. Mostly they were TV News cameras. But, as Harry Bell had forecast, P.D. Pethor had some of his people on duty, and one or two of them might be doing a bit of filming, also, for the Pethor archive. That would explain the scared silence of the crowd.

Scout Pethor and Matthew Gain walked down the centre of the wide, office-block street towards the Inquiry building surrounded by uniformed police: Peter Vincent Pethor, mostly known as Scout because he was born first of the twins, pathfinder. The police walked each side of them in line-ahead columns. There were gaps through which Scout and Gain could be seen and could have been shot at or stoned or spat at, but were not, as far as Kerry could tell. Probably these gaps were not deliberately left so wide to offer openings. If they were, no luck. The street was closed to traffic today, and hence more silence except for the eerie padding of shoes. Kerry did not know why, but the sound made her think of pilgrims out east on their urgent way to some shrine. As well as the footsteps there was, too, of course, the intermittent howling of Mrs Sabat, infinitely raw, half demented, maybe more. Oh, God, yes – more. How else could she have screamed those words?

The crowd had come to watch and stood behind a barrier on the left side of the street. Most of them stayed very quiet and very still. They knew about the cameras, all the cameras. Harry Bell had feared fighting if people tried to make anti-racist protests by rushing Scout Pethor and Gain, or at least by shouting at them, spitting at them. But the spectators seemed to sense it wisest not to offer themselves for later freeze-frame study as enemies of the clan on P.D. Pethor's private film. Christine Sabat would be there, though, and on every TV channel this evening. As soon as Mrs Sabat started yelling, Kerry had seen the cameras move in on her. The news teams might know who she was, guess who she was. She made a story. Possibly she wanted it. She had been a journalist and perhaps believed publicity a boon. And, naturally, there were times when it could be. This might not be one of them.

At least, though, she could go home to Detroit fairly soon and refine it all into a slice of writing done in distant safety. The people in the crowd had to stick around here and knew P.D. Pethor and his crew and brother would be sticking around, also, and could discover easily enough where they lived and worked and where their children went to school. Scout would scout. *If you haven't booked your return flight book it soon, Mrs Sabat. Get home to the nice remoteness of the word processor.* In whatever she wrote then, would Christine Sabat recall, reveal, the quaint evil of her thoughts and words today? Deranged evil? She wished her daughter had

122

been killed as desirable sexual victim, not simply as a hated black. *My daughter was fuckable.* They were tough with words, some of these writers, believed saying it, whatever it was, was the only way. Christ, did *mothers* say such things, though, even in Detroit? She meant, did she, that Angela was special, lovely, stood out, and should have been murdered on merit, not just for race: then there would have been at least an iota of the positive in her death?

And yet it was not only Mrs Sabat who thought like this. Kerry had met the same notion among other people since the murder, mainly black other people. They could understand it if a girl were killed as part of a sexual attack. It terrified them if Angela Sabat had been killed only because she was black. That meant vast, capricious hate which could reach any other black. This was why Angela Sabat had become a frightening symbol. Her death spoke a warning. It did not matter that she was from outside the community, foreign. People were massively affronted by her death because it seemed motiveless, almost random. Yes, almost.

Scout Pethor and Matthew Gain had glanced at Mrs Sabat when she started shouting, but that was all, a glance. They stayed blank-faced, even mild-looking. Did they have a policy of harmlessness for now, no matter what? Apart from that quick, instinctive turn towards her when she first bellowed they kept their eyes ahead and on the Inquiry building, like men driven by a mission, like men following a holy light, like pilgrims on their urgent way to a shrine.

Weeks ago they had announced in the media that they were eager to appear at the Inquiry and would gladly answer anything put to them: they wished to end for ever the notion that their acquittals had been wrong. This confidence and generosity enraged people. Scout and Gain knew themselves to be gloriously safe, could not be tried again for the killing of Angela Sabat. Scout and Gain would be entitled to cry 'double jeopardy': that sweet and absolute doctrine which said nobody was done twice on the same charge. Their cooperativeness was seen as crowing, their readiness as mockery. They were alive and free. The system had looked after them. Now, they were ready to look after the system because the system had declared itself powerless to hurt them. *'What's yours, Scout?' 'I'll have a double jeopardy, Matt.' 'Me too.'*

Kerry, an accelerated promotion part of the system, did not like the way it had worked. She wondered whether Vic, another part of the system, liked it. And Harry Bell? She thought he would be concerned most about whether the system could hurt *him*, because he and the system seemed to have failed

Angela Sabat. He was among the crowd somewhere, anxious in case things turned violent and by turning violent underlined how much the system and Harry Bell might have failed Angela Sabat. He was not in charge of the security of the street and the building and Scout Pethor and Gain. That was a uniform job. Harry, plainclothed and would-be unobtrusive, had come to see how bad things might get. It was a kind of facing up, a kind of terror, a kind of guilt, a kind of penance; also a kind of good indicator for Harry as to how seriously he must work at dropping the whole shit vat on Vic Othen, as though Harry hadn't already decided and started working at it. If you told super-intendents they could go fuck themselves, or almost told them, this was the way super-intendents would most likely respond. Even without that provocation, Harry, like all superintendents, would be thinking about retirement and the endearing prospect of a nose-clean pension. In periods of bother, the standard method of ensuring a clean nose was to shove all the dirt up someone else's, preferably an enemy's but, at a pinch, any-body's. At a pinch was where Harry was.

Vic, love, do you deserve this? The question is real, not rhetorical. Did you sterilise the murder site? When you, too, retire, will there be any stars in your coronet, or only thorns? Damned awkward to be in bed with, if we still find each other, in Mrs Sabat's noble term, fuckable. Of course, of course we will, won't we? You'll still be Vic, won't you? I'll still be Mrs Mark Tabor, won't I?

'I've got their faces now,' Christine Sabat said.

'What does that mean?'

'I've got their faces.'

'So you can describe them, in your article?' Kerry asked.

'These are a couple of guys who could kill and not let it get readable in their faces.'

'No, the court said they didn't kill,' Kerry replied. For the record.

'Their *looks* say they didn't kill,' Mrs Sabat said. 'They're really gifted.'

'If you were writing about them here you'd have to be careful what you said. Libel. You'll have to be careful, anyway. The *New Yorker* sells in Britain.'

'If I was asked which of them did it I'd have to pass,' Mrs Sabat replied. 'I mean, looking at the faces. But perhaps they both did it.'

'The court said neither of them did it.'

'And their clothes nice. Formal and nice,' Mrs Sabat said.

'That's for the Inquiry. They've been advised to look orderly and victimised.'

'Both dark. And not tall. A surprise. One could be Jewish, even. Gain Jewish? They don't seem *Master Race* at all. They're men, but like kids – as if they need looking after.

That cop – the one in the Inquiry – the one you juice up for – does he look after them?'

'Look, Mrs Sabat, I'm sympathetic – very – but don't say things like that about a serving detective, right?'

Did Vic look after them? Kerry would want to save him, anyway. But did he?

'Wow,' Mrs Sabat replied.

In the Inquiry today, the same geography first: Pord Corner bus stop, Bale Street, Lakin Street, the building site, as was. Scout, second on, after Gain and saying much the same as Matthew, could help the lawyer, Geddage, about the bus and Bale Street and even Lakin Street. The building site, no, he was sorry, he personally had no knowledge of the building site, except as a place he had, of course, noticed from a distance, but he, personally, had never entered it. And, as to Lakin Street, he and Matthew had certainly gone there that night in search of the girl, the girl being attractive and perhaps datable by him, personally, after preliminaries, or Matthew, but she could not be found. He realised now that she must have been afraid and bolted into one of the many restaurants, clubs or cinemas in Lakin Street. He, personally, very much regretted it if the lighthearted and, indeed, appreciative calls to Angela Sabat by him, personally, and Matt had been interpreted by her as threatening. He could understand how this might be so. This was a very beautiful young black girl on her own at night, and with two rather noisy white men following her. He, personally, regarded the behaviour of himself and Matthew Gain, with hindsight, as utterly out of order and thoughtless, especially given their ages: Scout forty-one, Matthew Gain thirty-two – not youths. They had not tried to think how the girl might regard their attentions. But that was all they were, admiring attentions, expressed in a rough-and-ready, rather boisterous fashion, admittedly, but no harm meant. After all, Scout was married and a father, just on a boys' night out. They did not realise at the time that she was American and, as a foreigner, might feel even more uncertain and troubled.

Yes, he did indeed recall the lady in the car who passed them in Bale Street. Yes, she did appear to show a lot of interest in him and Matthew Gain. He could not be certain why this was so. It might have been the shouting, yes. He did not mind admitting that now. Certainly she might have thought – but mistakenly – that they were menacing the girl. 'But, with the greatest respect, I, personally, I am afraid, thought she was so interested in us because she might be a cruising prostitute, although – no offence meant – so old, because this was an area where prostitutes do ply by car, especially now when, as in London, prostitutes here can be fined if they advertise in telephone boxes.' Had the lady only stopped and spoken to them everything would have been cleared up. They would have gathered immediately that she was not a prostitute, and she would have learned that, contrary to her impression, the two men in Bale Street meant no harm, were merely what is sometimes known, he believed, as 'laddish'.

No, he, personally, had no knowledge of how the police officer, Victor Othen, came to be informed before anyone else of an incident which had taken place in the Bale Street area. How could he have? Yes, he had a brother Philip David Pethor. He did not know whether his brother was acquainted with certain police officers. His brother met many folk in the course of business. With the greatest respect, this was surely a question for his brother, not himself, and his brother had not been asked to attend either the criminal trial or this Inquiry because no connection between his brother and the regrettable death of Angela Sabat had ever been established or even suggested in plain words. No, he had not been in touch with his brother on the night of the death of Angela Sabat, either face-to-face or by telephone or other means. They were close, as twins often were, but they were not in contact with each other every day, and sometimes not for weeks at a time. No, he would obviously not have been able to notify his brother there had been an incident in the Bale Street area, even if he had been in contact with him, because he, personally, did not know there had been an incident and certainly not a murder, the girl having been last seen by him and Matthew Gain entering Lakin Street alive and uninjured.

Having, he hoped, answered all questions with the frankness and fulness required, he would now, with the kind permission of the chairman of the Inquiry, Mr Nipp, and his colleagues, like to announce that he, personally, his brother, P.D. Pethor, and Matthew Gain wished to place at the disposal of the Inquiry a banker's draft for £20,000 to be offered as a reward for anyone who would come forward with worthwhile evidence about the murder, so that the real culprits might be brought to trial.

Scout took a wallet from the inside pocket of his double-breasted grey suit jacket. He put the draft on the table at which he had been sitting for the questioning and pushed it a few inches towards Bertie Nipp and the other tribunal members.

As Mrs Sabat had suggested, Scout looked unmarked by the roughnesses of a rough life. His skin was still childlike, without scarring of any kind. He wore his hair short, but stylishly shaped short, not hard-man short. His eyes were dark and lively and a decent way apart. They could grow friendly and caring. She had watched them do that when he mentioned the banker's draft. He had a straight, small nose, almost delicate, and his chin was strong but in proportion, no heaviness there to draw the face down and make it surly or lumpen. Kerry regarded it as the sort of chin that could wag about efficiently when the mouth was shouting filth at a black girl.

Mrs Sabat sat quietly during the whole of Matthew Gain's and Scout's appearances. That surprised Kerry. She had feared more outbursts. Mrs Sabat was entitled to outbursts, but Kerry would have had to try to smother them, anyway. Nobody moved to pick up the draft. Scout left it there when he returned to the public seats. Nipp and his chums could not touch it. After all, they were running an Inquiry to decide whether, because of police misbehaviour or incompetence, the killer, killers, of Angela Sabat had been allowed to get away. The draft suggested that the killer, killers, of Angela Sabat was, were, still out there and very *other*: not involved with Bertie's big-time Inquiry at all.

Eleven

A week later, Kerry secretly met P.D. Pethor in a stretch of woodland on the northern edge of the town much used for car romance. Of course secretly. She spotted no tail but just in case did all the anti-surveillance drills: up and down back streets fast, and also a couple of fast 360 degrees at roundabouts and back the way she had come. Clear.

Pethor must have switched off the cabin light of his car when he doused the rest and the interior stayed dark as she pulled open his passenger door and climbed in beside him. She adored shadow and entering somewhere unknown. God, the known was so played out once you had turned eight or nine years old. To people around, in the other cars, it must look like an affair, if people around in the other cars noticed anything but themselves. And she did get a bit of a tremor, no denying. All right, tremors were scarce lately, so collect them as and when. She did not think the fact that it was a big Mercedes, this year's registration, especially got her going. Someone running that kind of car wouldn't be woodlanding for his on-the-side sex life. He would take an hotel suite. Car, lateness, seclusion – they set up their own automatic responses in her.

Kerry could not really make him out very well at first, her eyes still used to driving here on headlights: just someone male, bulky, shirtsleeved, unrelaxed, leaning her way a bit in the driving seat, smelling of Boss? She had seen Pethor previously from a distance and on television news and in press pictures. He was middle height, square built, maybe moving a fraction towards fat, with thick, dark hair, his face snub, cheerful, unlined, big-browed. He and Scout were alike, though not identical, and it was P.D. who somehow had cornered the glamour. You would not necessarily see hood in him, any more than Mrs Sabat could see evil in Scout. That's what P.D. was, though. He dealt drugs in a major way, possibly even more major than Ferdy Nate. Like Ferdy, P.D. had been caught and shut away once or twice, though never anything to match the scale of his business. He always came back. The Mercedes helped show how well he came back. He ran other, straight businesses, too, for cover and laundering, again like Ferdy. It was getting to be a standard kind of commercial structure, and they'd be teaching it on Master of Business Administration courses soon.

This general idea Kerry had of his looks

she could now more or less confirm from close to, despite the darkness. He was turned towards her in welcome, smiling, wide-shouldered, his head and hair a few inches under the car ceiling – a sort of John Garfield in that original version of *The Postman Always Rings Twice* with Lana Turner, on TV occasionally – but, say, forty-plus, older than Garfield then. She could not remember ever considering whether Pethor had any sexual pull for her, which probably didn't mean he didn't, only that she could not remember. But climbing into a man's car like this – it was sure to give the question a prod. She could see there might be something to him: even in the dark she could see it, feel it. His voice was warm, though only friendly warm, not colonising. She was alert for that. He knew a lot about her and might think her cheap. She was choosy about who thought her cheap and who she was cheap with.

'Thanks for accepting the venue,' he said, as she closed the door behind herself. 'I had second thoughts afterwards. I don't know whether it offends you to come here?'

'I've been before.'

'Yes? I expect it's—'

'Often. Policing. There are robberies. People stretched out in these cars can be easy meat.'

'Easy meat.'

'They're not always in a state to give chase.

134

And muggers know such folk don't report thefts, because they're not supposed to be here. Plus beatings up. Husbands, boyfriends, wives, girlfriends, freelance thugs come looking. A near killing once. *Two* near killings: the car torched by a wife whose husband had a male tart with him. An old Super Snipe! Remember?'

It scared her and thrilled her to be with him now. This was herself on a solo. She still did not know what it was about, though she had thought and thought since P.D. telephoned her at home one night to fix the appointment. He had said it was a meeting he now regarded as inevitable.

'Oh?' she'd replied.

'Because of how they treated the banker's draft.'

'Ah, that.' Naturally, she had known about it, the full tale – everybody did by then – but hardly understood why he should want to see her, all the same. Never mind, never bloody mind: this was how *real* detection, top detection, worked, and if you were lucky and powerful – but especially if you were powerful – if you were lucky and powerful, interesting, murky people would ring and want to meet you and talk to you in private. Yes, solo. And some of what they talked to you about might be almost accurate and even usable. So, what made P.D. Pethor think she was powerful? And what could be in it for a solo detective? The basic case had come and gone, hadn't it, and could not come again? She had agreed to meet him wherever he liked, just the same – never considered not going.

Mark had taken the call first. 'May I ask who wants her?' he asked, and listened. 'Right. Mr. P.D. Pethor.' He spoke the name to Kerry and frowned. Frowning could make him look like an old map. It always irritated Mark when people other than friends or relatives came through on this unlisted number. He assumed Kerry had been handing it out to contacts. Sometimes Kerry did. But she had never given it to P.D. Pethor, nor to anyone in his companies. P.D. would have his ways. Mark passed the receiver to her, a hand over the mouthpiece. 'Is it really necessary to have one of the Pethors calling here, our home?' Mark liked the word home. He gave it holiness.

'Yes, it might be necessary,' she'd answered, then spoke into the phone: 'Kerry Lake.'

Voice geared to apology, Pethor had said: 'This is an intrusion?'

'Possibly.'

'Forgive me. I felt I had to talk to you, after this ... after this silliness over the banker's draft. I knew I must speak to someone sensible.'

'That's me. That's me?'

'Inevitable.'

'Oh?'

'I hear your name mentioned – nothing but good, nothing. I feel that anyone approved of by Vic Othen must be sensible. And he does approve of you, doesn't he? No question. So he should. It's touching – the way you were so very much *there* for him following harsh Inquiry sessions. This was therapy, no matter what others say. In fact, I refuse to hear it described as anything different. When I learned of that fine gesture do you know what I thought? I thought, this is a girl worth contacting.' He gave a big breath into the receiver, which might have been to signal certainty. 'But I definitely would not expect you to discuss Vic Othen now, while your husband might be in the room.' He went silent. So did Kerry. Then he had said: 'Yes, *silliness.*'

'That's how you see it?'

'Oh, absolutely. A whim.'

But the *silliness* and whim would be regarded by Pethor as more than that, what- ever he said and however he said it. The lightweight words were to make him seem controlled, unhysterical, though on the end of an outright and famous insult: Scout Pethor had received the cash draft back in the post, special delivery, the day after offer- ing it at the Inquiry. This rejection of the gift was efficiently leaked and all the media gave big coverage. Kerry read it in the *Daily*

Telegraph and the local morning paper. She had also glimpsed a tabloid headline at the newsagent's: 'Stuff Your Loot, Scout!'

On the phone she had told P.D.: 'To accept or decline the draft must be entirely a decision for Mr Nipp, the chairman. It's not a matter where an ordinary detective sergeant would have any influence.'

'He *is* still in the room, is he – hubbie? Yes, you just keep talking about whatever seems safe. I'll adjust. Vic's only incidental to all this, and I don't see any further need even to mention him if it is an embarrassment to you. And I can certainly see it might be. An entanglement. I thought a one-to-one meeting, somewhere entirely discreet, for both our sakes?'

'An Inquiry virtually makes its own rules, Mr Pethor,' Kerry replied.

'There's enough controversy already about who talked to whom and when, isn't there?' Pethor said.

'Some sensitivity, right,' Kerry replied.

Yes, a bucketful of sensitivity. As soon as she read in the Press of the returned draft she had realised the Pethors and Matty Gain would spit flame: the refusal pissed on them, calculatedly pissed on them. Wanting to get civic they had been told instead to slide back to their slime pit. This rejection was Bertie Nipp speaking loud from his judgmental soul. This was Bertie Nipp acting pure. But, obviously, the Pethors and Gain would never believe any lawyer knew purity, not *really* knew it, as one might know a friend or a pet; not even if the lawyer had been moved up in his elderliness and grandeur and hypertension to chair an Inquiry. Or particularly if the lawyer had beem moved up in his elderliness and grandeur and hypertension to chair an Inquiry. The Pethors and Gain would regard all Inquiries as politics. And politics and purity lived on different sides of the island and never met except at funerals.

Near the end of that phone call, Pethor had started talking about likely spots for their meeting: 'I don't like those supermarket car park rendezvouses, do you, Kerry – may I? "Detective Sergeant" is so heavy and forbidding – nor do I like dodging around the pillars in dark multi-storeys: *All The President's Men* finished that for me. I'm sure you remember Deep Throat? Deep Throat?'

'A formal letter to the Inquiry asking why the panel rejected the sum might elicit an answer, Mr Pethor, though there is probably no obligation on the members to account for their decisions,' she replied. Kerry had glanced at Mark, held the receiver away from her for a moment and made a boredom face. He did not respond. So, bugger him. The work had to go on.

Her mind had kept busy as Pethor named various possible sites and then dismissed them. Those three must have known it was a risk to offer the cash in public. They had invited open rebuff. There was a kind of mad or desperate guts to it, and a kind of mad or desperate arrogance. People would see the twenty grand as combined bribe, sop, smoke-screen, self-advertisement. But, although the three would have half expected it to be turned down – maybe more than half – Kerry had realised at once that this was not going to lessen their rage and sense of hurt. P.D. Pethor especially would not forgive such a slight. It was a slight projected big and with relish on TV and radio news, front paged in two broadsheets, and prominent on page one or five or seven in all the tabloids and *The Times* and *Guardian*. Probably the whole money had come from P.D., or one of his businesses, and almost certainly would not have been chargeable against tax. This twenty grand was a large and large-hearted gesture, and Bertie Nipp had contemptuously nipped the hand that tried to feed the law and order cause. This was how P.D. would see things.

Yes, but how was *she* concerned?

Eventually, Pethor had grunted with a kind of exasperation and said: 'Oh, look ... I ask myself, Kerry, where and when would two cars parked close to each other not cause much curiosity – where is it, as it were, *normal?* And the answer I get – finally get, and possibly a slightly distasteful one, but I hope not – the answer I get is any area used at night by lovers. There will be some cars standing alone, of course, but also pairs of vehicles, where the relationship entails arriving and leaving separately. That *does* happen, I think. Let's say eleven o'clock tonight at Old Drovers' Lane, shall we? Lord knows how long this bosky spot will be able to resist redevelopment. Don't misunderstand me, please, but are you familiar by any chance with Old Drovers' Lane late at night?'

'Just phrase it as a question to Mr Nipp, not an aggressive complaint, saying that you are baffled by the decision to ignore your donation and asking whether there is some reason for it that you cannot see.' The call could end now. The hooking had been done, her, him. 'Not at all,' she said. 'I am happy to have been of use, Mr Pethor.'

'My car is a silver-grey Merc.'

'Right.'

'These are bewildering times, Kerry.'

She had longed to put the phone down then, but felt he was still not finished. 'Yes, bewildering,' she replied. She enjoyed this word. It brought an echo: their local paper had reported Scout Pethor as saying he was 'bewildered and distressed and, yes, I must admit, a little angered' upon opening the envelope at home and finding the spurned gift. He had explained to the reporter he was naturally expecting a receipt and perhaps a

141

thank you from the Inquiry chairman, or the police or even the Home Office. Instead, Scout told the paper, 'There was no letter with it, no explanation or acknowledgement, nothing. But anyone could appreciate what this communication's message added up to. Its message was, "We don't want your money." Is this the way for supposed supporters of lawful behaviour to behave themselves? I'm afraid I cannot think so.'

The newspaper had let him run and run and Scout went on: 'My wife, Charlotte, and two children, Liz, ten, and Alex, seven, were disturbed at my appearance when I returned to the breakfast table carrying the envelope. They could see from my pallor that I had suffered an appalling shock. Liz asked, "What is it, father?" I replied only that, "In life one must learn to expect setbacks, Liz, dear, even from those one most looked up to and trusted." ' Oh, Liz, ten, how she must have grieved with her daddy.

Still there, on the telephone, P.D. Pethor had said: 'And you're driving a white Corsa these days, aren't you, S reg, the figures 712 or something close? But, look, I wouldn't want you to think we've been watching you.'

'Yes you would,' she replied.

'But why? Oh, to scare you?' he asked.

'Right.'

'This is nonsense, believe me.'

'No.'

'Bell might put surveillance on to Vic and you, but would I?'

'Sure.'

'They won't follow you to this little meeting, will they?' he asked. 'But no, you're too sharp. I'll be there in good time. I wouldn't want you hanging about such a place alone.'

'Right then,' she replied.

Kerry had felt elated. It was the kind of call, the kind of furtive fixing, she had always yearned for, schemed for. She tried not to let Mark see her excitement and pleasure, though. So, why the concealment? Oh, Mark would have been suspicious of Pethor's motives in calling. He suspected any kind of private contact between Kerry as police officer and people like Pethor – either openly crooked or probably crooked but so far never caught. In her earlier days as a detective, several of Kerry's child informants would occasionally telephone. Mark had detested that. He would probably detest it more when the caller was someone dubious and season-ed, like Pethor, someone with a name which smelled so badly since the Sabat killing. It had smelled before, too, but somehow P.D. managed to keep going, and find a place in the outfit for Scout.

In any case, Kerry had known she was more or less manipulated into secrecy by the way Pethor spoke, and by the references to

Vic. She supposed those were meant to get some leverage on her, if any were needed. *Let me tell you what I know about your sex life, Kerry. Absolutely no need for it to go any further. We can have an understanding.* Leverage *wasn't* needed, though. Pethor's approach brought her status. He hoped for something special from her. Perhaps he wanted to move his confidential talking away from Vic and on to someone younger, for the long term. She rated. This she already knew, of course. Of bloody course. But it was good to get it endorsed. She would put up with the mystery of *how* she rated. This was movement. She thought – no, nothing so precise – she *sensed* she might be getting herself tugged into the dark end of the Sabat case, although the Sabat case was nominally closed. Good. Great.

In the Mercedes, Pethor said: 'Advice.'

'If I can.'

'I'm not likely to put up with what's happened, am I, Kerry?'

'Return of the reward money?'

'I could tell you things about Bertie Nipp.'

'This would have been a panel decision, if not higher.'

'I'll remake the offer, but independent of them,' Pethor replied.

'A private reward?'

'With a big launching party, covered by the media, so people know and can respond. See anything against that?'

'Do you think people will come forward?'

'Why not?' Pethor asked.

'They've heard of you.'

'Heard what?'

'Heard of you.'

'I own companies, decent companies. My brother is part of that, properly employed. Is something wrong? You're an expert, so tell me, Kerry, is something wrong about that?'

'Oh, only you're a fucking crook,' Kerry replied, 'the decent businesses a handy show. Your brother could be a killer. Racist killer?'

'No court has ever said so. I haven't been in a court for years. Scout was in a court but acquitted.'

'That could be our fault.'

'Which?'

'Both.'

She could understand why he might refuse to abandon the reward project. When you scraped away all the flim-flam from Scout about shock, broken trust, disappointment, humiliation, image, there was something grim and dangerous for the Pethors and Gain in rejection of their gift. If the twenty grand reward had been officially offered it might have signified that Scout and Matt Gain were now generally recognised as guiltless. After all, the reward nominated that eternally convenient item, *Someone Else*. Bertie Nipp spotted this, of course. True, their trial had already said Scout and Matthew Gain were guiltless, but this did not guarantee public acceptance of it. Bertie or the police or the Home Secretary could have moved matters a step towards that public acceptance, and towards greater physical safety for Scout and Gain, by taking the banker's draft and devoting it to the interests of justice. It had not been taken, it had been instantly chucked out and quietly laughed at, and the suggestion, therefore, must be that the money was filthy and the intention in offering it corrupt and absurd.

So, the Pethors and Gain looked ridiculous. And there was worse: Scout and Matthew Gain might remain targets. Many people – most – regarded Angela Sabat's murder as more than the killing of a girl. For them, it said gross and simple racism. Perhaps they were right. They saw the standard legal apparatus as too feeble and incompetent to avenge that death; or too bent to avenge it. Who would worry if Scout and/or Matthew Gain were found nicely slaughtered? Possibly knocked about a bit before that, too. Well, P.D. would worry about his twin. Was that why he had called and fixed the meeting? He *did* want advice?

'Do you think it's enough?' Pethor asked.

'What?'

'Twenty grand.'

'Enough to what?' she said.

'To bring information, of course.'

'Is there any?'

'I have to hope. We all have to hope,' he said.

'Is the money enough to look real – is that what you mean?' Kerry replied.

'Perhaps others will come in, add to it. That's how some rewards work, isn't it? Several parties. They build and build.' He was excited by the idea and his voice boomed in the high-grade metal box. She saw he was used to success – you bet he was used to success – had the spark and push to make businesses grow, some legit even.

'Is that why you're talking to me? I'm supposed to help get others interested – give cred – because I'm a police officer?'

'Two or three other firms,' he said. 'That's all. Between us we could pile up important coin. Perhaps a hundred grand. I could go to thirty, maybe. To hell with Bertie Nipp.'

'The other firms are to make it seem they believe in you and Scout?'

'They *would* believe in us. That's the point, isn't it? They'd be showing they know Scout is being victimised post-trial by disgusting rumour. Vendetta. Some people loathe our family.'

'I don't know why.'

'Oh, and it would ease things for others, besides Scout, Matthew and me.'

'Which others?' *Which other?* She knew the

answer. Vic. She wondered about him. Perhaps he would have preferred it if the draft had been graciously received and transformed into a reward. This would have helped end the criticism of the police for how they handled the investigation, and the criticism of Vic in person for possibly being in some crook's pocket. Well, no mystery: P.D. Pethor's pocket. Kerry would have to ask Vic his views, wouldn't she? She had not seen him lately, not even around headquarters. Perhaps he was lying low because of the minders, lying low with old-bones Julie, *such* a bracing bloody thought. How could he behave to Kerry like that after the Coronet? Betrayal hurt so damn much.

Pethor said: 'If there are unpleasant rumours about me and Scout it doesn't stop there, does it? You're bound to be concerned for Vic, a fine and complete man even now, and entitled to fade away honourably. Do you know Julie? But listen, Kerry: we float this big reward, it brings in the information we are all looking for, the police make the arrest or arrests – the *proper* arrests, this time – and all the miserable accusations against Vic and against Scout and Matt and against me are shown to be crass and cruel, and Vic can proceed undisgraced, unpenalised to a good retirement, or continue in his extraordinary career. That would be easier for you, too. It's surely more comfortable to run

148

a relationship with someone no longer a subject of slur and evil speculation. I hate to think of some skivvy at the Coronet looking at him out of the corner of her eye. A silver-haired man with a first-class suit and faltering lungs deserves better, deserves courtesy.'

Yes, but do you have a hold on Vic, and did you phone on the night and ask him to check the Sabat death site because you knew your brother was involved up to the elbows?

This was another of those questions Kerry only thought, did not speak. There would be a denial and possibly onward transmission of the question to Vic. But Vic must not think she doubted him. That could drive him even more than now towards the flaking Julie for his support and consolation.

Her eyes had adjusted and she could see Pethor better: 'Hey, have you got a hard-on?' she asked, brushing her knuckles once across the stick-up tepee in his navy slacks. He smiled and tried to look guilty instead of smug. He said: 'Sorry. This kind of place. Perhaps this kind of situation?' He moved minimally towards her, one shirtsleeve about to reach for her arm or shoulder. 'Look, Kerry, I—'

'Get rid of it,' she said, but not touching him again. 'Think of something dulling – hay bales or the Welsh Assembly. It's *not* that kind of situation. Do I fuck villains in a German car?'

'There are all kinds of villains.'

'I don't fuck your kind.'

'What do you do with my kind?' he said, pulling back against the door.

'I listen, because I thought you were trying a bit of strongarm, a bit of blackmail, and I needed to assess. And I listen because every detective ought to have a voice from the sewers, even if the voice is already talking to someone else.'

'Which someone else would that be?' he asked.

'You'd be my first. I'm an informant-world virgin – adults, that is. But I can't help you with the private reward scheme. It's dead mad anyway.'

'Is yours like what they call an *open* marriage?' he replied. 'Doesn't Mark bother? But would the career like it – the double love interest, and one of them another officer? Might Julie make aggro? Met her? She's quite grown up, and possessive and belligerent – the way they are, on the down slope. But you wouldn't know yet, not for ... Well, I'd say not for years. Yes, quite probably years.'

'Nobody's going to bring you any genuine information from outside, because there isn't any.'

'I thought a high-profile presentation of our new reward, you see. I was wondering if your hubbie's firm would cater for the shindig, when we announce. They do a brill liver pâté, I hear.'

'But I do like the notion,' she said.

'Which?'

'Saying "Up yours" to Bertie and the rest.'

Twelve

Kerry went alone to a couple of parties.

P.D.'s bash for the launch of the private reward was done just like that, as if it were a slipway launch: there was the mocked up bow of a ship and P.D. himself swung the bottle of champagne on the end of a red, white and blue rope. As the bottle shattered he declared rousingly, 'I name this ship, *Justice*, and may God and the wonderful British legal system protect all who sail in her.' *JUSTICE* was written, too, in large white capitals on each bow. Applause rattled and kept on rattling for the cameras and press. Pethor had said earlier that he had invited the Queen to perform the ceremony but she'd been too busy, still trying to sort out her family. Although mostly loathsome he could do humour, would make a joke that seemed to mock himself a bit.

Pethor had failed to jack the amount up to

£100,000, but it was £50,000 now, which meant that, supposing he had boosted his own contribution to £30,000, he must have raised £20,000 from sympathetic companies. Or P.D. and his team might have done a bit of leaning. By all accounts he was at least as good at that as at jokiness. Scout and Matthew Gain were present, of course, and the Pethors' wet-eyed parents and many supporters. Splinterface, the pop sextet, played, and Cadence and Wally Katt sang. P.D. Pethor announced that all of them were performing free, 'Their welcome way of contributing to our cause – the cause of justice.' Possibly P.D. had done something for Splinterface and the singers before they were top billing and this was claque payback.

But as she half listened to Wally do his clangorous job on 'Body Hopscotch' Kerry's mind vamoosed for a while to another party she had attended earlier that week. It puzzled her, it alarmed her, it preoccupied her even tonight, as Wally howled and Scout and Matt Gain beamed out upon the crowd, affable and impish and entirely unprosecutable for Angela Sabat's death. This first party took place in what she continued to think of as the blue house: that bleak, pretty rectangle on the trial map showing where Angela Sabat's body was found. A young black man played the piano, really played – delicacy, pacing, some effective quiet bits as well as the required spells of frenzied banging – and not 'Für Elise'. Poulenc?

A man of about sixty, thin-bearded, thin-bodied, thin-faced, and drinking what looked like milk from a brandy goblet, had sneaked up to Kerry and said: 'What I always ask myself about a party is, what is it *for*?' His fingers were next thing to total bone. Perhaps he was trying to build himself up.

'For?' Kerry replied. 'People enjoying themselves.'

'But *for*,' he said. He did a wave with his free, flimsy hand, indicating the clusters of talking, laughing, drinking people, and stared about. There were big abstracts on a couple of the walls, mostly devoted to blue, turquoise and navy rectangles of different sizes, and separated by circles and near-circles in glistening silver-grey. Kerry thought the rectangles were probably mountains, the more circular bits lakes. Possibly the pictures were versions of spots in North Wales or Switzerland. They seemed to be originals, not prints. Had Ferdy turned collector? Or perhaps it was Mrs Ferdy. 'I wouldn't say dangerous, but orchestrated,' the man with the brandy goblet said.

'The piano playing?'

'A concoction – the crowd.' He had a think for a while. 'I said I wouldn't say dangerous, but, yes, on a recount, I would. The death of someone could be arranged here, perhaps more than one. Are you a neighbour, too?'

'Work acquaintance.'

'Of?'

'Mrs Sabat.'

'Oh? Should I know you?'

'Kerry,' Kerry had said.

'I see. Neville. Nev. I met one neighbour already. The lady in powder blue by the china cabinet. She's at a loss. A bit afraid. That's reasonable in a crew like this. Where's her man? This is a real mixture.'

'You're not a neighbour?' Kerry asked.

'When I say what is it *for* – getting the neighbours in would be reason for a party, yes. Introduce oneself to them. But it *has* to be for more than that, some of these faces. And the suits.'

'More how?'

'Those suits are meaningful.' Nev had sipped at his drink, and seemed to ponder again. 'Yes, a mix. I approve. That's what a party needs, a mix. People getting put in touch with other people. That's what I'd say this party is *for*.'

'Most parties are.'

'I don't mean sex – though some of that, I expect. First-class clothing comes off as easily as any other. You lining yourself something up? People do these days. One doesn't necessarily object. But this clambake tonight – more concerned with business. Yes, call it business.'

'What business?' Kerry asked.

'You know about this room?' he asked. 'That's what I mean when I say business.'

'What?'

'This room,' he replied. His accent was educated London, with traces of preserved cockney for democracy's sake. 'People meeting in this room, partying now in this very room, and the mother present. This room gets a message over, wouldn't you say? I can look around this room and spot folk who would hear that kind of message. I think you can, too. Not tear-jerking. Nothing crude. A girl dead in here, yes, and the feel of it still in the air, yes, yes, despite the wallpaper and sapele floor. But not to bring on weeping or a big mourning show of any kind. This is a party, for God's sake. The fact of it, though – of the death: this would get it into the minds of guests here, don't you think? Motivational? More than would happen just by reading about it. And it's a while after, isn't it? Things read could fade. Here, now – a shot of the vivid.' He stuck his head forward over the glass of whatever it was, like a chicken prospecting. 'A drinks trolley is parked on the spot. That's what I'm told – Angela's exact spot. Emblematic drinks trolley, saying that life and boozing go on, regardless. No objection to that. But people notice. They're not going to mention it, except someone like me to someone like you,

155

which is a sort of *privileged* conversation, wouldn't you say? But *they* wouldn't do it, because they think it would be dark and cruel to bring it up. It puts a mark on their minds, however. To the point. My invitation didn't come from the hostess herself but from Christine Sabat.'

'You knew her in London? She spoke of friends there.'

'Colleagues. Rivals, I suppose. She's got a flair.'

'Journalistic?'

'Mixing.'

'Yes.'

'This hostess, Mrs Lydia Nate – Christine establishes good links with her. She's staying in the house now, you know. Mrs Nate said it would save hotel expenses. A good gesture, the house being what the house is. Was. This is why I said business. Mrs Nate would want to help her, and beyond just having her here to lodge. Mrs Nate knows capable people. Her man knows capable people. All right, he's away, but influence can get out.'

'What does that mean – *capable*?'

'Able to handle an assignment. Willing to.'

'What assignment? Help her how?' Kerry asked.

'A function like this is bound to have a *purpose*. It's what gives a party its true groin stir, much more than the pairing off, though, as I said, a quota of that, too, of course. I see you looking around, warming to some. Very inclement types wearing these handmade suits, shit in a crystal vase. Friends of the male Nate, as I say: business associates capable of handling a matter. All right, they're white, but just the same they might do things on the street for Christine if the prompt came through Mrs Nate, which would be the same as coming through Nate himself. He's a honcho. I did some research when I heard where we were invited to. Those boys meet her here, in this room, it's influential. Bound to be. They wouldn't care if the targets were white, not if the order came from Mr Nate, now that his wife's got a sisterly friendship going with Christine. If you have a black wife you'll support things black, won't you? Especially if your wife has a smart and grieving black lady friend whose kid was found dead in your fledgling house. You, personally, like a bit of thug in your men? I can hear it in your breathing. It says, Knock me about a bit possessively – or, at least, Tell me tales of baseball battings in a profitable cause. This is what I'm getting at – the charm of the mix.'

'My invitation came through Mrs Sabat, too,' Kerry said.

'Well, I expect so. She's very American, very all-embracing. It's communal thinking. I doubt whether she knows what's really going on here. No, I'm sure she doesn't. There's a culture divide.'

He began to move away. 'What *is* going on here?' Kerry said, shouting over the Poulenc or similar. He did not stop. She felt pathetic. She was a local cop, familiar with the ground and the people and the room and the house, and this London wizard comes in and picks up, allegedly picks up, all sorts of tremors she's missed, the way a foreigner like Mrs Sabat missed them, allegedly missed them. Kerry could not be sure that what looked like milk in his glass was milk. She could not be sure whether he was drunk or thoughtful. He walked all right and was welcomed into a group on the other side of the room: lots of laughing and handshaking. Would he put the jinx on that laughter by telling them without telling them about the dangers here, and demanding to know the *purpose* of the shindig? Maybe some of the people he had joined now were part of the danger. She could see very fine suits there, possibly handmade, and a couple of the men's faces did look – what were his words? – *capable*, and not too clement. Were they dossier faces? She tried to visualise them above a lengthy printed number, but did not think she recognised any. This was the kind of party many in London would prize – dainty clothes, classy music, ten-for-twopence abstracts, but big, confident. The small stink of crookedness would be relished, and the violent cachet of

158

the place.

The pianist finished and a disc took over. People began to dance. Kerry believed she recognised stuff from Travis's *The Man Who* album, a bit sad-sounding, or at least wistful. That was all right. Perhaps it suited. As Neville said, the room and the house and the occasion and the drinks trolley had some built-in sadness, and, behind one or two of the brill double-breasteds and capable faces, their owners might be feeling, as well as other things, wistful. Which other things? Vengeful? – under the influence of the room and the house and the occasion and the drinks trolley and what came off it. Neville had it right: this *was* an influential room.

Mrs Sabat, brilliant and slim in a pink trouser suit and high, high black shoes, had now edged her way through to Kerry. 'Some party,' Kerry said.

'I suggested to Lydia it would be a sort of peace gesture to ask neighbours who complained about the music – mine – to come in for a drink,' she replied. 'And more music! It's how we'd do things in the States.'

'The man with the milk said it was probably your idea.'

'Oh, Nev. It's not *all* milk. Milk for his ulcers, the rest for him. Yes, the US approach. Maybe the situation needed that sort of simple strategy. And I suggested she ask some of her own friends and Ferdy's. They know a lot of folk. I was sure they'd behave all right. I mean, this room.' She tightened her lips for a second. That was the only sign of pain. 'It speaks, doesn't it?'

'Nev said that.'

'He would. Atmosphere. Journalists are on the watch for it, like a woman for slurs.'

'You, too?'

'Oh, a bit. And then I said to Lydia I'd ask some old acquaintances of mine – Nev, Evelyn, Penny and so on.'

'A mix.'

'Another move in banishing the horrors of this house,' Mrs Sabat said. 'I'm in favour.'

'Nev said he felt danger here.'

'Oh, Nev! He feels danger everywhere. He's searching for it. He's a reporter. So, the ulcers.' She put a hand on Kerry's, took her drink and put the glass on the trolley. 'Let's dance,' she said. 'It's something I need to do. And the man situation – not great. It's going to be tough finding satisfaction tonight. Considered that? Most come accompanied. Lydia's already nailed the only really inter-esting-looking solo guy. Well, not exactly solo. He came with the dame in the powder blue, who's no opposition.'

'By the china cabinet?'

'But Lydia has sort of *worked* on him?'

'Nev said the lady in the powder blue is afraid.'

'I'm afraid she's right to be afraid. Lydia's

moved in there, and fast. Leaving the rest of us rather...'

'There's always Nev,' Kerry replied.

'Nev is sixty, dear. And I hate the smell of milk on a man's breath.'

'Have you run into that a lot?'

'It's like getting yokel-fucked in a Hardy novel.' She started to dance.

Kerry held her arm and made her wait. 'Are some of these people here for you to meet, get to know for business purposes – maybe help you?'

'Which people?'

'The ones in suits.'

'Help me? I told you, they've almost all brought their own women with them. And class pussy some of it. Young. These people in suits know I had a daughter as old as their girlfriends.'

'No, I mean *help* you.'

'Who can help me? Angela's dead. Where the drinks trolley is.'

'Yes, Nev said that.'

'He'd spot it. That's a useful detail. Atmos.'

'For you as well?'

'Maybe.'

Atmos. Later in the week, there was some of that at the Pethor party, too. The occasion was staged in the Ronceval, one of P.D.'s night clubs in the centre. He offered free entry until 10 p.m. to the function, which guaranteed a crowd to look supportive in the

161

TV coverage and press pictures. After the ceremony with the champagne came 'Body Hopscotch' and a couple of numbers from Cadence. Then, as three bar staff with brushes and dustpans gathered the glass fragments, P.D., Scout and Matthew Gain went up into the three-ply version of the sailing ship's bow. It had been put together by Ronceval staff, with mock portholes, mock anchor, trailing ropes, the whole ensemble. The three men had a giant cheque for £50,000 with them, and held it high over their heads and above the gunwale for a while, so people could see, and for pictures. Provisionally, it was made out to ANY LOVER OF THE TRUTH, and signed by P.D., Scout and Matthew 'for and on behalf of THE FRIENDS OF JUSTICE MOVE-MENT'.

Scout made a speech: 'This cheque – I don't say anything against it – well, would I, you'll ask, when I contributed to the fine sum on offer? – but this cheque is not the full tale, nor anything like. We know – *know* – myself, Matthew and my brother, Philip, we *know* that there are many who would wish to help in the detection of whoever killed Angela Sabat. The money – even such an amount as this – the money is of secondary concern. People will come forward with information about that terrible killing, not because they want the reward money, but because they

162

have a love for the law and its honest imple-
mentation, and for fairness, decency and
honour. We offer this reward only as a means
of triggering new thoughts about this awful
crime and, by the amount, try to signify how
vile it was. We have no blame for those who
declined to offer our reward in the first
instance. They have their strange rules, their
odd quibbles. Anyway, they have enabled us
to enlarge the cash available to its present
attractive state.

'Perhaps some folk out there, reading of
this friendly get together tonight, or watching film of it on television, will remember
relevant matters which until now have lain
neglected. May we plead with you, if you do
find you know something, or have heard
something, about the Angela Sabat death,
that you will at once contact the police. We
have a plain-clothes police officer with us
here tonight – Detective Sergeant Kerry
Lake – and I am sure that she will endorse
what I say.'

Kerry nodded. What else? But, Christ, it
made her look as if she were in alliance with
those three – Scout, Matthew, P.D. That's
why Scout had mentioned her, naturally.
Lacking the sexual glow of P.D., Scout came
over now only as someone who could lie,
turn rough, turn gentle, turn civic whenever
one of these or a combination might help
him and his family and confederates.

Laser beams flicked and darted. The music began again. P.D. came down out of the boat and stood with what seemed to be a girl-friend. She was stupendously non-bimbo; white, navy suit, silver cravat, tall, elegant and restless-looking: the way beauties would stare at some distant, unobvious point, as if they knew real life was going on very-else-fucking-where and felt sure they would be absolutely in it, but for the bath mat they were with. The woman had joined in the applause with the rest at due places and, each time, she had afterwards gazed at her ring-less, neat hands as though unable to believe they had been up to anything so showy. These were hands made for lovely china and acme credit cards. And, as to hands, how would she like to hear that Kerry had done a quick car grope of Pethor and that Pethor would have responded, had been pre-responding, and hence the grope? Probably she would flute, 'Really? Vehicular?' Kerry could certainly see how he might pull even a woman of this calibre. His black curly hair clung tight to his scalp and made him seem neat, well-packaged, complete though shortish. He had cheek and resilience and loyalty to his clan. These went some way. No further, though, did they? Did they?

Thirteen

At the Ronceval's buffet table Kerry saw that Matthew Gain wanted some private time with her. 'Aren't I great, great, great?' she murmured to herself. 'I have the gift, the lovely flair that makes folk talk to me and me alone. All top detectives get it.'

'I'm a fool, fool, fool,' Kerry murmured to herself. 'I survey a murder aftermath and until now see only two men, the Pethor twins. Arsehole, there are three.'

In a dead voice whisper, Gain said: 'Come to my parents' house.' He gave an address. 'And, please, don't speak about this to ... don't speak to anyone. They'll kill me. It's in the agenda.'

'Who? What agenda?' Even hoods had learned to speak jargon.

'The reward. All that. Now, for Christ's sake, say something loud and safe about the cheque or the good ship *Justice*. Be open, jolly.'

He must have spotted P.D. and his girlfriend nearing, and Kerry summoned up a slice of public chatter: 'Oh, sure, Matthew, but I thought the three of you looked like a scene from HMS Pinafore.'

'This is Kerry Lake, Susan,' P.D. said. *'Detective Sergeant* Kerry Lake. Despite that, she's had an education. Kerry, you don't know Sue Phelps.' He threw his arms about to semaphore confusion. 'Or perhaps I still haven't got it right and should introduce Kerry as Mrs Mark Tabor. Hubby's a director of our caterers tonight.'

'Really?' Sue replied, unfascinated.

'But, as a careerist, Kerry keeps her own name,' P.D. said. 'That's how it goes, doesn't it, Kerry?'

'Won't you keep *your* own name when you marry, Susan?' Kerry replied.

'Oh, married,' she said. 'I've heard of that game.'

'Kerry may have done something to intercede for us about the catering,' P.D. said. 'I don't *know* but I suspect. Sue, you'd be surprised to hear that not every company would want to take on this function.'

'No, I'm not surprised. I can see that, darling.' She put a long, wholesome smile P.D.'s way. 'You're giving the finger to the system, aren't you, Phil, you and your brother and Matthew? Firms might fear to seem tied up with such a trio. Guilt sticks.'

Definitely non-bimbo.

'Not *guilt*,' P.D. said. 'We don't like that word, do we, Matthew?'

'Well, stuff what *you* like, Phil, Matthew,' she replied, with more of the smile. 'That's how outside businesses would see your launch party. This reward shit. But, all right, maybe it's a giggle, too. You used some influence, did you, Kerry? Phil's won you over to the indomitable Pethor cause, has he? He's good at that. Well, I hope you're grateful, Phil. Fine nosh.'

In fact, Kerry had tried no persuasion on Mark one way or the other. He was ferociously against the Ronceval contract. Mark wanted no business links with villainy. Probably he had it right. But Mark's boss, Stephen Comble, overruled him and all his ferocity. Stephen always went for what looked correct – simple and correct. And what looked simple and correct to him now was that Scout and Matthew Gain had been acquitted after proper process by a British court and were therefore British pure. You couldn't say better. Correctness also told Stephen that P.D.'s offer of the reward was a positive civic act and should not be shunned. It was the private sector helping the public. Mark had been sure to stay away. Kerry said to Susan Phelps: 'Used some influence? Oh, the catering. Only a business matter, after all.'

'There's business and business, isn't there?' Susan replied. 'The reward offer is business, possibly clever, possibly only crafty. I'm not certain. Do I understand it properly? How about you, Kerry? Do *you* understand it?'

Did she? Kerry said: 'I see it as—'

'Does any bugger anywhere really believe P.D. Pethor has suddenly gone all *pro bono fucking publico?*'

'Susan had an education, too,' P.D. said.

'I mean, P.D. Pethor selfless? Selfless! Do I hear right? Do you, Kerry?' Susan stared down towards the other end of the table. 'That genuine caviar, not lumpfish row? Really?' she exclaimed. 'And you're feeding them free tonight, Phil? It *has* to be business.' Susan began to wolf from the table, moving food direct to her mouth, not bothering with a plate or cutlery. She made a kind of gradual, unslackening progress which would take her to the caviar before the club crowd had the lot.

Kerry went with her. Matthew followed. Kerry said: 'What do you do, Susan, or are you—?'

'Or am I what – a subsidised pet for P.D?'

'Are you?'

'Jealous? I teach slow learners,' she said, around the slab of food in her mouth. 'Are you gobsmacked?'

Kerry was but said: 'Why?'

'If people think of me working at all they expect me to be in some frippery job like getting commodity placements in TV drama or flogging superior timeshare.'

'Yes.'

'Mind you, I did say *superior* timeshare. They have the grace to think I'm not total offal.'

'I'm sure.'

'It's lovely work, mine. But some slow learners won't learn.'

'No?'

Matthew Gain said: 'Some will.'

In the morning, when Kerry called at the address he had given her, Gain's mother opened the door and stared behind Kerry both ways along the street. 'By yourself?' she said.

'That's what your son wanted.'

'Yes, but *are* you?'

'Of course.' She had done her anti-minder drill but thought it was superfluous now. They had been called off, off *her*, at any rate.

It was a big, modern detached house in grounds, not just gardens, probably five or six bedrooms, and most likely at least three bathrooms, plus bags of en suites. Mrs Gain was about fifty-two, short, undoubtedly pretty once, tight-mouthed, tight-eyed, burly-to-fat, gentle-voiced, her hair blonded with skill, middle-length, expensively cut. You would not see haircuts like that on a bus. She led the way in. 'They'll execute Matt, you know.'

It was spoken without mania, even without

anger. To Mrs Gain it was the obvious. 'He said the same,' Kerry replied. '*Who* will execute him?'

'You know who, twice,' she said. There was a weariness to her voice now, as though she resented having to explain what should be clear. Did she think Kerry deliberately refused to understand?

But Kerry said: 'No, I don't know. Am I dumb?'

'Maybe. Yes, maybe,' Mrs Gain replied. 'He'll be a scapegoat. Know the Bible? The animal that carried the guilt for the tribe and was sacrificed to keep God sweet.'

'That's ludicrous,' Kerry replied. Was it? After all, didn't she fear the same might happen to Vic?

Mrs Gain led her into a large sitting room. Matthew Gain was already there. The three of them sat down. The furniture was fairly decent repro, the sort of stuff you might see backgrounded in a picture of some very old Hollywood actor posing for an *at home* feature and wanting to look un-tinseltown. Kerry didn't mind it. Mock-old pieces show-ed people despised modern mass-produced, but lacked the tedious gall to go for real antique woodwormery.

Gain said: 'I've told you, Mum, I changed my mind. This is not very bright.'

'What?' Kerry replied.

'Talking to you,' Matthew said. 'You're not

with us, can't be. You'll spill to him.'

'Matthew thinks you're hot for P.D., pants hot,' Mrs Gain said. 'Like all the rest.'

God, people's mothers. They said things so damn straight.

'I watched you with him at the Ronceval after we spoke,' Matthew said.

'So?'

'Some clicking between you?' Mrs Gain asked. She gave it a lot of contempt. 'P.D. does pull.'

'It's nonsense. He was with a beautiful girlfriend,' Kerry answered.

'So? As you'd say,' Mrs Gain replied. 'These things can still go on, underneath the obvious.'

'Susan Phelps picked it up and didn't like it,' Matthew said.

'I've never seen any woman so confident,' Kerry answered.

'I know Sue,' Matthew said. 'I saw her different. Edgy, scared of you.'

'Because I'm a cop?' Kerry asked.

'Because you're a woman,' Gain replied.

'Suddenly Matthew's worried you'll pillow talk to P.D. – making things worse, if they could be,' Mrs Gain said. All at once, she seemed about to break, and for a second Kerry thought Mrs Gain would start to cry. There was a terrible fear in her face. Maybe to give herself some time, she stood and went out of the room, perhaps to the kitchen. She came back immediately with a bottle of white wine. It was as though she would not allow Kerry and Gain a chance to speak privately. That was fine by Kerry. To her, the wine looked plonkish, but she knew nothing about wine and could only make her judgements by the garishness or not of the label. This one was garish. Kerry liked small labels with not much more on them than the name of the wine in plain capital letters, and she would drink that and assume it was good even if it cost £2.99 a bottle. Mrs Gain brought three plain wine glasses from a cupboard and poured. 'Us talking to you – P.D. would see it as betrayal,' she said. 'I believe that risk must be accepted. Time's the thing now. There's not much of it.' Her voice seemed back to matter-of-factness. There were no longer signs of disintegration, only dread.

'No shared pillows,' Kerry replied. 'Not with P.D.'

'Matthew says you're ... well, *active* – liberated, liberal, married or not.'

'It's the buzz,' Gain said.

'Let's keep this talk sensible, shall we?' Kerry replied. 'I don't want my life tooth-combed by you two, thanks.'

'I can see you might be,' Mrs Gain said.

'What?' Kerry replied.

'Active,' Mrs Gain said. 'You've got the face, the body, the raw gleam.'

Kerry thought, Do I put up with this crap?

Oh, let's offer her a bit of what she's looking for, laugh at her: 'I touched his dick once, through clothing. That's all.'

'Ah,' Mrs Gain said. 'Intentional?'

'With the back of my hand,' Kerry said.

'Could you show me?' Mrs Gain asked.

A mistake to respond to her? Had farce taken over? Christ, they were here to talk about her son's possible death, weren't they, not a lust spasm in some sleep-around crook? Kerry moved her right arm in a small arc, knuckles downwards.

'And back again?' Mrs Gain asked.

'I said once.'

'Excuse me, but did he have a hard-on?' Mrs Gain asked.

'That's why I touched it.'

'They're much more inspiring hard. You didn't go further?'

'I was discouraging him,' Kerry replied.

'By touching him up?' Mrs Gain asked.

'I told you, Mother, there's an intimacy,' Gain said.

'Touching, not up,' Kerry said. She grew impatient. 'Look, what's it about – the scape-goating?'

'But he's up already. He gets a hard-on just by looking at you?' Mrs Gain asked. 'This is what Matthew means about things between the two of you, I expect.'

'The circumstances were special,' Kerry replied.

'Of course, they often are,' Mrs Gain said. 'Excuse me again, but ... well, any moisture through the material?'

Jesus, the mad, graphic doggedness. But behind it was true anxiety, a real determination to discover whether Kerry had something going with P.D. and might be part of the move against Mrs Gain's son. 'Knuckling was the end of it,' Kerry replied.

'The special circumstances – locale, time, secludedness – would they have ... forgive me, but might they have allowed you to ... well ... fuck him there and then – supposing you'd craved it?'

'Certainly,' Kerry said.

'And you didn't?'

'What?' Kerry asked.

'Crave it or fuck him?'

'No.'

'Which?'

'Neither,' Kerry replied.

'It would be more telling if you *did* crave it but didn't fuck him, despite the conducive circumstances. It would show immunity.'

'Not if I craved.'

'It would show you can fight it.'

'Sorry.'

'All the same, this *is* promising, Matthew. She may be all right.'

'If we believe her.'

'I think I do now,' Mrs Gain replied. 'Touch P.D.'s dick and get away with it, and when the girl looks made for play, like Kerry! That's so incredible it's got to be credible.'

'Thank you, Mrs Gain,' Kerry said. 'How do you mean, execute Matthew?'

'How do I mean?' she grunted. 'Well, I mean kill him,' she said. 'He's not family, not Pethor.'

'But what would be in it for them?' Kerry asked.

'P.D. won't just ditch his hopes of giving you one,' Mrs Gain replied. She shook her head, weighty with wisdom. 'He'll be back. Touch a man's dick, even through a garment – they'd all see that as a commitment. This is the trouble, if the word's out that a woman's having more than one. Men think availability. God, I had so many sniffing around me when younger. Only a little younger.'

'It won't happen. You can talk to me and it stops with me – not even passed to colleagues if you don't want it.'

'No,' Matthew replied. 'Don't, Mother.' He stood, as if regretting Kerry's visit, as if ending it.

'We've got nobody else, Matthew,' Mrs Gain said, her words like a lash.

'Deal with it ourselves,' he replied.

'You really think so?' It wasn't a question. It was a rebuttal. 'Against P.D. and Scout? You're brave to say it, no question. And mad. There's a scenario here, Kerry. Please see it. Please.' Mrs Gain's face was down into her glass and the final, sad word seemed to bounce out of there with a faint, lingering whistle sound: Pleassssse. The wine was not undrinkable.

Agenda. Scenario. 'Where's the scenario?' Kerry asked.

'In the reward offer.'

'But Matthew's part of the offer.'

'Matthew *acts* part of it. Of course he does. He has to think safety.'

'Where's *Mr* Gain?' Kerry replied.

'You think we need a man?' Mrs Gain said.

'Where is he?'

'Do you want the official answer or the other?' Mrs Gain said.

'Dad couldn't handle it – all this, the trial, press, neighbours turning against us. It might not have been so bad for him if I wasn't still living at home. Christ, *should* I still be living at home? I'm gone thirty.'

Did he want sympathy? Kerry tried everything to restrict that.

Mrs Gain said: 'My husband's on long-term secondment for his firm in New Zealand, establishing a network. Alternatively, he's in a bedsitter in Exeter. The mortgage still gets paid and I have a cheque monthly for Weetabix for two. He's very honourable.'

'Did you kill, help kill, Angela Sabat, Matthew?' Kerry replied. 'Well, of course you did.' She found it nauseating to call him by his first name.

'Matthew could have run a career if he hadn't turned out such a street-level prick,' Mrs Gain said. 'I blame skateboarding. The start. His sister's manager of an arboretum.'

'People superglued into the past,' Matthew said. 'My mother – always talking about careers. Things are not like that any more. OK, my sister knows about trees. Are trees everything? We've moved ahead.'

'Did P.D. get the death site cleared up for you and Scout?'

'They have a different what's called mindset, you see, people of Matthew's age,' Mrs Gain said. 'But if they become a nuisance they can still get their balls cut off and shoved down their throats to choke them to death. Matt's a nuisance to them now. Well, Kerry, you're about his age group, I suppose. How's your mindset?'

'She went cop, didn't she?' Matthew said. 'That's her mindset.'

Kerry said: 'Matthew, last night I thought you were going to warn me against telling Detective Constable Vic Othen about this meeting. "Please, don't speak about this to..." But you backed away. Why? It turned into, "Don't speak to anyone".' It was the only question she really wanted to ask.

'Why should they let Matthew live?' Mrs Gain replied. 'We're dealing with twins here – that mysterious bond. Not just family. Twins. You think they're going to mess about looking after Matthew?'

'I understood there was a bond between the *three* of them,' Kerry said. 'Scout and Matthew from killing Angela Sabat. P.D. from taking care of his brother, which would also mean taking care of Matthew.'

'Don't they teach people in detective academy to think past the obvious?' Mrs Gain replied. She was standing near what was supposed to be a chiffonier, a chiffonier circa 1999, veneer mahogany on top quality filling. Kerry and Matthew had grey-blue armchairs.

'She's leading you on, Mother.'

'That's all right. This way we might get somewhere. The house is not easy to defend. We need help.'

'She can't give it and she wouldn't anyway,' Matthew said. He was built like his mother, squat, almost bulbous, heavy-legged, wrists wide. His voice seemed like hers, too, mild and tentative, though Kerry could imagine its volume upped for yelling hate at a black girl. Kerry could imagine it, too, muttering a bit of late, soft-heart, ashamed comfort as the black girl died. His face was round and fleshy, anxious now and distrustful, a face expecting treachery. If his mother wanted to get him into a career it should be football management or stockbroking.

'The *scenario*?' Kerry said.

'It's grim,' Mrs Gain replied.

Kerry said: 'You mean the Pethors will pretend the reward brings in information about Matthew – for instance, that he did it alone, maybe after he and Scout broke up that night?'

'So you *do* see things,' Mrs Gain said.

'Then the Pethors let the word circulate and suddenly Matthew's found dead, as if by some avenger of a race killing,' Kerry said.

'Very much *as if*', Mrs Gain said.

'And it's unsolvable – too many suspects, all black,' Kerry said.

'That's how it would look,' Mrs Gain replied.

Kerry said: 'The load would be off Scout, off the Pethors both. Scout's no longer a possible target. The Pethor businesses are freed from the slaughter's awkward smell. The Angela Sabat slaughter, that is. They wouldn't catch any from the slaughter of Matthew. They wouldn't be involved, would they?'

'They wouldn't even have to spend any of the reward,' Mrs Gain said. 'They could not disclose where the information came from, could they? Bloody confidentiality. They'd make twenty grand. What firm is going to ask for their contribution back from the Pethors?'

'Do you *know* this?' Kerry asked.

'How *can* she know it?'

'I know it because I feel it,' Mrs Gain said.

179

'Not enough,' Kerry replied.

'It's enough for me. Enough for Matthew.' She lifted her head and put her face on full open view to Kerry, agonised, demanding: 'Save him. He looks like he doesn't deserve it but save him.'

People talk to me, to me alone. I'm great. How do I save the sod? Do I want to save the sod?

'But, Matthew, you – have you real evidence they'll kill you?'

'It's what I'd do if I was one of them,' he said.

'No, that's not evidence.'

'As Mum said, it's enough for me.'

'Would they do it themselves, or hire in?' Kerry asked.

'You can't help at all, can you?' he replied.

'Matthew, don't. We need her.'

'I asked her if she can help, didn't I?' he replied.

'You asked her as though you didn't want it. Will she if she can?' Mrs Gain said. It was spoken quietly, almost throwaway, like a piece of gentle musing.

Kerry asked: 'Were you saying to me at the Ronceval, or *trying* to say to me, that talking to Vic would be the same as talking to P.D.?'

'Was I?' Matthew said.

Fourteen

She wanted to talk to Vic. Well, no, not just talk. Of course not just talk. She wanted him in a car where she had met P.D. Pethor at that dark, woodland, romancing spot, Old Drovers' Lane. It had to be there. The idea grew obsessive, was pathetic, egomaniac, woolly – she knew this. Just the same, she needed something to wipe out the niggling imprint of her rendezvous with P.D.

She felt lowered a bit, sickened a bit, by that nothing encounter now: his insolent hard-on, her brief, knuckle hello to it. Mrs Gain's demands for detail troubled Kerry: *Any moisture through the material?* Prurient? Comic? Sharp? What was she asking – had Kerry been capable of exciting him enough to get his blood really moving? Did Mrs Gain doubt Kerry's attractiveness? Anyway, had she cared, did she care now? She found, yes, she did bloody care a little, at least a little, and this infuriated and confused her. Had some rotten, random corner of her actually fancied P.D. Pethor? You John Garfield, me Lana. Had the girlfriend's radar registered something was on, as Matt Gain suggested? Did Kerry's own radar half pick up a coolness in her? God! So, no mystery that Kerry wanted full-out, jonnock, blazing love with Vic Othen, at the identical piece of parking ground if possible. That might chase off all earlier inconvenient sex shadows.

Would it be no more than making use of Vic? Perhaps. So, make use of him, for once. Everyone used somebody else sometimes. It was not always like that between them, nothing like: they loved each other, regardless of divided interests, and generally knew how to look after each other. Now, though, she required special, quick help. She was ashamed. No wonder lust won a place in the seven deadlies. It had no boundaries, no decency, no fear of the absurd. Never mind: honest adultery would put her to rights. She never thought of seeking consolation with Mark. Possibly she should have. Possibly she wished she could. Mark would not do, though. Sorry, sorry, sorry, Mark.

She did, also, want to talk to Vic about work things, material Mark could certainly not have helped with. This was absolutely secondary, no question, but a factor all the same. She had to discuss what Gain and his mother said. Was Matthew really lined up to be slaughtered in the fine interests of peace – peace for the Pethors? And if he was, how would Vic react? This might tell her things about him which he would never tell her direct, but which she felt entitled to know. The relationship was worth that, wasn't it? Kerry would break from him finally, wouldn't she, if forced to recognise he was corrupt? Wouldn't she? She could put up with the venerable sodding Julie and his age and ciggies and occasional poncines about his clothes and hair, but not corruption, could she? Vic offered all sorts of other lovely things, obviously, or why had she wanted him and sort of stuck with him? But corruption would annihilate all this, wouldn't it?

Wouldn't it? She was not as certain as she occasionally liked to think, and maybe *ought* to think. In the back of her car now, both of them naked except for his black silk-and-cotton mixture calf-length socks, she felt a brilliant, uncompromising tenderness towards Vic, and she knew part of it came from the suspicion that he might be weak, fallible – corrupt. If he was, he would be needy, wouldn't he, and she knew about needs, could sympathise? God, had she started to get motherly, motherly to someone nearly twice her age? A man bare except for longish socks was always going to look pitiable, even in the near dark of the car. But her feelings for him were not sock-based, went much further than that. Her feelings were also different from when she had rushed him off to the Coronet after that torrentially shitty

183

Inquiry day. Then, she had simply thought he needed reminding in the best way she could manage that life was more than being clobbered. The best way she could manage was love, mind love, bed love.

Now, her head hard against the door, feet touching the car ceiling for angle and depth, and the corner of a radio cassette jabbing her behind, she wanted to take and take, *was* taking and taking, but longed to give as well, *was* giving. This was where a rigid dick ought to be, not under trouser cloth. Vic's, anyway. It wasn't something to be hedge-hopped with the back of a hand, it had to be welcomed and niched, and not at all required to leave early. Vic's, anyway. She brought her feet down so she could fold herself around his hips, donate Vic a leg cuddle that would tell him he was forever prized and never alone, and never linked only to the cobwebbed Julie, either, no matter how heavily he had fallen into dirtiness, if he had. There were some impulses you did not hinder, because one day they might start failing to turn up.

Vic had been doing something with a body wash around his chest and shoulders, a pricey body wash, most probably, with a refined, lemony edge to the smell. This gave no real opposition to the Marlborough breath, but to try seemed a loving and lovable gesture. There were moments like this when she knew she would never break

184

from Vic and *could* never break from Vic. Knew? More or less. Was pretty sure, at present, anyway. She lunged up at him with her mouth and bit his upper lip. The moustache would hide from Julie any damage, and so fucking what if it didn't? God, there had been a time when she rarely swore, not word, not thought. Perhaps it was a restraint she'd automatically adopted for dealing with child informants. Occasionally, this self-control had broken down even then. It hardly operated at all now. She was playing with the big boys and girls.

If his moustache failed to conceal the teeth marks he could say a stroppy prisoner had been at him. They did bite sometimes, especially if they were handcuffed and couldn't hit you. Shags in cars were not the sometimes decorous joinings of the double bed. You had to expect savagery. *He* had to. And he could dish it out, thank God – to Julie as well, the bastard!

'You're not bleeding,' she said.

'Have another go.'

'No, it's a one-off. Otherwise it interferes with the rhythm. I want the rogering rhythm.'

'So why bite?'

'Sometimes I want to bite more than I want the rhythm,' she said. 'The biting is to show I'll always be here for you and sod what they say about you.'

'Who?'

'The polity.'

'Do I know them? What do they say?'

'The biting is a sort of territory thing,' she replied, 'like a cat cocking its tail up.'

'I'm your territory?'

'And I'm yours.'

'I didn't bite *you*.'

'You're fucking me.'

'I thought *you* were fucking *me*,' he said.

'You're not seeing it from where I am, or feeling it from where I am.'

'I'll accept that,' he said.

'No, *I'll* accept that.'

'Graciously.'

'Can you shut up now? I want to concentrate.'

'I like it when you concentrate. I can feel it.'

'Where?' she asked.

'In my liver, sphincter, scalp, elbows, earlobes, cock.'

'That's a start.'

'I—'

'So, shut up, will you? Just keep the joy going, the unparallelled love going. And no dopy puns about not going but coming.'

'Coming will come.'

'Only in due course,' she said.

'Certainly.'

'This is a big plus from your being old.'

'I see it more as mature.'

'If you like,' she replied.

'And widely experienced.'

'Fuck you, Vic.'

'Yes, you do. So shut up. I want to concentrate.'

'I can feel you concentrating,' she said.

'Where?'

'Liver, sphincter, scalp, elbows, earlobes, cunt.'

'Good. Never think of that as passive.'

'I don't.'

'Always it's full of alertness and instigation.'

'You're telling me?' she replied.

'We must be made for each other.'

'We are, but we're with someone else.'

'I'd noticed that,' he said.

'So shut up, just love me, Vic, and send the sweet, moist signal.'

'Only in due course,' he said.

'Certainly.'

'Now.'

'Is that a question?'

'No,' he yelled.

'No, all right, then, all right, really all right.' And then, after a while, she said: 'No, it wasn't a question, was it?'

They didn't dress, but she leaned over from the back to the ignition and started the engine, then put the heater on. Vic, watching and drawing enormously on a cigarette, said: 'Some arse.'

'The car's designed to show it off in this

type of situation: listed in the literature as standard, not an extra.'

'I'll fax them to say it works, given the right arse, of course.'

'They're not.'

'I am,' Vic replied.

'You know how to appreciate.'

The darkness outside was pretty good and, apart from Vic's Peugeot, there were no other vehicles really near. Vic had said at the start that he had ditched the minders. The Peugeot would give her some cover. Kerry went out and brought a hamper from the boot. She felt a little rain on her shoulders and back, and it was very chilly. Mud tugged at her feet. They picnicked on the rear seat with wine, scotch eggs, prawns and bread. 'Why here?' Vic asked. She had made a point of bumping into him at headquarters and told him the place and time.

'People at the Coronet may have been asked to give Harry Bell a call if we turn up there again.'

'Yes, but why *here*?' Vic said.

'Ambience.'

'We deserve better.'

'We do, but we're not going to get it, yet,' she replied.

'Down among the young motorised lovers – I'm being rejuvenated?' he asked.

'You could do with that.'

'Bollocks. I can teach them things.'

188

'About sock styles?' she said.

'We deserve better, but it was lovely, is lovely. I've never felt so close.'

'I wanted that, the closeness,' she said, and fed him a couple of the more runtish prawns so as not to breed greed and a gut.

'Closeness is always going to be there.'

'I think so,' she said.

He chewed for a while and she was aware of him peering at her face off and on. 'But some part of the job is slaying you, yes?'

'It can't make a difference between us, Vic.'

'I expect it can,' he replied.

'The reward,' she said.

'You're afraid they'll use it to do Matthew Gain?'

'How come you know this idea's around?'

'I hear ideas that are around. It's my main flair,' he said. 'How did *you* know about it?'

'Are you still talking to P.D.?' she replied.

'He told you?'

'How do you mean?' Then Vic did a fair imitation of Pethor's thick tones. She could make out prawn carcass on one of his teeth. ' "Oh, Vic, I'm going to fake some anon info via the reward and subsequently get Matthew nicely dead because the tip will be that he's the only killer and therefore liable to end up tit-for-tat killed by person or persons beautifully unknown." '

She laughed, then said: 'Yes, all right, crazy.' But she wanted to howl at him those deep-down, shattering, intimate, unintimate questions. Did he take from Pethor, work for Pethor, swap good turns with Pethor for informant services given? Did Vic clear up little problems for Pethor and his brother, little problems such as evidence around the Angela Sabat death site? Was he into the reward project with P.D. because it would put things right for almost everyone, including himself, though not Matthew Gain? Wasn't there about the reward offer and the uses it could be put to a cleverness that might be beyond even P.D. and would require the brain and long-career know-how of someone like Vic? There was no one like Vic. So, all right, the brain and long career know-how of Vic, then.

But she found she could not speak such thoughts. Yes, she was entitled, but she still could not. Tenderness blocked them, and she was glad. It proved the job had not quite swallowed her yet. Questions like those would destroy something she had just said with delight was sure to go on and on, and which she believed would go on and on, despite that age-match piece he had living in at home. How could Kerry tear the essence out of someone who had made engulfing love with her minutes ago and who sat now with her naked, or as near as damn it, huddled and trusting in the back of a small car, gloriously sharing a symbolic common crust and a plain-labelled bottle of Oz red which had cost almost the full fiver and tasted distinguished even in plastic cups?

'No, I don't talk to P.D. any longer,' Vic said. 'I couldn't. It's been blown that he voiced to me, hasn't it?'

'Voiced to you about what?' she asked.

'About crimes, actual or intended.'

'About the Sabat death immediately after?'

'Not that. He'd know I wouldn't help.'

'Would he?' she replied.

'There's more than one voice who talks to me,' he said.

'Is there?'

'P.D. talked to me, when he did, about the general picture. So, he's probably in more peril than Matthew Gain ever will be, and from more directions.'

'Could you fuck me again?' she replied. 'Now.'

'Is that a question?' she asked.

'No,' he said, pushing the food débris and the bottle on to the front seat out of the way.

'No, it's not, is it?' she said.

Fifteen

No phrase from Harry Bell's mouth necessarily meant what it seemed to say. No phrase from his mouth necessarily meant anything actually definable at all. As an undergraduate before she joined the police Kerry had learned about something called subtext. Although she had forgotten most of the academic froth that went with it, she recalled the essentials. You examined a piece of writing or chat and tried to work out what was *really* being said, not by the words but behind the words: before jargon boomed, people used to call this 'reading between the lines' and 'nod, nod, wink, wink'. Well, Harry Bell's talk was often all subtext. Perhaps the talk of every superintendent or above was likely to be all subtext.

But, instead of this now being a harmless little university conundrum, she knew Harry's subtexts might be about a possible future death – possible future *deaths* – on this manor, plus some deeply unwanted disclosures about herself. Kerry could have done with a tutor-guide to help her through the massed unspokens of this one-to-one meeting with Harry in his office. There was a doctorate for somebody in making Harry intelligible – and accountable later if things went wrong because of what he had said. Or not actually *said* but had *seemed* to be saying. No somebody was around, however. Any decoding she had to do herself. And, of course, people like Harry could protest afterwards that your decoding was totally haywire if shit flew because of it. Perhaps Staff College had a special course on The Ancient Art of Evasiveness and Keeping Your Nose Clean. One day she might find out. *Did I say that, Kerry? Truly? I don't think so.* This was the simple, clear beauty of subtexts: subtexts might mean all or absolutely fuck-all, and who could say which, when?

'I've spoken to our lawyers, Kerry,' Bell began. 'We can't stop P.D. offering the reward. He doesn't even have to do it via us. P.D. would have got the nod from his own lawyers, naturally. This means any information will go to him direct in the first place. Then he passes it on, if it suits.'

Kerry said: 'There can't be any information, can there, sir? Those two killed Angela Sabat. We know pretty well *how* they did it. Can anyone come forward with new material?'

'Well, quite. Of course, of course. And yet, Kerry...'

'The court says the opposite.'

'The court tells us these men are innocent. We have to listen, we even have to concur, or where is the absolute respect we owe our British legal heritage? We are police officers. Not to be naive or ponderous, but we live by the law, or by nothing. If *we* do not give such respect are we not inviting chaos, inciting chaos?'

'Courts mess up sometimes.'

'Certainly. But we require another court to tell us that, don't we – the Appeal Court, the House of Lords, the European Court, the judgment seat? You could argue that this sounds quaint – one court may have shown itself fallible, so we assume the next court we ask is *in*fallible! Yet this has to be the system we live by or we have *no* system, no civilisation.'

'Do *you* think we'll get anything new on Angela Sabat because of the reward, sir?'

'I believe an open mind is called for, as in so much police work, Kerry.'

'If information does come, it might be provided to P.D. on a no-names-for-disclosure basis.'

'Certainly.'

'That means P.D. could manufacture the material himself. He doesn't have to produce a source,' Kerry said.

'Right.'

'We—'

'Naturally, I've heard the theory that Matty Gain might be set up for a revenge hit by spreading rumour based on a make-believe tip,' Bell said. 'One of the reasons I wanted to see you this morning. Likely, do you think?'

'Possible.'

'Was it spoken of at the Ronceval launch party?'

'No.'

'No. An idiotic question. Who's going to mention something like that? But you *had* heard it?'

'It's around.'

'What *did* you hear at the Ronceval?'

'Not much. The public pieties.'

'You met P.D.?'

'Briefly.'

'A charmer, isn't he? The hair and eyes. Women get wowed, I gather, despite everything. Lookalike of some long-gone toughie film star? Not Bogart or Edward G. Not George Raft. Hang on, I'm getting there. In the earlier version of *The*—'

'P.D. was with his girlfriend. Very lovely.'

'I expect so. I don't suppose it would matter.'

'How do you mean, sir, matter?'

'Whereas Scout lacks most of that, I'm told – the glow and pull. And yet a twin. Remarkable, really.'

'I expect Scout concentrates on killing blacks.'

'Garfield, James Garfield? John Garfield?'

'No, don't know him,' Kerry said.

'Too early for you, I expect, although he turns up on TV. Explosively sexual.'

'Is that the one who plays Sonny Corleone in *The Godfather*, the one with the big dick who satisfies a bridesmaid against the bathroom door?'

'That's James Caan.'

'Sorry.'

'I wondered if P.D. spoke of Mrs Sabat,' Bell said.

'He's not likely to know her, is he, sir? She wouldn't want contact.'

'That's why I mentioned his charm. A bridge, maybe.'

'Used on Mrs Sabat? Oh, I—'

'Have I been stupid, insensitive? Sorry, Kerry. Jealousy's a horrible feeling, I know.'

'Jealousy? For God's sake, Mr—'

'Mrs. Sabat's still young enough, isn't she, as I recall her?'

'For what?'

'To look around. To respond. This is what I was saying about P.D. being able to get to women who on the face of it should hate and or despise him. Sex simplifies a lot of situations, Kerry, and complicates them. Well, who am I giving lessons to, for heaven's sake! P.D. is certainly active. He gets down to Old Drovers' Lane at night in the Mercedes. You know Old Drovers' Lane, of course – what it's used for. All sorts there. I'm not saying Mrs Sabat. Good Lord, no, I'm not saying that. But all kinds of other unexpected folk. Class, job, marital state no bar – especially not marital state, or people wouldn't need the secrecy, would they, Kerry? And yet why do I say unexpected? Anyone can crave a bit of outdoor passion and a midnight picnic in the buff. But, no – not Mrs Sabat. Not at this stage. I was wondering only whether some sort of contact between them.'

'I don't think so. Why?'

'She's a journalist and is thinking about writing on things here. Wouldn't she have to talk to everyone? As a mother she might not wish it, I agree. But she's not *only* a mother. P.D. is part of the tale. And so, perhaps, she will meet him or has met him already to ask questions, soak up some impressions. Does she find that one of the impressions she's soaked up is of a successful, nicely dressed, apparently amiable, attractive young man?'

'I don't—'

'Then, as part of this new friendship or more, he might whisper to Mrs Sabat what he has heard, allegedly heard, from reward chasers about Matthew Gain. *It was Matt what done it, Mrs Sabat.* This would help him two ways, wouldn't it, Kerry? First, it clears his brother and therefore makes P.D. altogether sweet in her eyes as well. People don't like to be thought badly of, even people like P.D. Second, we know, don't we, that Mrs Sabat has built a nice friendship with Ferdy Nate's lady? This may be why P.D. accelerated the reward offer. It seemed to come very suddenly, wouldn't you say? P.D. is probably scared of Ferdy, even though Ferdy is locked up. Many are scared of Ferdy. Most are. As we know, he has notable friends outside. Wasn't there a party where a lot turned up? So, do we get a procedure like this: P.D. tells Mrs Sabat what the unidentified voice or voices have revealed to him about Matthew; Mrs Sabat tells Mrs Ferdy Nate; Mrs Ferdy Nate tells Ferdy about her new chum's terrible grievance against Matthew Gain; Ferdy puts out an order or two; Matthew Gain is hit – a killing more or less undetectable because the person, persons, who do it will have no previous connection with Matthew, no special motive. My view, Kerry, is that if someone deemed trustworthy and with an open ear called on Matthew Gain and his mother they would describe to her, or him, a fear very much along these lines. What do you think?'

'I—'

'And, more importantly, what do we do about it? I'd be *so* reluctant to start treating Mrs Sabat as a possible accessory to murder, wouldn't you? Hasn't this poor woman seen enough suffering? I don't want to chuck more harassment at her, do I? And on what basis could we act? I've given you what I regard as a very credible bit of speculation. That's what it is, though – fancy. I don't see what I can do, merely because Matthew Gain is afraid, supposing he is. We don't know this, since nobody has spoken to him that I'm aware of. And if I were to start making moves which depended in part for their justification on P.D.'s drawing power over women, I'm going to have to outline to the Chief or the Deputy the rather grubby history of a place like Old Drovers' Lane, and I don't know whether any of us would want that, would we?'

Sixteen

Decoding Harry. Kerry tried to do some of this while he was talking and then more later, when she could think quietly and without the need to watch her defences. Of course, when he was talking she had the actual words. Later, it was a memory job. She took no notes, made no recording: you did not go wired up to meet your boss. But her recall had always been good.

'I've spoken to our lawyers, Kerry. We can't stop P.D. offering the reward. He doesn't even *have to do it via us. P.D. would have got the nod from his own lawyers, naturally. This means any information will go to him direct in the first place. Then he passes it on, if it suits.'*

To anyone who did not know Harry and did not know the situation right through, that might have sounded like a sad admission of defeat: P.D. had worked a coup and Bell saw no way to counter it or recover. But Kerry thought she detected also a slice of satisfaction in Harry's analysis. He wanted the reward to be offered, didn't he, and wanted all the results that might come from it? The standard police reaction to such a brazen ploy by P.D. was naturally bound to be stern disapproval, and Harry's words formally gave that. At the same time, she suspected he was saying but not saying, 'Thank God we can't stop him, Kerry.' His large, usually benign-looking face appeared haggard and frustrated as he spoke. Harry could do special effects. Kerry had seen them before. He ought to be in amateur dramatics.

'Naturally, I've heard the theory that Matty Gain might be set up for a revenge hit by spreading rumour based on a make-believe tip. One of the reasons I wanted to see you this morning. Likely, do you think?'

The gorgeous essence. What did Harry want her to answer? She had said 'Possible.' Would that do? On the face of it he was asking whether she thought Matthew Gain

200

should be protected. That might be a proper official police response to the rumours. Gain was a citizen and like any citizen entitled to be kept safe. But Matthew Gain dead and blamed for Angela Sabat's killing would resolve a lot of dismal aftermath for Harry, woudn't it? A kind of justice would have been done – a wild kind and an uncheckable kind. Allegations of a police cover-up because of P.D. Pethor's rough influence would no longer have the hellish edge they had now, because no Pethor would have been involved in the Angela Sabat murder.

It had always been part of Scout Pethor and Matthew Gain's defence that they left each other shortly after losing Angela Sabat up towards Lakin Street, but left each other to go home. Was it possible that Gain had not gone home immediately, but somehow managed to locate Angela Sabat, on his own, and had been spotted with her by P.D.'s eternally undisclosable source? Was Gain the kind who would by himself kill a girl for no apparent motive – not sex, not robbery, but just because she was black? He might be racist, probably was – they had done some background on him and Scout before the trial, of course – but this didn't mean he would turn solo killer. It was laughably flimsy evidence against him, if there were any question of bringing Matthew to court now. There was not. He had been before a court and was acquitted: Gain and Scout sailed in the magnificent, unsinkable vessel *Double Jeopardy*, not the vessel called *Justice*. And, in the scenario that Harry might have in mind, Matthew would be safely revenge-dead, anyway, and unable to come up with contradictions. There would be some sort of absolution for Harry, in time for his retirement. And some sort of absolution for Vic, in time for his: even Kerry could feel the attractions in that.

'Garfield, James Garfield. John Garfield.'

Of course, throughout almost the whole of their talk, Harry was indicating that he knew about her trips to Old Drovers' Lane. Perhaps she had been stupid to think she'd dodged the minders. And perhaps Vic had been stupid to think *he* had. There was a further possibility, and a terrifying one. How would it be if Pethor had carefully picked that rendezvous spot, despite all the apparent dithering, and then breathed a word about it in the right direction, Harry being very much the right direction? There'd been no sex to speak of, not with Pethor – naturally there hadn't been – but if you were in a car at night with a man at Old Drovers' Lane, it could be made to look as if you had a case to answer, and that's how Harry made it look. He was telling her Pethor excited women and that if she was pulled it would be very understandable. She thought she'd spotted the

202

resemblance to John Garfield for herself. But others must have noticed it, too.

And so, because she could see the way Harry's talk was going, she denied even having heard of Garfield. To admit she saw the likeness would have been to admit she recognised P.D.'s dark glamour. Harry was telling her, was he, to keep quiet about the rumoured dangers for Matthew Gain in the reward offer, or her unkempt love life might be given some exposure? She had not disclosed that she had seen Gain and his mother, because Gain wanted it confidential, and Kerry wanted it confidential herself. Private knowledge could be an asset. But this knowledge clearly was not private. Somehow that visit had been logged by Harry, too.

As to the rest of what Harry said she did not know how much of it, if any, might be feasible. Was Mrs Sabat implicated in the stage-by-stage scheme that might bring Gain's death – Mrs Sabat, Lydia Nate, Ferdy Nate, one or more of Ferdy's hard lads? Did Kerry swallow this? Had she really given some twitch of jealousy when Harry suggested P.D. and Mrs Sabat might have something going? Oh, God, no. Surely not. Had Harry mentioned Mrs Sabat's possible involvement as another way of telling Kerry to do nothing to hinder or reveal the progress of things? Perhaps he was sincere when he said he dreaded having to harass Mrs Sabat. Yes, perhaps. Perhaps he thought Kerry would share that considerateness. Perhaps, too, Harry truly accepted as he'd said that if a court had declared two men innocent they must be regarded as innocent and the search kept going for those who did the crime they were cleared of. Yes, perhaps. It was the usual thing when Kerry tried to decode Harry that she felt more confused, troubled and frightened at the end.

Seventeen

Two bullets, they thought, possibly three, though they had not found the third yet. One clipped the face from the left, taking most of it away and spreading it on the wall. In what remained, all the neck bits were on show and the top of the spinal column. The other shot smashed a water bottle which was still dripping slowly when Kerry arrived. The third, if there was one, might have gone into the shed structure somewhere, or anywhere in the garden; perhaps even anywhere in next door's garden. Kerry, Vic Othen and Harry Bell went together to talk to people in adjoining houses.

One neighbour said she had heard 'three

rapid bangs, like a Chinese New Year fire-cracker on TV'. Her partner said she had been asleep and was awoken by 'two explosion-type noises, but I might have missed one or more of them while unconscious'. Both admitted they had always been anxious about living next to Scout Pethor, though he had never behaved anything other than courteously, which made a change from some.

Harry Bell whispered to Kerry in obvious confusion over the death: 'Christ, where does this come from?' She tried a bit more decoding. Might it mean Harry considered a proper, laid-down scenario existed for any future violence and that it involved Matt Gain as objective, not Scout? For God's sake, Scout was supposed to be a beneficiary. Did this killing show Harry that serious, un-accounted-for forces operated who did not know about the plans, or who knew about them but did not care? That was more likely and more alarming. Did Harry suddenly see terrible symptoms of that chaos he had talked about the other day? Would it turn out that there was no nice, convenient system to play along with, after all? Instead, he heard of 'three rapid bangs' or 'two explosion-type noises' and an utterly unscheduled, bloodily messy, instant slaughter. Not even the number of shots could be agreed on. This really was breakdown.

'Were you sleeping together?' Vic asked the neighbours. He spoke it tentatively, delicately.

'Pardon?'

'If you were in different rooms the sounds might seem different,' Vic said.

'Together,' the small, thin woman replied. Her dark hair was cut gamine. She wore a cheap-looking floral dress, like a child's. She was enjoying the excitement and her eyes dodged about between Kerry, Vic, Bell and the other woman as if seeking the one with the most to thrill her. Kerry thought the time given each equalled out.

'Possibly you're a lighter sleeper than your friend and were woken earlier,' Vic said. 'Any sounds before the shots – say someone, or more than one, moving about outside? Possibly even a voice, voices. This might have been what woke you.'

'Voices?'

'Conceivably,' Vic said. 'If there was more than one they might have spoken – guidance – moving about in what could be strange territory in the dark. It might be useful.'

'This was quite early to be in bed and asleep,' Harry Bell said. 'Before eleven p.m.'

'We don't keep late hours. Marj and I both have to be up at six a.m. for work.'

'I'd take the day off,' Vic replied. 'The night's half gone.'

'And when you heard the two or three shots

what did you do?' Kerry asked.

'Well, I didn't think at once, or even at all, at that stage, *shots*,' Marj replied. She was in a long denim skirt and denim waistcoat over a black T-shirt. You'd expect beads with an outfit like that, though possibly not at two a.m. after being roused from sleep. Her voice was clipped, careful. About the same height as the other woman, she was heavier, squarer. They would both be in their late twenties.

' "Explosion-type noises",' Kerry said.

'Shots is not going to be the first thing one thinks, is it, in a fairly quiet street? Even living next door to Mr Pethor and in the present situation,' Marj said.

'Situation?' Harry Bell asked.

'Well, I wouldn't say this if he were here, obviously—'

'No, he isn't, obviously,' Bell replied.

'Many still blamed him for the girl's murder, didn't they, despite the not guilty verdict?' Marj said.

'I've heard some did,' Harry replied.

'There was talk that he and the other one might be – well, talk they might be targets.'

'Really?' Bell replied. 'Targets? Vengeance targets, wholly illegally?'

He meant, didn't he, did he, that *one* of them might have been selected as a vengeance target, he would go along with this, endorse this, but not Scout, for God's sake, or where was system, civilisation?

'Marj woke up and I think we lay there for a while, just listening.'

'We did, Simone.'

'We both had an idea something was seriously wrong, but we did not know how, what,' Simone said. 'No, I don't believe either of us was thinking gunfire, at that stage, although I'd always—'

'We were quite used to some noises from Mr Pethor's garden late, of course.'

'Oh, yes, if we heard movement out there, or someone opening the shed, maybe, it would not disturb Marj and me, or even wake us, because it's normal, you see,' Simone said.

'Sometimes he would be quite late feeding them,' Marj said. 'I'd hear him walk down the garden, and then the thump, thump, thump of their back paws, sort of beating them, because they were excited about getting the food.' She was seated on a chair at the side of the bed and illustrated the sound by banging her heels on the carpet insistently seven or eight times.

'After the shooting?' Kerry said. 'We'll call it that now, because we know that's what it was. Noises then? People running? Any shouting?'

'Some shouting later,' Simone said.

'How much later?' Kerry asked.

'A few minutes,' Simone replied.

'Minutes?' Vic asked. 'Not seconds?'

'It would be minutes, yes,' Simone said.

'Yes, minutes,' Marj said.

'This is when we got out of bed to look from the window,' Simone said.

'Both of you?' Harry asked.

'Support,' Marj said. 'We were really anxious by then.'

'You had to walk across the landing from the front bedroom to this one at the back to look down on Pethor's garden?' Vic said.

'We didn't put any lights on,' Marj replied. 'That's what I meant, support.'

Kerry had a vision of them edging their way to the rear of the house in darkness, holding hands, Simone probably in front, scared but curious. Naked? Nightdressed? She thought of the two women as brave. Was that patronising? Did she pity them for the absence of a man at the time? This would be gross. You never knew when your prejudices would pop into the open.

The lights were on now. Vic said: 'So, the two of you get to this rear bedroom window and are looking down. What do you see?'

'Hey, all at once I recollect,' Simone said.

'Yes?' Vic said.

'Yes, I was puzzled, I mean really, really baffled, trying to work out how I knew your face. You're the one who was in the press and on TV re the Sabat case, aren't you?' Simone replied. She was pointing at Vic with the index fingers of both hands like a two-gun cowboy. Maybe this needed some decoding, too. Kerry thought she heard there a question beyond the one asked. Perhaps Simone wanted to discover how a detective who was under inquiry for his behaviour on the night of that murder – the start of 'the situation' – how this detective could still be working on aspects of the same 'situation'. She said: 'Do you know what I think, I think it was you who found the black girl's body.'

Kerry said: 'Someone who knows a case from the beginning is—'

She had been going to say 'priceless', but turned it into 'irreplaceable'.

'Absolutely,' Harry Bell said.

'Does it bother you?' Vic asked.

'No, no,' Simone replied. 'Just an, as it were, observation. Entirely.' And that, Kerry thought, meant, One cop is as bad as another. I wouldn't trust any. Kerry could understand this: didn't she wonder herself about Harry, was not even sure how Vic would be feeling about this attack on a Pethor.

The five of them were in the back bedroom of Marj and Simone's house. Kerry, Vic, Harry and Simone had grouped at the window. Marj left her chair and joined them and they all looked down at Scout's back garden and the big wooden shed. It was just after two a.m. Kerry, Vic and Harry Bell had

210

been out there a couple of hours ago and, even in the darkness, Kerry had seen that the garden itself was beautifully tended and arranged, shortest flowers in the front, tallest at the back. There was a rectangular cement pond where the water looked very spruce, and a curved patio with tubbed plants on it up near the house.

'The door of the shed was open and the electric light on in there, like now,' Marj said, 'but at first I could see nobody.' Then she split the word, with a central pause: 'I mean no body. And nobody.'

'We watched for a while and still nothing,' Simone said.

'Nothing in the garden or the neighbouring gardens?' Vic asked.

'Not that we could see,' Simone said. 'We certainly did quite a survey – well, as you would expect, letting our eyes travel across the—'

'So we decided everything was all right,' Marj said.

'Perhaps people letting off fireworks somewhere,' Simone said. 'That's what we thought. Not the season, but people do. If we were in the garden sometimes we'd see Mr Pethor go into the shed and leave the door open. It's big, used to be a garage for two cars. He'd be out of sight at the far end of it.'

'Well, we were going back to bed when we heard the shouting. A man's voice. Perhaps

211

Mr Pethor. Hard to be sure. We were on the landing.'

'You returned to the window?' Harry Bell asked. Did he want them to have returned to the window?

'We did, but it was the same, as far as we could see,' Marj said. 'The door to the shed still open, a rectangle of light out on to the garden, but nobody there. When we first heard the shouting it seemed to come from down the garden, maybe from the shed, but now we could hear voices in the house, the Pethor house. I assumed it was Mr Pethor and that he'd run in from the garden.'

'Not shouting now, but loud. And angry, maybe scared,' Simone said.

'The words?' Vic said.

'A jumble. Not everything intelligible,' Marj replied. 'But questions. At first, from the shed, "What? Who are you?" Almost a scream.'

' "Who *the fuck* are you?" ' Simone said.

'Yes, that,' Marj said.

'No other voice? No answers?' Vic asked.

'Not that we heard.'

'And then more swearing,' Marj said.

'The words?' Vic said.

'The usual,' Marj replied.

'Which?'

'Fucking bastards. Fucking wankers,' Simone said, 'Really yelled – rage and terror. Perhaps more rage than terror, although I—'

212

'Pethor shouting, screaming?' Vic asked.

'We think so,' Marj said.

'Nothing specific in the swearing?' Bell said.

'Specific?' Marj asked.

'Do you mean did he call them *black* fucking bastards?' Simone asked.

'Why do you say that?' Bell said.

'It's what you would expect, isn't it?' Simone replied. 'If there was a vengeance shooting for Angela Sabat's death, wouldn't it be reasonable to suppose this?'

'Yes, that sort of thing,' Bell said.

'No,' Marj replied. 'No such words. It's important?'

'We need the full incident,' Vic said.

'When the noise was from inside the house, it was just noise, no words we could make out,' Marj said.

'Only the anger and fear,' Kerry said.

'That tone, yes,' Marj replied.

'I've often commented it would happen somehow like this, Mr Pethor's habits being known,' Simone said. 'I explained to Marj, didn't I, Marj, that if I were going to do a hit on him, I'd come at night to the rear gardens of these houses and—' She turned towards Vic: 'You said "strange territory" for whoever it was. I have to wonder about that. Perhaps someone, more than one, has been around here to watch Mr Pethor and see the shape of things. Didn't I say to Marj long ago that if I was—'

'The thing about Simone is she does talk and talk occasionally,' Marj said. 'I don't mind it. Well, obviously. Would we be together? Simone's different from me, from most people. *We've* come to think restraint is the same as intelligence. We're bred up to self-censorship. A hell of a lot of what Simone says is crap. But so it would be for anyone who talked as much as she does. *She* says it, *we* hold back. We might have said it, too, if we had been talkers not hoarders. And are we really any brighter because we have been taught what *not* to say?'

'You're doing a fair whack of talking yourself, Marj, aren't you – I mean now?' Simone snarled. 'Anyway, did I get it right?'

'Exactly what I'm saying,' Marj replied. 'There'll be all the crap, but a jewel in it now and then.

'We dressed and went down to see if we could help. We're crouched right down like soldiers under fire. A laugh.' She giggled.

'But, we might really have been under fire, mightn't we? At the bottom of our garden we are quite close to the shed and we straightened up there. And over the fence we could see through the open door the body and the blood everywhere,' Simone said. 'Appalling. You've seen it for yourselves. I was just going to get over the fence when we heard the cars, the police cars in the street, men in baseball

214

caps and dark outfits and carrying guns. Someone must have dialled 999. Another neighbour, I suppose. So we weren't so silly or panicky to think something serious was going on there.'

'Yes, another neighbour,' Bell said.

'And then you people arrive,' Simone said.

'You've given us a very good picture of things,' Vic said.

Simone asked: 'Have you spoken to Mr Pethor and his wife? And there are children in the house, also. Awful, really.'

'Briefly,' Bell said. 'We'll see them again now.'

'How police work, isn't it?' Simone replied. 'Keep calling, checking, see if what people told you last time is the same as what they tell you this time. Who does Mr Pethor say it was – who does he say he *thinks* it was?'

'They needed time to recover,' Kerry said.

'Thanks, Marj, Simone,' Vic said. 'We might have to come back and talk to you again.'

'Such a surprise!' Simone replied.

'Get some sleep now,' Bell said.

'Oh, I don't think I could,' Simone answered. 'If once I've been disturbed I—'

'Let's try,' Marj said.

Eighteen

'She was in a hutch at exactly head height,' Scout said. 'That's *my* head height. I've got more than twenty hutches in that shed, some stacked on top of others. This is more than a hobby, this is my little industry, you know.' He was the older twin but must have taught himself how to act disarming and modest. Perhaps, while he was concentrating on that, P.D. went past him in the business game. Of course, Scout might not have been so disarming and modest in the Bale Street and Lakin Street area at night. 'The does are Flemish Giant, the bucks Old English,' he said. 'Scientific breeding. I hear what you say, Mr Bell, and I appreciate you have to think of all the possibilities. But please don't tell me this was people firing just to kill one of my rabbits as a scare ploy. I mean deliberately to kill only a rabbit, sort of merely symbolic.'

'It's how it's done sometimes, Scout,' Bell replied. 'A pet gets killed as a warning. That film with Michael Douglas. A bunny, as a matter of fact. Killed and cooked.'

'*Fatal Attraction*,' Kerry said. 'And an old Peter Sellers picture that comes on TV, where thugs smash his aquarium and kill all the pet guppies.'

'These are no pets, no bunnies. I breed them for restaurants, I breed them for show,' Scout said. 'It doesn't reach my soul if one of them's shot.'

'Except the fright,' Kerry said.

'They're beautiful,' Vic said.

'They're earners,' Scout replied. 'Anyone would be frightened – to see the head of a creature just go like that when it's right alongside me – what, seven or eight inches from my face? To my mind, it would be an experience not many have had – a rabbit with its nose and mouth nibbling away the nice way they do, and then suddenly all of it's gone and there's just the, well, trunk left. That what they call it, the trunk?'

'That would be it,' Bell replied.

'This is blood and bits of bone on my own skin, blinding me, I'm that close. No warning. It was for me. Maybe I moved, just in time, not planned, just did. What have they got to warn me about?'

'Why for you?' Kerry asked.

Scout gave her some genuine stare. He had dark-brown, rough-house eyes that had seen quite a bit one way and the other. Also, Kerry thought they were eyes he knew how to control, and which would have shown absolutely no surprise at the acquittal verdict no matter how surprised he was. He said: 'I'm in favour of girls getting on in the police – notebooks, truncheons, everything like that, driving the big fast cars.'

'Great,' Kerry said.

The gentleness broke briefly, though: 'You fucking well know why it would be meant for me,' Scout replied. 'This is someone, or more than one – some mad and evil people – saying bollocks to the court, bollocks to *not guilty*, we'll do the job on him regardless. We know his routine. Wait till he's feeding his flock, he's all soft and unalert then.'

'This was appalling,' Bell said.

'Yeah, appalling,' Scout said. 'Just as long as you know *how* appalling, Mr Bell, and as long as you can tell those above even you. I need them aware of it at the very highest levels, the policy levels. This would show why the reward is necessary, I think you'll agree. I went to ground, obviously, when the shooting started. That much I know about gunfire, from war films – get flat. And I keep still. I act dead. I suppose they see my face is nothing but blood and bone chippings and they think they've done me. They might imagine those chippings are cranium pieces – *my* cranium, not the rabbit's – with perhaps brain adhering. They're in a rush, aren't they? They know neighbours will have heard the shots – no silencer, I'd say. So, there'll be a 999 call and police guns around shortly. The people who tried to do me want to disappear soonest.' He became sad and respectful. 'I've got to say thank God for the rabbit, I know this – the way its individual head exploded, exactly that, and the blood not just in the hutch but thrown outwards on to me and the shed wall. This is a big animal – well, a Flemish *Giant* – big head, and big body for meat. You mate them with the small-boned Old English male and you have an ideal kitchen item, huge haunches like a Rubens picture. Such a head blown off from such a range, this is going to reach everywhere, poor thing. All right, perhaps I *can* get sentimental: I don't like to think of a rabbit being brought into the world for that kind of bullet stopping.'

'It's just a cover trade, isn't it – the rabbit industry?' Kerry said.

'You're blinded by the blood and fragments, so you don't see anyone?' Bell asked.

'This was complete closedown. Not a hope.'

'Voices? Footsteps?' Vic said.

'No voices. But after a while the sound of running.'

'Going away from you?' Bell asked. 'Obviously.'

'How many?' Kerry said. 'More than one?'

'Difficult,' Scout replied. 'My ears were still affected by the firing. But, yes, probably more than one.'

'More than two?' Kerry asked.

'Ah, this is what I mean,' Scout replied, smiling, tolerant, 'It's right women officers should be encouraged to become detectives and take part in all kinds of inquiries – not just stuck in woodentop uniform jobs. Of course, you know my brother, don't you, Detective Sergeant Lake? He's got that wide, comfortable Merc.'

Scout had the same thick, dark hair as P.D. but was plumper in the face and body. Possibly he ate Flemish Giants' haunches. There was a bad absence of John Garfield burn to him. Maybe he had decided P.D. could look after most of the sex game while Scout concentrated on social amiability, other than when he was around the Bale Street and Lakin Street district at night. Occasionally his breathing sounded like an old man's, worked-for and bubbly, but Kerry recognised that this could be shock, if the tale was right. It would confuse anyone to get face-wrapped by rabbit blood when on a routine feed mission.

'So the blood etcetera – that's why there was no immediate shouting?' Bell said.

'There was no shouting because I'm dead, aren't I?'

'How long were you lying there?' Bell asked.

'Can I answer something like that? Be

220

fucking reasonable, Mr Bell, will you? My mind was nowhere.' Now, he spoke even the 'fucking' with mildness, a pleaful 'fucking', his features also pleaful. His features would never reach charm but now and then they could suggest suffering.

'Your mind was able to tell you to lie down and act shot,' Kerry said.

'I'm not timing things. About two or three minutes?'

'Then what?' Kerry asked.

'Maybe a car starts and pulls away. This is at a distance. They might have run to it, I don't know. Or it could be nothing to do with it. After another wait I can't hear anything that sounds like an enemy, so I risk moving one hand, one arm. I try to clear my eyes with my fingers, picking the stuff out. This is still a gamble. I don't know – someone could be standing there, watching me. I'm scared, though, because I can hear dripping and I think I might have been hit somewhere and am bleeding badly. I need to see. So, I risk it and in a bit I get my eyes workable more or less and the first thing I spot is that the dripping noise is blood from the hutch and water from the smashed bottle that used to feed the rabbit's bowl. I'm seeing only bit by slow bit and everything is red, obviously, red misty.'

'Like anger,' Kerry said.

'Anger certainly came to me in a moment,'

221

Scout replied. 'You're quick. I can see why my brother would— I'm really happy Mr Bell brought you.'

'And it's now you start to yell?' Vic asked.

'I'm still down there, but, yes, I start shouting then. Like Detective Sergeant Lake says, I'm suddenly more angry than afraid. That's how it always is with me. I can't stay scared for long. I've got to correct.' Again the switch to a kind of aggression, the voice sharpening. 'Who is it that can make me cling to the floor of a damn rabbit shed? This is Scout Pethor scrabbling like that. There's the family name. All right, it's not Windsor or Sainsbury but it means something. It needs looking after.'

'Who'd want to be humiliated in front of his own Giants, female Giants?' Kerry asked.

'This is why you shouted "Who are you? Who the fuck are you?" is it?' Bell asked.

'Did I?'

'The neighbours say,' Bell replied.

'Including the swearing? I'm sorry about that, in this neighbourhood,' Pethor said. 'Thoughtlessness. Perhaps excusable. Then when I stand up and see the body, I'm even more angry. I don't know if you can imagine it – the state of the fur. As I said just now these animals are not pets. I don't have names for them, anything like that, even if I could have recognised this one, things being as they were. But I also said I can feel something for them. Naturally. It was rough to see a doe like that, shattered, incomplete. I don't think I understood just then that it must have been me he was going for, they were going for. The anger was just from seeing this headless body. Who did it? Yes, who the fuck, if you like. And I kept telling myself it all had to be cleared up because the children often look in here before school or afterwards. I think I knew, though, that it couldn't be – that you would have to see it as it was, the hutch at head height especially, my head height and the body still present.'

'You were going to call us?' Kerry asked.

'Well, of course. This was a shooting in a respectable quiet street. It had to be reported. This is not Moss Side, Manchester. I was just going to ring when the first officers arrived.'

They were talking in Scout's pleasant sitting room. His wife was upstairs with the children, who had been awakened by all the din and now needed calming and to be persuaded back to sleep. Scout had made tea and they sat with mugs on easy chairs and a sofa. He added rum to the tea. On the walls were what looked to Kerry like very well done flower pictures, bright, accurate, nicely framed in light-coloured wood. Did Scout know about flower art as well as Reubens? Long, velvet, dark-green curtains were drawn and gave the room a rich peacefulness. This was the kind of room you would want to take honest care of and where you might sit meditatively and regret killing a black.

Scout said: 'I think I had my hand on the phone to call when I heard the first police. I hadn't even washed or changed my clothes. There'll be blood on the receiver, I should think. If there's one thing I can't stand it's a stained telephone receiver. That's always seemed to me to soil the wonderful principle of communication the telephone might be said to represent. I must have still been a foul sight when the officers arrived.'

'Yes, they said about the blood,' Bell replied. 'They thought you were hurt.'

'Sorry for appearing so gross,' Scout said. 'And possibly walked into the carpet.' Ashamed, he pointed to a line of dark marks. 'I galloped from the shed to the house – there could have still been people around, I wasn't sure – I'd heard the running and the car, but maybe someone was left behind, so I went fast. Charlotte was at the kitchen door looking down the garden, anxious, having heard the shots, and as soon as I told her what had happened, really yelling with anger and, yes, some fright, I suppose, she said to call the police. I would have done it, anyway, despite – despite all that went on during the case.' He sighed. 'Mr Bell, I don't say that hasn't affected me. I'm not being personal, but I can't think of the police as a worthwhile organisation the way I used to before all that. Can't think of the organisation as always straight up. I'd be very watchful in any contact with you and yours now, Mr Bell – sorry, but I think you'll understand; it's natural, isn't it? But when it comes to something like a wilful shooting on one's own property, I wouldn't know what to do except call the police and seek their – your – help. Perhaps this is inconsistent.'

Bell said: 'We'll certainly do—'

'I can see the difficulties, of course,' Scout replied. 'It's the motive, isn't it? Detectives can usually narrow down the number of suspects according to motive. But now? There are all sorts out there who might imagine in their off-balance, poisonous minds they have a reason for resentment, aren't there? People who'd fancy themselves as holy avengers, yes, *holy*, incited by some of the media – thinking they were doing work the system has fallen short on.'

'There could be quite a range, it's true,' Bell said.

Kerry stood up and walked to the telephone. 'Yes, bloody,' she said. 'As if it has been used to beat someone to death. But I don't suppose it would be possible these days with these featherweight modern plastic sets. What do *you* think, Scout? A falling away in quality everywhere. Have you called P.D. about all this?'

225

'Ah, yes, as I said, you know P.D., don't you? And so does Detective Constable Othen, of course.'

'P.D.'s prominent, in his way,' Kerry said.

'I spoke to him, naturally. My brother, my twin.'

'Sometimes twins know things about each other by a sort of telepathy, I gather,' Kerry said.

'He didn't come here. Not at once,' Scout replied. 'I expect he'll look in before morning. He knows we're all right – Charlotte, myself and the kids. He got some friends together and was going to search the streets for the intruders. Priorities. P.D. has always been very good on those.'

'That sounds worrying,' Kerry said. 'When it comes to streets, the Pethors are—'

'Obviously, if they found anyone they'd hand them over immediately,' Scout replied. 'We definitely have faith in British courts, haven't we, no matter how our views on the police have been shaken?'

'They might run into our patrols,' Bell said.

'There are reservations about the police as an organisation – though not all officers personally, obviously – but, yes, P.D. and I share those reservations, naturally. Yet I feel he would enjoy cooperating on a matter like this,' Scout said. 'He's always keen to be constructive. Isn't the reward proof of that?'

'Is it?' Kerry asked.

Scout's wife, Charlotte, appeared in the door. She wore a long cream-and-gold housecoat. She was tall, perhaps taller than Scout, broad-faced, pale, hostile-looking and very straight-backed. Perhaps Scout supplied the amiability in their arrangement. She said: 'Couldn't you do better than mugs for the guests, Peter?' Kerry found it weird to hear him called by his real name, one of his charge-sheet names, Peter Vincent Pethor.

'They're not guests, darling. They're policemen – oh, and policewoman.'

'They don't give a shit you were shot up, do they?' she replied, not coming any further into the room.

'I shouldn't think so,' Scout said. 'And so, no quality china for them, as retaliation.'

'He *wasn't* shot up, was he?' Kerry said. 'It was a nameless, faceless understudy caught in mid-nibble. Scout's here for you, Charlotte, intact and spruce – as spruce as he'll ever be, good intentions a-throb.'

Scout said: 'As a matter of fact, Detective Sergeant Lake knows P.D. and so does Detective Constable Othen.'

'Oh, P.D.,' Charlotte said. 'Sometimes I can't make out whose side he's on.'

'Sides?' Scout replied. 'There are no sides, surely. There is truth, there is fairness, there is *live and let live*. I feel that except for a few very twisted folk we are all in favour of those qualities, Charlie. Definitely all of us in

227

this room.'

'Of course there are sides,' she said.

'What I would never allege, for instance, is that Mrs Sabat was in any way connected with that murderous attack tonight,' Scout replied. 'Clearly, I don't mean that anyone would ever suspect her of actually accompanying the attacker or attackers and taking part, even if she *is* from Detroit. That would be crazy. But there *is* the closeness with Ferdy Nate's Lydia, isn't there? As I hear. I believe Mrs Sabat is actually living in the Nate property, a property with terrible associations for Mrs Sabat, of course. Yet, I do not at all say Mrs Sabat would press Lydia to get Ferdy involved in this situation, Ferdy and some of his people. Ferdy certainly had – and has – the sort of men who could carry out a shooting like tonight's. But I want to stress that I do not think this is what occurred.'

'You don't? Why not?' Charlotte asked. 'It might suit Ferdy businesswise to have you gone. All right, you're not P.D. but you *are* a Pethor.'

'He's been telling us,' Kerry said.

'Other disturbed, perhaps diseased, folk did it,' Scout replied. He punched down hard at the sofa and grew damn positive all at once. 'Do you know what I would like, Mr Bell, Charlie, everyone? Do you?'

'Oh, God, Peter, an idea?' Charlotte said.

'I'd like Mrs Sabat to come here, come to this house, see us as we live our lives, and, in particular, I suppose, see how *I* personally live my very minor but very satisfying life – the garden, the rabbits.'

'Oh, stuff it, Scout,' Charlottè said. 'She thinks you killed her daughter. Is she going to pay a social visit. She was shouting at you in the street, remember.'

'Yes, I do remember,' Scout replied. 'Angry that the girl hadn't been raped. This was shocking, indeed. A mother about her own child.'

'That's not how to put it,' Kerry said. 'She was angry that the killing had been apparently causeless, possibly absolute race hate. Just raw evil.'

Charlotte said: 'Do you think I'd still be with him – do you think the kids and I would still be with him if there was the least bit of truth in it, rape or no rape?'

'You and the kids *are* still with him,' Kerry replied.

'I didn't mind him having an all boys night out once in a while because I was always sure he ... Do you think I don't know him?' Charlotte said.

'Do you think you do?' Kerry replied.

'Oh, this talk of evil,' Scout said. 'Detective Sergeant Lake, your job's not about good and evil, it's about the law and offences against it. And offences against it have to be proved or they are not offences. But, whatever – I'm ready to learn, I hope. Might she come?'

'You're nuts,' Charlotte said. 'You've got trauma after the episode.'

Bell said: 'I suppose she might. She's hoping to write something about it all. She would need to talk to as many people involved as possible. That's how writers think.'

'They'll meet anyone for copy,' Kerry said. 'Anyone.'

'So what's in it for the police?' Charlotte asked. She had half turned away to leave, apparently upset by Scout's idea. But she came back. 'What's in it for you, Mr Bell?'

Yes, what was in it for Harry?

'Kerry's our link with Mrs Sabat,' Bell said.

'Do you think she'd come, Detective Sergeant Lake?' Scout asked.

'She might.'

'Could you try to persuade her?' Scout said. Excitement ran through him like a breeze in a wheat field. He had to stand and walk a few steps. His chubby face gleamed. Once or twice he deliberately clipped the heel of one of his trainers with the toe of the other. He must have changed his shoes to create no more marks on the russet carpet, which went more or less all right with the curtains.

'What's in it for them? What's in it for Detective Lake?' Charlotte asked.

'We could invite the media,' Scout said. 'It would show pleasant reconciliation and might prompt people to come forward and claim some or all of the reward for new information. You're very silent, Detective Constable Othen.'

'Yes, I am, aren't I?' Vic replied.

Nineteen

Yes, he was, wasn't he?

In that sweetly schemed room, Kerry again had her vision of Vic dead, those three vengeful, downward knife blows in the neck for his role in covering up, and then the eleven minutes it took him to get to the end. *Oh God, Vic, let me save you, look after you, your silver hair, your silver moustache, your dear unconscionable lungs. I am the new, the strong, the inflight high flier.* His safety was her only mission.

As ever, the eleven minutes was only a notional eleven minutes, just as Vic's death was only notional, a piece of grotesque imagination, so far. Kerry's mind actually gave her the knifing tableau and the eleven minutes in not much more than two or three this time. Its intensity dazed her. The experience was shorter than usual because people in the room were still talking, interrupting her private viewing of the slaughter – that is, Vic's fantasised slaughter, not the actual death of a wide-thighed Giant. The room had quite a jaunty odour, a mélange of tea, rabbit blood, Charlotte's middling-expensive scent, and rum. Kerry wondered whether it had brought on a kind of light-headedness and pitched her into doomy clairvoyance again. There was no cigarette smoke. Vic in other people's houses could sometimes decide on restraint. He was a gent, a nicotine gent. So far he had prevented tobacco from leaving any yellowy-brown stain on the silver of his moustache. Could she have taken that?

'Is this all we're going to get out of you, Detective Constable Othen?' Scout asked. 'But why?'

Bell said: 'Oh, Vic's not one for—'

'I think Vic's going over it in his head, what happened out there, the stages of it, getting them clear – the way you told things, Scout,' Kerry replied. 'It's how detectives work, officially known as reprise. Vic's flair is reprise.' Christ, she felt she had to speak for him, as if he were dead, or on the way.

'That's it,' Vic said, 'Reprise.'

'You're saying it was not like Peter described?' Charlotte asked Kerry.

'Of course it was like Peter described,' she

replied. 'Can't I see the footmarks?' Charlotte's scent had begun to get drowned by the opposition now, especially the rich rabbit-blood smell, plus there was the distance from Kerry, and a long day's wear and tear.

'Come in and sit down, Charlie,' Scout said. 'They're all right.'

She stayed at the doorway. 'How can they be all right?'

'Within reason,' Scout replied.

'*She* thinks it was set up,' Charlotte said.

'Set up?' Bell replied.

'How could it be?' Scout asked.

'Set up,' Charlotte said.

'How could it be?' Kerry said. 'What for?'

'Both Detective Sergeant Lake and Detective Constable Othen know P.D.,' Scout replied.

'Oh, Christ, you've said that.'

'No need for blasphemy, Charlie,' Scout answered. 'I know I've said it, but I want you to take note of it. Have you?'

'What do you mean?' Charlotte asked. 'That this meeting and the visit by these three are only formalities?'

Bell said: 'Formalities? I don't think so. Gunfire in a suburban garden – hardly a formality. A death, even if only, fortunately, a rabbit.' Harry had concocted a phase when he looked and sounded supremely benign. He could spot what was needed. Harry might not be a comet, but he was not a plod, either.

'I mean it's well-intentioned, this confer-ence,' Scout replied. 'Favourable.'

'We have a duty,' Bell said.

'I'm trying to work out the pattern,' Charlotte said. 'It's not the usual one for police – hard and soft interrogators. Here, it's gabby interrogators, trappist interrogator. What's the *real* function of Mr Ancient of Days?' She pointed a thumb at Vic.

This was not a bad question. It was not a bad question about almost anybody – what was his, her, *real* function. What is that man for? – as a child asked about Randolph Churchill. But it was especially smart to ask it about Vic tonight. What had destroyed him?

Hang on, who said he was destroyed? Because of the frequency of the visions where he died she possible *expected* that he would sometimes appear as if blotted out. Did she imagine her lurid dreams controlled Vic? More egomania. Maybe he had decided he knew what the rabbit shooting signified and did not feel any more talk about it was wanted or wise. And if he *had* decided, would he tell her? *Could* he tell her, without giving away something he needed kept private? He might have only turned up at the shooting to look after his own secret interests. There were plenty.

'Is it Allure you're wearing, Charlotte?'

Kerry said.

The obvious explanation for Vic's presence here tonight was that the incident fell within his job as Community Role Coordinator: a special title they'd cooked up so he could be paid more than a constable's wage. Did CRC cover rabbit murders? But perhaps there were those other reasons for his arrival. Not much to do with Vic was simple, as CRC or just as Vic.

'Some people must think you did kill the girl, after all, Scout,' Kerry said.

'I hate that name,' Charlotte said. 'It's like khaki socks.'

'Some people must think you did kill the girl, after all, Scout,' Kerry said. 'They regard the reward as a ploy and distraction.'

'We'll try and give a bit of protection,' Bell said. 'It will have to be unobtrusive. The press would get ratty if we provided obvious bodyguards, in the circumstances.'

'Which?' Charlotte asked.

'The Angela aftermath, thicko,' Kerry replied.

'Are you saying the police can't do what they are obliged to do? They won't look after Peter and the rest of us, despite a gun attack? And this is because some carefully encouraged rumour still says Peter killed a girl and shouldn't be living free?'

'Like that, yes,' Kerry said. 'Some rumour gets near. Think what the *Daily Express* would make of it if we turned all caring about Scout. And some MPs.'

'*What* would they make of it? There are children here.'

'And Scout's here,' Kerry replied. 'Remember the screams over the cost of guarding Salman Rushdie? Folk can be selective about who's to be kept alive. It's horrible sometimes. In the case of Rushdie it's horrible. Scout's case? I doubt it.'

'Next time Peter could be killed,' Charlotte said.

She sounded genuinely worried. Well, Scout was Scout but he was hers. Kerry could sympathise with Charlotte. 'Vary the hours of your visits to the rabbitry, Scout,' Kerry replied. 'Would it interfere with their digestion, haunches and mental well-being if the feed came a bit irregularly? P.D. might give you second billing on the reward: Who killed Angela Sabat? And who tried to kill Scout Pethor, *mon semblable, mon frére*?'

It was nearly four thirty a.m. by the time Kerry reached home. She moved very quietly and tried to slip unnoticed into bed with Mark. 'I wasn't sleeping,' he said and turned towards her. 'Has it been bad for you?'

'Some shitty charade,' she said. 'Some playlet.'

'Confidential?'

'What pisses me off is that a gawky Slav-faced woman could tell I thought it phoney.

Do I give out signals, for God's sake?'

'Who was there, wherever it was? I mean, which police?'

'Just me and Harry Bell.'

'Bell himself? Big, big, big stuff?'

'He fancies the nitty gritty now and then. Why couldn't you sleep?' she asked.

He pushed against her, wanting to be held, nursed a bit. She knew the signs, didn't mind them too much. Marriage was marriage. *Wilt thou cocoon this man when angst sets up camp in him? I'll do better than that.* She drew her shortie nightdress up so he could rest his head on her breasts and then put her arms around him.

'Things in the company,' he said.

'Your job?'

'I was wrong to try to block catering for the reward launch.'

'Who says?'

'Well, Stephen says, obviously. He over-ruled me, didn't he?'

'You had a view. So what?' Kerry replied.

'It's a view that didn't chime with the chair-man's.'

'He's giving trouble?'

'In his mild, very principled, very rational way.' Mark said. He yawned and his lower lip touched her nipple, a helpful, warming accident. She could have done with more of that. 'He wonders where I was "com-ing from". That's one of his psychobabble phrases these days. It means, How the hell can you disagree with me? He said he's worried about my "jumbling of the sentimental and the ethical-stroke-legal", hints this is a potentially grave drawback in a member of one of his boards.'

'The prick,' Kerry replied. 'What's it mean?'

'In his view it's *"merely* sentimental and in a sense subversive" to feel resentment against the Pethors, seeing that Scout Pethor has been cleared, ethically-stroke-legally cleared. "Irrational". That's one of Stephen's gravest criticisms of anybody.'

'Scout Pethor did it,' Kerry replied. 'He and Gain did it.'

'Tell Stephen that. Tell the courts that. Then tell the courts to tell Stephen, special delivery.'

'He wanted the business,' Kerry said, 'Another outlet for his *vol-au-vents.*'

'*I* should have wanted the business. That's his view.'

'So where's he fucking *coming from*, Naivesville?'

'He's a good and serious man, Kerry.'

'And can be a good and serious prat.'

'He believes in what he calls "the institutions of this country". More than believes in: he "cherishes" them. One of the institutions is the law and the presumption of innocence.'

She let a hand slide down Mark's crazily

tense body and tried to fondle his worries away for a time. In a while he moved gently on top of her and she gripped him hard with her legs, her hands firm on his back. She would let him know he was wanted and perhaps always would be in some form, regardless of palace battles in the Comble firm. It was a decent and lovely thing to comfort your men when you could. 'Let's bring a bit of peace and love and blankness to you,' she said.

'You can always do that, Kerry.'

Yes, she could, she could. She was not able to hold this physical arrangement for very long, her feet touching over his behind, but Mark had always needed to be caringly embraced, by arms or legs or job or social rating, and she wanted him restored and resolute. She wanted him as she knew him. A husband who folded in a dispute about snacks she could not visualise as her long-term sidekick.

Twenty

In the morning, very early, Matthew Gain telephoned. The call woke her, but not Mark. Perhaps she really had fucked him brainless, careless, frightless. Good, she wanted him to rest. He needed rebuilding. Sometimes the sweet benison of lovemaking did operate like this. He was entirely without movement, a sleep beyond anything boredom or run-of-the-mill exhaustion could bring. Just the same, a long conversation on the phone might disturb Mark and, although she could have answered on the bedside extension, Kerry got up quickly and went to the handset in the living room. She felt sure the call was for her. Naked and shivering a little, Kerry asked Gain to wait while she pulled last night's tablecloth off and swathed herself. It had been used for meals a fair bit, and she'd smell of baked beans and saveloys, not Allure. Sometimes you'd doubt this was the home of a catering director, even one whose job was shaky.

'Did you hear about it?' Gain said, when she picked up the receiver.

'The rabbit?'

'I've got to see you again. Not my home, though. Listen, I'm trusting you. Half trusting you. I can't believe you're shagging P.D.'

'Kindly.'

'When I say I can't believe it, that's what I mean. I *can't*, because if I do I've got nobody, nobody I can talk to. Nobody that's safe. Safe-ish. Except my mother, and what use is she? Plus a few friends. So, what I'm saying, I've *got* to believe in you – not girlfriending P.D., and not in it with any other cop either.'

'How do you mean, in it?'

'In it. Or even a tie-up with Ferdy Nate and his people. I heard you're nice and cosy with Mrs Sabat.'

'I'm ordered to look after her.'

'And Mrs Sabat is cosy with Ferdy's lady now. And, of course, Ferdy's lady talks to Ferdy.'

'Scout would like to meet Mrs Sabat,' Kerry replied.

'Naturally he would. That's to show her how sweet he is, and how he could never have done that to her daughter, so it must be someone else. And aren't the reward claims going to say who the someone else is? Or that's the tale Scout and his brother will spread. Scout will show her the shed and try to make her weep about his suffering and the terrible death of Brer Rabbit. She's a writer, isn't she? This will give some touching

241

paragraphs.'

'How did you hear so early?' she asked.

'P.D. rang. He said he was worried about me. Yes, *worried*. He said, if they were having a go at Scout they might have a go at me. Like thorough. Supposed to be considerate of him to alert me. *Oh, thank you, P.D.*'

'Perhaps it makes sense,' Kerry replied.

'Is my phone bugged?'

'Why would it be, an innocent man?'

'And not your place for the meeting. Somewhere private.'

Not Old Drovers' Lane. 'Sometimes I use—'

'He says he's going to put protection on me – on me and Scout. "You're at risk, Matty." ' He did a fair, poisonous imitation of P.D., the way Mark sometimes did harsh mimicry. ' "A vengeance campaign, Matty. What we've all foreseen. It will be blind-eyed by the authorities, naturally. Thank God we've had a bloodshed warning." He says the police won't supply guards because of public opinion. And because you'd like us taken out, anyway. You don't care who does it.'

'It's difficult. Politically it's difficult.'

'P.D. had it beautifully worked out. What you would expect.' He tried more impersonation: ' "The Press would be asking, *Why fuss over this piece of shit, either piece of shit? Whatever they get they had coming. The court couldn't nail them but justice has.* We must

242

counter this villainous inhumanity, Matthew, at least until our reward produces the names of the true killer or killers." '

'Yes, some people *would* think of you as a piece of shit,' Kerry replied.

'I can wear that. My mother believes in me, and there are several others.'

'That right?' Kerry asked. 'Which several?'

'Of course, the fucking reward will produce the name of one piece of shit only. That's Matty. This is what he'll say – or *not* say in public, just put around in whispers.'

'It's possible,' Kerry said.

'Protection, I mean, what's it mean? I mean, what does protection mean?' Gain's words tangled. His voice had slid down to a squeak, sometimes a terrified mutter. The frantic repetition must be to make certain she heard.

'He's got some people who could do that kind of duty,' Kerry said.

He grew louder. 'I know he's got some people who could do that kind of duty. This is what I mean, isn't it?'

'What?'

'His people.'

'He's been out with some of them during the night hunting the rabbit killers.'

'He said he was sorry but he didn't find anyone despite "remarkably extensive trawls",' Gain replied. 'That surprise you?'

'Too big a delay?'

'That surprise you he didn't find anyone?' Gain replied. 'Is it people looking for them-fucking-selves?'

'What?' Kerry said.

'Ah, you think so, too? Some rabbit dead, Scout untouched. What's it mean? Or, look, I'm talking absolutely open to you, taking the piss out of his voice, everything. You're definitely not in a romance situation with him, are you? Was it really only knuckling him through the cloth down the Drovers', a put-down to him, not a come-on? And then, seeing it from a different side, you could be in it with the others.'

'Which?'

'That Bell. Or Vic Othen. Ferdy? Do you really see it like he tells it?'

'Who?' Kerry asked.

'P.D. Some rabbit dead, Scout untouched.'

'What about meeting on the sands at Pinon Point?'

'You fucking mad?'

'Out of season,' Kerry replied. 'There'll be nobody. Maybe a couple of oldies walking the dog. I've used it for rendezvous with—'

'I want somewhere with people. I want witnesses. I'm exposed on the sands.'

'I'll be with you.'

'You'll be with me until you're not with me. You could suddenly vamoose, leave me solo.'

'Why would I?'

'Tactics? Are you part of it? Or maybe I

244

don't mean part of it yourself, not in full, but knowing someone who's part of it. Afterwards, I'm left on the sands. The tide tidies me away, like a charwoman.'

'How could it happen? This would be midday, for God's sake,' Kerry replied. 'A resort.'

He went quiet, perhaps thinking about it. Then he said: 'My mother and I were going to get out. What's here, except aggro? Many shun us.'

'That right?'

'Really away. Even Scotland. They hate the English but my mother had a Scotch aunty. Genuine. You couldn't understand a word the Scotch bitch said. I'd like some cottage in the mountains, bottled gas, battery TV, a grand view over moors to see what fuckers were coming and if they're jailhouse faces. Or Mexico. Hot, but there's sun barrier stuff. But now this protection. That what it's called these days? Can we run if he's got protection watching? Protection – what's it mean? You believe that?'

'What? Scotland? Mexico? Why not?'

'No, do you believe it misses Scout and takes the head right off?'

'How do you know it took the head right off?'

'This is P.D. telling me, isn't it? What does it mean, the head right off? I'm no fucking rabbit, you know. My mother was woken up by the bell – a call before dawn like that.

What is it they say?'

'Who?'

'British Telecom. They say, "It's good to talk." I don't know. It depends – depends what the talk *is*. My mother's awake and here's P.D. talking to me about the head right off, eyes, teeth, nose flying everywhere like confetti. Is this honest behaviour or truly considerate? My mother asks me later, "What was the call, Matthew, darling?" It's a reasonable question when the call's at that time. So, what do I tell her?'

'Wrong number.'

'I've been talking to him for ages, listening. Do I say to my mother, "Mr P.D. Pethor rang to tell me urgently of a Flemish Giant's brutal death?" She doesn't know a thing about rabbits. It wouldn't seem sensible to her for P.D. to phone at all about a dead rabbit and especially not at dawn. Rabbits get killed all the time, wild and tame. Think of the roads and butchers' shops.'

'Where is she now?'

'Who? The doe? I should think your people have her. Forensic? She's an exhibit, isn't she? They'll freeze her headless for the jury. This is proof there were real bullets around. P.D. needs that.'

'No, your mother.'

'My mother? Look, keep my dear mother out of this, right? That's what I'm saying – a mother should not have to be involved in things of this sort.'

'Overhearing now?'

'She's downstairs. It's OK, the nosy cow. I had to tell her it was P.D. on the phone and about the shooting. It's going to be in the papers and on TV News. I didn't say the head shot right off. Sometimes the media go easy on rough details. She might get edgy.'

'Why would P.D. tell you about the head off?'

'So I accept protection, isn't it? The head gone shows it's not a prank. I'm supposed to be grateful, and my mother.'

'You're not?'

'We're like prisoners, fool. And then one day or night the protection has a lapse, doesn't it? And it's my head off because there are no rabbits around our property. Yes, all right, where you said, noon,' Gain replied. 'You'll definitely be alone?'

'You want that?'

'Of course I fucking want it. Too many people in all this already.'

'All what?' Kerry asked.

'Twelve noon.'

'How will you manage it, if you've got protection? They won't let you go. Or they'll want to come.'

'They're not here yet. Why it's got to be immediate. What about you?'

'What?' Kerry replied.

'Have you got protection?'

'Why should I?'

'Have you?' he asked.

'I'll take care of it.' And she hoped she'd be able to take care of it, if it was back.

She spread the cloth on the table ready for breakfast and returned to bed. It was still only seven twenty a.m. Mark did stir, but nothing much. He was on his side facing away from Kerry. She put an arm around him and drew herself close. He felt solid, formidable, someone who might be able to take care of himself, eventually. No, not fair, not fair – contemptuous. Mark was strong. He'd been hit off balance for a moment, that's all, by the noble idiot, Comble. It could all be rectified. She prized being married to a company director.

After a while she licked about four inches of Mark's backbone, working slowly up towards the neck five times. It was a kind of intimacy, one of the lesser kinds yet useful. She found a comfort in it – in the completeness of Mark, after so much talk about a head blown away. There were more interesting bits of a man to get at the end of your tongue but this would be fine for now. Oddly, Vic's sweat always tasted better than Mark's. Perhaps cigarette smoke, once it had been through all the processes and pores, came out pasteurised. Vic's had a flavour between cashew nuts and Edam. But Mark's sweat was not intolerable. Perhaps it oozed now from his sublimated frets and she swallowed eagerly as though this could clear him of all interior pain, and give his usual poise and happy bombast a chance again.

'I'll speak to Stephen Comble,' she said. His sweat greased her throat and, she thought, gave her voice a sort of majestic depth, at least for this time in the morning. He grunted. She could not be sure whether he took in what she said. 'I'll ask Comble if he really wants his firm connected with three pieces of shit like the Pethors and Gain. Well, his firm's already connected with them because he insisted on providing the launch grub. But I'll tell him he should do penance for this and recognise that one of his junior directors, Mark Tabor, knew by instinct that any such association was unsavoury and to be avoided.'

'What?' Mark mumbled. He was coming to.

'He'll take it from me.'

'What?'

'Clarification.'

'Who?'

'Comble. He can be a jerk but not a one hundred per cent jerk, and he'll acknowledge his error. He enjoys acting the gent.'

'Who?' Slowly, Mark turned to face her. She thought he looked terrible, like someone worry gets a grip on the moment sleep ends, eyes jumpy, breath short, jaw unhinged.

She'd seen better sights woken up in cardboard boxes under the viaduct.

'Whose error?' he asked.

'Comble's. I'll tell him.'

'What?'

'That the fuck-up he was responsible for is not totally irreparable, but close. I'll make it positive, don't get anxious.'

'Who?'

'Comble.'

'Stephen?'

'He'll appreciate the advice from someone with my special knowledge,' Kerry replied.

'Oh, Jesus,' Mark said.

'I know how to be delicate.'

'Oh, Jesus.'

'And yet clear.'

Of course, she thought, Matty had it so right. If Kerry was cuddling up with P.D. now and then, and talking to him, or if she was what Gain called 'part of it' – part of some police conspiracy and/or Ferdy Nate conspiracy – Pinon Sands would be a wondrous spot to lead Gain on a nice little walk. Here he might meet folk he did not want to meet, and where she would bolt or drop flat at the due moment, out of the line of fire. It could even be possible as he suggested that the tide would dispose of him at least for a while, if the interception took place at a proper spot and before high water. The best proper spot would be on the other side of Pinon Point, a high headland which you rounded to reach a small sand-fringed, rocky bay backed by sheer cliffs. Even in the season few people went here when the tide was well up, afraid they'd get cut off. Gunshots, silenced or not, might go unnoticed.

But Kerry was not putting out to P.D., not in any way, and was not 'part of it', either. She might know people who were 'part of it' but could not be sure. This was not something you asked Harry Bell or Vic, unless you already knew the answer. It was not something she even *wanted* to ask Vic, though she would, if she knew the answer. If she knew the answer, to ask him would be a chance for Vic to make things slightly less awful by admitting it, and by admitting it to her only, not to any Inquiry or Bell or creaking Julie. Above all not to Julie: this would be frank, emotional bonding stuff between Kerry and Vic. If she knew the answer and asked him he would naturally realise that she knew the answer, and he might then admit it, supposing he cared what she thought of him. Would that be enough for her? Would she still want him in that case, regardless, or almost regardless? The taste of his sweat and the indestructibility so far of his body were endearing, but did she have limits? Stand by your man? Stand by *one* of your men? Stand by one of your men even if you shared him with someone else?

Kerry loved this whole slice of coast: the gangs of flapping oystercatchers and gulls, the bang of the breakers and the dancing haze above them, the brown and black jaggedness of the cliffs. There was a great stretch of beach and then the small, tide-affected bay around the headland, part sand at the sea's edge, part low, fat, volcanic-looking rocks, backed by the unclimbable cliffs and two small caves. Kerry knew it all well. Now and then she had used Pinon Sands to talk with one of the child inform-ants, who lived with her parents in a round-the-year caravan park nearby and could walk to the sands. The child had felt relaxed here – vital with kids. It was not always a business spot for Kerry. Sometimes she would walk the beach with Mark. Sometimes she would come alone, and maybe think for a long while about him or Vic or the damned near misses on the lottery or the glorious dark subtleties of the job, and the need to keep the job dark and subtle and ultimately more or less wholesome.

Gain turned up in a long navy raincoat and wearing a big-brimmed black trilby. The trilby was what she thought of as a Yeats hat. She did not say that because it would make her sound poleaxed by education. That *did* happen to people, and it was pathetic: out-side a couple of lecture theatres and class-rooms, who the fuck had heard of Yeats?

The outfit suited Gain. They said squat people should not wear hats, and certainly not big hats, for fear they'd look like drawing pins; but Gain's trilby gave him an authentic touch of formality and quaintness. Despite what he'd told Kerry, he probably did not like being considered a piece of shit: he had bought the hat to bring himself racy grandeur, and it almost worked. Hard to imagine someone like this slaughtering a black girl on a whim, though Kerry *could* imagine it. Whims could come to all sorts in the street late after drinks or smokes or snorts, or drinks *and* smokes or snorts, and with an influential chum. Gain also wore large, plain sunglasses, and these, with the hat brim, did a reasonable job of concealing his face. When she used to meet the child informant here, Kerry had felt terrible anxieties throughout in case they were spotted, even though the girl herself was at ease. Obviously, Kerry could not worry like that about Gain, except she did not want any attempt on him until he had told her whatever he had to tell.

They walked unhurriedly along the sand towards Pinon Point. Occasionally, Gain would turn right around and make a few of his steps backwards so he could ensure a 360 degree survey. He reminded her of a spinning top. Kerry did not think there was anyone to trouble him. She felt pretty certain she had brought no minders. True, she had felt like that before now, and been wrong. But today she had thoroughly checked the street again before she left and had done continual mirror work in the car. Perhaps Harry really had pulled them off. He might think he knew enough.

The beach was more or less as she had promised. She saw three people strolling, two with dogs, and all of them at least retirement age and unlikely to have heavy careers with P.D.

'Get us out,' Gain said. 'Why I needed to see you.'

'Who?'

'Mother and me. This is a very dear lady I have to cherish and keep safe. She is my priority.'

'Out where?'

'Like I said, Scotland, Mexico. Anywhere.'

'You were going to arrange that for yourselves.'

'I told you, it's impossible now, if there's protection. I didn't want to give much away on the phone. You say not bugged, but of course you'd say it.'

'I can't get you out,' Kerry replied.

'Like a supergrass.'

'You're not a supergrass.'

'A supergrass you can fix up with a new name, driving licence, home, the whole identity. I've heard of it. That's all we need.'

'You should just have gone today early if you're scared, before the protection moves in.'

'Of course I'm bloody scared. You know what happened last night.'

'A rabbit got killed.'

'I said to her this morning, straight after I spoke to you, "Mother, we leave, now. Now." I'd have broken this date. Sorry, but I'm talking urgencies. "One case each and what we can throw into the car." Of course, the blind, soft cow won't do it. Like I said, she hears of a rabbit's death and thinks only about a rabbit. At that age they've given up vision. Plus, and a very big plus, she thinks my father is going to come back to that place one day, one day soon, and he'll want to find her there or he'll fuck off again, maybe for ever. That's *her* view. My view is he's already fucked off for ever and he likes it where he is – New Zealand, Exeter, toss a coin. Basically, she's in love with all those bedrooms and bathrooms. She thinks we'd be in rough lodgings or a hut.'

'It's a lovely house.'

'Look, I'm not saying finance. I know you run a fund for grasses, payments, exit money. But we can look after that for ourselves. Just get us out, make us disappear. There's a proper machinery for it, isn't there?'

'Grasses, supergrasses we owe something to,' Kerry replied. 'They've helped us. You?

As you said, you're just a piece of shit. I'm sorry for your mother.'

His words crackled in the ozone: 'I'm guiltless. It's official. You owe me as well, and her. We're in danger. You have a duty.'

'I don't pack that kind of power, anyway,' Kerry replied.

'I know you know what happened last night.'

'A rabbit got killed.'

They rounded the headland into the small, rocky bay. Gain obviously did not like it, felt encompassed and offered-up. His eye-sweeps became more agitated, all directions still. 'Fucking caves?' he said.

'They're shallow. You'd spot anyone'.

There were several nervy silences. Kerry could see nobody now. 'Scout knew they were coming,' he said. 'He nominated which rabbit. He picked one with a head that would really give a message when it was shot off.'

'A message? Who to?' Kerry asked.

'Everyone. In general. They want people to think the gun party were popping at Scout and hit the rabbit by mistake.'

'Who do?'

'Who do you think? Then, when they come to do me, they don't hit any rabbit, they hit me, but P.D. can say, "Oh, my God, this must be the same vengeance outfit who attacked my dear brother, Scout." Some might suspect P.D. wants to get rid of me as a scapegoat, so everything can return to peace and good business. But now he's got the answer, hasn't he? He says, "Would I be likely to send a posse to do my own twin?" He says, "Surely these two shootings are linked?" '

'Staged?'

'Don't pretend you hadn't realised or I'll really think you're helping them.'

'Scout says—'

'Oh, Scout says he was French-kissing the rabbit – as close as that – when it got shot. So nearly him! Of course he bloody does. Scenario, not fact. He probably shot that fucking creature himself. Maybe it was past childbearing. Get Forensic to look at its ovaries. Found any neighbours who saw or heard other people in the garden? They heard shooting. Yes, because there *was* shooting. Scenario shooting.' Waving his hand towards the bay, he said: 'I'm not happy here. Well, I'm not *happy* anywhere. But let's get back around the point. I feel like I'm in a box.'

Twenty-One

Just before they rounded Pinon Point on their way back, Gain said: 'You wait a bit, will you? I'll go ahead to the car.'

'I thought you didn't want to be on your own.'

'I don't want to be on my own, but I don't want to be seen talking to you. Choices. I'll do the open beach bit by myself now. If there was going to be any bang-banging it would have been here.' He waved again at the little bay. 'Listen, I'm in favour of nature, don't think I'm not – cliffs, rocks, crabs in the pools, birds, the whole coast scene, it's important to show how life began. I mean Life. But it's just the way it all comes together in there.'

'Nature can be like that.'

'And a life could end.'

'It didn't,' Kerry said.

Briefly, he looked as if he might hit her for the smartness of the answer. She could have understood that. 'So, you definitely can't help us get clear – won't help us get clear?' he said.

'My best to your mother,' Kerry replied.

He shifted his feet so he could stand very square in front of her. She thought he looked strong, pitiable and odious. 'Forget about being a cop, all that, for a second,' he said. A wind spattered the side of Kerry's face with sand, stinging her ears and neck. 'Look at it like at a situation, like anyone would look at a situation. Can you just leave me to get blasted? Never mind law, but I mean, what about the Christian side of things – items like mercy, humanity?'

'You've heard of them?'

'Where's your womanliness, your tenderness?'

'Was that hat specially made?' she replied. 'Is it bulletproof?'

'You *are* shagging P.D.,' Gain replied, his voice not much more than a hopeless gasp. 'So why isn't he here, waiting for me? Didn't you put me on a plate for him?' Gain turned and went on to the main beach, a bit crouched, hands in the pockets of the long raincoat. Did he have something in there? Did he know guns? She tried to remember his dossier. The wind would be blowing direct at him now and he kept his head low, maybe to stop the hat getting whipped off. As long as you did not know him you could see something elemental, filmic, about his solitariness and the determination of his trudge. Kerry recalled pictures of explorers battling across

Arctic wastelands.

If someone, more than one, suddenly came out of the dunes and took a shot at Gain or went for him with knives, what would she do? She had no gun herself, of course. Perhaps she'd go back and take another walk across the little bay. More of that blind-eyeing he had spoken of? Matthew Gain done would be Matthew Gain done, no matter who did him, and a lot better than the trial court had managed, especially if the tide did clear him away and gave his corpse a bit of a banging on the rocks. One down, one to go. What would Vic make of that?

Kerry stayed at the point until she saw him move up from the beach to the road and drive away in his Citroen. Then she followed. Something like the same distantly scattered walkers were visible now, people and a couple of dogs. In addition, a young girl came running towards Kerry very fast, helped by the wind behind her, and flailing her arms in a sort of clownish send-up of trained sprinting. She was shouting something and in a second Kerry realised it was her own name. She recognised her one-time grass from the caravan park, Josie Cosse. Josie had always liked to fool. Kerry used to try to make her more serious, less vain, more cautious, but ultimately gave up.

'With Matty Gain were you? I watched the two of you from one of my secret spots but I wasn't sure. Then when he was walking back I decided yes. So many TV pictures of him – well, there *were*, when the case was on.' A change moved in on her voice. It grew urgent and touched by bliss. Her round, porky, cheery face grew *more* cheery. 'Did Mr P.D. Pethor send you two with the money? Is it there, Kerry? Not the *whole* lump? Honestly? All? No, really? Oh, is it, is it there? It is, it is!' She almost sang and capered about on the sand in front of Kerry, her features alight with some sort of triumph, Kerry did not understand what. 'Come back with me,' the child cried. 'Show me where, exactly where. We've got to get it before the tide. This is how I planned things.'

Josie grabbed Kerry's hand and began to tug her towards the little bay again. 'I expect you knew it was me, did you? My playground and my realm. That's what you used to call the beach, and it is. Still. Why I picked it, isn't it?'

'What money?' Kerry replied.

'Are you working for Mr P.D. Pethor now? On the side, that is, of course. And on the quiet, obviously. You haven't given up being a detective, have you, but this is an extra little job, with Mr P.D. Pethor, is it?' The urgency and excitement still clanged in her tone. She had to shout above the wind. Now and then bits of spit flew from her lips. 'What's he like? I only spoke to him on the telephone. A looker? And he's loaded, yes? Well, a fifty grand reward. That's *got* to be loaded, even if some is from other firms. Think of the gowns for that! When I heard the buzz you was having it off with him, I thought he must be a real looker, and loaded, or you wouldn't bother, you being you, Kerry, and with plenty of other romance, as is well known, as well as married. Has he bought you gowns? This with Mr Pethor is only now and then, is it? Old Drovers' Lane. There's a lot of it there. But you do some work for him as well.'

Kerry let the child draw her back towards the bay. They went around the point. The sea was a couple of feet away. Josie released Kerry's hand and ran to one of the caves and rushed in. The cliff face was great slabs of wavy stratified rock – orange, grey, brown – looking like heavily laid on paint in one of those Sutherland pictures of the coastline. God, this was a back-to-front way of seeing things, wasn't it? The paint in the pictures looked like rock, not the reverse. The rock definitely came first. Was her mind slipping?

By the time Kerry reached the cave, Josie was on her way out and passed her, still running. She looked flustered now and the joy and assurance had gone from her voice. 'This is the cave that I told him,' she said. 'Have you done it wrong? The one on the right, I said.' She stopped for a second and faced the caves, then raised her right arm a little. 'Yes, that's the right.' She dashed into the other cave, though, and Kerry, starting to follow, heard Josie scream, loud and booming, from inside: 'Where? Where, Kerry? Oh, where is it?' A couple of gulls, disturbed by the yell, left their spot halfway up the cliff and flew agitatedly towards the sea. Josie came running out of this second cave and passed Kerry. The girl hurried back to the other. 'Have you kept it, you two? It's not fair if you kept it? I'll give you a cut, Kerry, I will, but it's not fair if you two have kept it all.'

Kerry turned around and stood in the mouth of the first cave, the one to the right. Josie had climbed up some rocks at the side and was sweeping her hand along a ledge on the cave wall about five feet up. 'Is it there?' she shrieked. 'I can't see. I'm not tall enough to see. Did you put it up there? Did you forget I wouldn't be tall enough to see, you silly?' She turned and stared at Kerry and tried a laugh. It was almost a sob, though.

Kerry said: 'What are you looking for?'

The words seemed to reach Josie and shock her. 'Why were you here, Kerry, the two of you? Was it just to spy, just to see who did it? Didn't you bring any?'

'What?'

'Money.'

'What money?'

'You know what fucking money, you thieving bitch!' Josie shouted.

'We should get back. The tide's nearly up.'

'I know about tides, don't I? My realm.'

'Let's get out,' Kerry said.

'If the tide comes up and you've left it here somewhere it will be gone. The sea gets right into these caves, fills them.'

'Yes, so let's get out.'

'But if—'

'There's nothing here. We've left nothing here,' Kerry said. 'Why should we?'

'Not *all* the fifty grand. I don't expect all. But some. There has to be *some*!' Again it was a scream. 'He said some. Here?' She tried to move her hand along the ledge again but was weary or in despair.

Kerry stepped into the cave and took her by her arm. Perhaps by now Kerry did understand what Josie was saying. And, if she did, there were two urgent reasons for getting away quickly, not just the sea. Josie let herself be led out. When they reached the point they had to take their shoes off and wade during a pause between breakers. On the main beach again, Kerry said: 'You've offered Mr Pethor some information?'

'For the reward,' Josie said.

'And you asked him to leave the payment in the cave?'

'The right cave, facing.'

'What information?'

'Didn't he send you, you and Matty to bring it?'

'What information?' Kerry replied. They put their shoes on. 'We should hurry. You said a time?'

'Just before the tide, so there'd be nobody else in the bay.'

'Does Pethor know who you are?'

'I did a grown-up voice on the phone. It's like in kidnappings. What's called *the drop* – where they leave the ransom. Have you heard of *the drop*, Kerry? Being police, I expect you have. Somewhere where there's nobody around, so they won't be revealed and caught.'

'What information?'

'About the black girl who's dead.'

'Yes, but what?'

'Valuable information. I know about information, because of when I worked with you.'

'What information? You weren't in Bale Street or Lakin Street that night, were you, or on the building site? Were you up the town so late?'

'Information,' she replied. 'He said it was great. I could tell he was *really* thrilled. You know, when people *mean* it and are not just being polite.'

'You made it up, did you?' Kerry asked. 'You saw the reward advertised and the number to ring and you wanted a slice? You were being clever. *Thought* you were being clever. I remember you as clever.'

'Yes.' But she said it as if she wondered.

'Here's Mr Pethor now. Keep quiet. We'll hope he thinks this is a spot where I meet my informants secretly. And it used to be.'

'Of course it did. You're really not romancing him, then?' Josie replied.

P.D., in a navy tracksuit, was jogging down towards the bay.

'Perhaps he's bringing the money personal, from gratitude,' Josie said.

'Forget it, idiot. It's too late to leave it there. He wants to see who's hanging around till the tide makes it impossible, hoping to collect.'

'No, he might, he might have it,' she whispered ferociously. 'There's pockets in them tracksuits. Look for a bulge – not a lunchbox bulge, a money bulge.

'He doesn't want information.'

'What?'

'He'll supply his own information.'

'But there's a reward.'

'Is there? There's an announcement.'

Pethor stopped in front of them. He wore a red bobble hat with the tracksuit and very old trainers. 'One of your rendezvous points, Sergeant?' he asked. His breathing was easy, despite the trotting.

'One of yours?' she said.

'The little girl's a grass and has been telling you about some big matter like bicycle thieves?'

'Yes, the film,' Kerry replied. 'She's the

movie critic of the *Sunday Times*. You're sharp. And fit.'

'I like to look after my body,' he said.

'I don't blame you. Rumour says it's the only one you've got. And a lot of people would like to snuff it out.'

He continued his run down towards the point. Josie said: 'Yes, he *is* dishy. Are you sure you – just a quickie, down Old Drovers' Lane? But why do you talk to him so rude?'

This is how they were, these children who had wandered at some time into informing. They were worldly and they were half-baked. They were knowing and they were crazily romantic. They thought sex could be at work almost anywhere, and on that they were, of course, correct. They thought that if things were not running on sex they were running on money, and on that they might be correct, too. They believed that with luck and in-genuity and cheek they could land some of this money for themselves, and so they might dream up tales and try to sell them as real. Josie's grassing had been like that. Most kids' grassing was like it. You weighed and measur-ed everything they told you before you paid out or acted on what they said. They thought double-dealing was the norm, and, again, they might be correct. They might even be correct in deciding that there was no great gulf fixed between the real and the imagined. The real was what you could persuade a court to accept. Now, Josie was trying the same make-believe skills for a much bigger fee. Or for *perhaps* a much bigger fee. She had all the techniques for setting up the operation and collecting, including what she'd learned from kidnap reports. Her only lack was basic grown-up sense to tell her the operation was impossible and P.D.'s reward offer a device.

'Did you notice, he looked at me a lot,' Josie said. She had posed a bit, pushing her lips out and her teenage breasts.

'Yes, he's wondering.'

'Some people think I'm eighteen, when I'm in all my good gear and made up. I didn't put anything good on today because of the sea and that.' She wore jeans and an old beige sweater and looked what she was, fourteen, possibly just fifteen by now. 'But when I'm smart—'

'A gown?' Kerry asked.

Josie gazed appreciatively after P.D. 'Businessmen have to run because of getting a pot. But he's all right, isn't he?'

'He's wondering if you were Madam Anon on the phone,' Kerry said.

'Who?'

'The mystery witness.'

'What would he do?' Some squeakiness invaded her voice. She was troubled.

'Lie low for a while, will you? Don't go stalking him. He might come again tomorrow to check.'

Josie looked angry. 'Would I throw myself at him?'

'Would you? But don't. He's only interested in you for one reason and it's not romance. Or sex.'

'Are you jealous, Kerry?'

'Keep away from him,' she replied. 'What was the yarn you gave him for the reward?'

'Oh, it was brill, brill,' she said. 'I wrote it down and read it, so it all added up. A payphone, no tracing, like you trained me to do.'

'Did you describe someone seen in the murder area to him?'

'Like that, yes. Acting suspicious. Not Matt Gain or Scout Pethor. Mr Pethor doesn't want to hear it was them, does he? Of course not.'

'Who did you describe?'

She waited a few seconds, then said: 'Only the headmaster.' She looked up at Kerry, her brow suddenly taut with guilt. 'God, Mr Pethor won't start searching for him?'

'He knows it's rubbish. He knows who killed Angela Sabat. He knows who he's going to line up for it. He doesn't need your help and he won't be paying for your help, true or phoney. So promise you won't go looking for that money again tomorrow.'

'I wouldn't think you were a slapper just because you had it off with him on a one nighter, Kerry. I mean, if you did. Many women get carried away by their feelings. It's famous.'

'You won't phone him again, will you?'

'Why would I?'

'To ask him where the money was.'

'Do you think he'd bring it next time?'

'What next time?'

'I mean now he's seen me.'

'He doesn't know he's seen you.'

'Perhaps he does,' Josie said.

Yes, perhaps he did. 'What next time?' Kerry asked.

'Whenever. Say tomorrow.'

'Don't ring. There's nothing.'

'Are you sure, Kerry? You *really* don't want me to see him, do you?'

'No, I don't,' Kerry replied.

'I should think he's too busy to come down here again in person tomorrow, anyway,' Josie said. 'You needn't get what they call it – possessive.'

Twenty-Two

Of course, just before high tide next day Kerry went back to the little bay and the caves. A duty. A compulsion. Why was she so alarmed about this kid? Josie amounted to a sideshoot, nothing more, didn't she? A random intruder powered by nuisance. She could have no bearing on Kerry's main and unswerving objective – to make sure, try to make sure, that Vic stayed undamaged in his job and repute, and above all undamaged in his old, treacherous, fuckable body. He must not finish up with three vengeance knife blows in the neck. They were out there some-where waiting, weren't they?

God, that again. Was her fear mad? Had dimwit thinking and diseased visions taken over Kerry's brain, destroyed all that preci-sion, coolness, balance she used to kid herself was hers, and had managed to kid others was hers, at school, Oxford and on the high-flier police course? P.D. was not going to hurt Josie, was he? Was he? All right, Josie had tried to con some money out of the reward project in her dopey, grasping way. Many others craving quick funds would probably have a go at that. It wouldn't surprise or anger P.D. Did he care? He wasn't looking for real information. He knew it did not exist. All rubbish that came in he would listen to politely and discard. He might be supplying his own rubbish soon, to set up Matthew Gain, if Matthew Gain had things right, and Kerry thought he probably did. A murder was being arranged, another one, an aftermath murder, and, as P.D. hoped, a cleansing murder, a let-bygones-be-bygones murder. A rabbit first, then Matty.

Josie might be down here again today. So might P.D. Oh, Josie a certainty. She had probably made a repeat call on the reward number to ask why no money was left. She would do this even though Kerry had warned her against, or perhaps *because* Kerry had warned her against: had put the notion into Josie's mind. From their earlier dealings, Kerry knew that Josie was private enterprise, Josie was Small Business Initiative. She believed in personal commitment, and about being ever positive in the hunt for profits. Oh, yes, Josie would get here, looking for a second chance of landing the cash, and possibly for a second chance of wagging her boobs and flourishing her lips at P.D., if he turned up to see who was making the calls. Kerry felt what she'd often felt when dealing with youngsters – a terrible responsibility for

Josie's safety, possibly for her life. Maybe it was panicky and excessive. Just the same, Kerry knew she had to be present. Damn it, did she want to wag her own boobs at P.D.?

This time, entering the right-hand cave on a brighter, colder day at the coast, she immediately saw the money had arrived. Or at least she saw that *something* was there: a sealed envelope inside a plastic cover and clearly visible on a rock at the back of the cave. She was Ali Baba? Kerry picked up the package and took it to near the entrance where there was better light. Carefully, but without hesitation, she opened the envelope. It was addressed to The Unknown Witness. She could pass for that. There was a typed letter on Pethor company notepaper with the payment, also addressed to 'Unknown Witness'. The letter came from the envelope first and Kerry read it at once because, as she unfolded it, she was appalled to glimpse her name mentioned there.

The letter explained why the money was in cheque form. It also explained why the cheque was made out to Kerry Lake.

This is a formality for security reasons only. I am confident that Detective Sergeant Lake, whom I believe you know, will cash the cheque and pass the money to you. I expect you have done other transactions with her and know she is very honest. Thank you for your great work in helping me to track down the killer or killers of Angela Sabat. The information you provided was not full enough to earn the complete reward but, as you will see, I have sent £100 (one hundred pounds) and I trust you will find this satisfactory. Yours truly, P.D. Pethor.

Kerry's first instinct was to destroy all of it at once, cheque, letter and envelope. Then she would attempt to disappear across the beach and back to her car, unseen by Josie or by P.D. Pethor, supposing they both came – and Kerry *did* suppose they would both come. She felt ravaged by confusion, could not see what was happening here, nor what she *wanted* to happen. Holding the papers in her hand she went out from the cave and back to the headland. From there she could examine the main beach. As yesterday, there was a scattering of elderly walkers, but she made out nobody who looked like Josie or P.D. The wind had fallen today and the sand haze was gone. If she tore up the cheque and letter and scattered the bits on the sea like flowers at a shipboard funeral would the tide bring them all back and lay everything on the beach? Josie had the kind of eyes that would probably single out immediately one of the fragments with Pethor's signature on it, or the one hundred pounds in words or figures.

She went back to the cave and replaced the

cheque and letter in the envelope and resealed it as well as she could. Then she put the envelope in the plastic cover and placed it all on the rock under a pebble. She couldn't deprive the child of her earnings, could she? Would it amount to theft? If Josie did come, she might be too eager to get at the reward to notice that the envelope had been opened. Kerry went to the cave's mouth, found a decently flat rock to sit on and waited for her. Josie needed some more warnings, some more protection.

After a few minutes, the urge to annihilate the package came again and Kerry abruptly stood up, ready to go and get it. Only destruction made sense. She had had time to think properly now and believed she could see what Pethor hoped to do. By treating Josie's tip seriously he made the reward offer seem serious, too, didn't he? By making the cheque out to Kerry he ensured there would be a bank record that he had paid part of the reward – not much of a part, but possibly enough to encourage the tipster to look for more information. He had been quick to use what he had learned yesterday: that the un-known witness was a child who knew Kerry Lake. P.D. had talked about grassing on bicycle thieves but saw what really went on. The payment was meant to dispel rumours that he had only devised the reward cam-paign as his means of isolating Matty Gain, and to end public hate towards Scout and towards the name Pethor, personal and business. P.D. would appear as an unselfish and genuine worker for the great general good. That would be worth a hundred pounds to him.

Christ, if Kerry did not get rid of the cheque she would become a kind of accomplice in the plot against Gain. She was a police officer, yet would help prepare a killing. How had she drifted here? This was bad, but was still not what disturbed her most. Above all she loathed the certainty that by assisting in the death of Gain she might also assist in making Scout safe and his brother and his dirty businesses stronger and apparently sprucer. In the name of God, what kind of policing was that? It was the sort of puzzle she longed to take to Vic. Although he had next to no education, his mind could brilliantly unpick the moral subtleties of almost any situation, as long as unpicking them did not expose him in some way: that would be the difference between Vic and an Oxford tutor – Vic's moral philosophy was practical, learned on the job and self-interested. But Vic was not easy to reach these days and even if she reached him she was not sure which topics he'd feel safe with now.

Kerry would have to deal with this herself and alone and had begun to move towards the package to destroy it when Josie cried with soaring, slightly uncertain joy: 'Oh, Kerry, you did bring it, did you, did you? How lovely; lovely, lovely!' She ran into the cave past Kerry and pulled the envelope from the plastic cover, and then the cheque and the letter from the envelope. She read the cheque first, frowned momentarily, but after another second smiled, a make-the-best-of-it smile. Afterwards she examined the letter. Now, her voice boomed with absolute, assured delight and was thrown back and forth between the high wet walls of the cave, a wondrously echoing congratulation: 'You *are* shagging him, are you, Kerry, and on a regular basis so he trusts you to do such work on his behalf and pays through you? I think that's *really* nice. This must be a true affair.' She was in a blazer, shirt and tan slacks today, a neat outfit, and had heavy make-up on. Perhaps she wanted to look eighteen, in case P.D. reappeared. But she said: 'I'm sorry if I was talking yesterday like he was *available*. Silly. Unkind and silly and childish, I can see that now if you're – if there's a proper love affair, not just a quick bang at Old Drovers'. I *knew* it would be more than that if it was you, Kerry, because of your depth. I wouldn't have a hope, would I, just a kid, although mature for her age?' She waved the letter happily: 'Did he tell you what he has done? Did he show you this cheque and the letter? No? He's made the cheque out to you, because of precautions. That's in case someone else came in here and saw it by mistake and if it was just cash they could walk off and keep it. But now this cheque has to be taken to the bank, your bank, me not having a bank yet, and he says in the letter that he knows you will pay it over to me because you are so honest and I think this is really true. This is what I mean – he *really* knows you.' She held out the cheque to Kerry. Kerry took it. 'Thanks, Kerry,' she said. 'I think you should have twenty for yourself. You deserve a cut. Just give me eighty, all right?'

'No, not all right. The lot's yours.'

'Or has he already given you a good fee? And I'm definitely not going to put it around that you're having it off with Mr Pethor, because this could be upsetting for your hubbie and that other officer you know, the oldie, but never mind. Many grown up women need more than one man at once, I've heard of this, it's quite normal, don't be ashamed. I don't know if I'll be like that or happy with just one.' They moved out of the cave and around the headland. Today, the sea still had a few feet to come. P.D. was not in sight. He had been and withdrawn. Kerry tried to work out if she was disappointed. Josie said: 'The headmaster *will* be all right, won't he? It was just he's easy to describe, you know? Big nose, glasses, big gut. I did alter it a bit, the description. I said dark hair but he's ginger-bald. I didn't want anyone to track him down and give him misery. He's not so bad. He never ever tries anything, girls or boys, and he has lots of chances doing pastoral one-to-ones, patting kids to encourage them and that. I never heard of one pat going into hormone areas. It would be rotten if he was vengeanced because of total shit some anon voice gave Mr Pethor.'

'*Sold* Mr Pethor.'

'You taught me how some stuff was worth a bit.'

'Real stuff, not total shit.'

'Yes, well, there's not so much real stuff about lately,' Josie replied.

Twenty-Three

Apparently Ferdy Nate had heard in prison about the proposed meeting between Mrs Sabat and Scout Pethor at Scout's house and thought it was great. 'He wants me to go with her, if that's all right,' Lydia Nate told Kerry. 'He phoned me.'

'Great how?' Kerry replied.

'*Fucking* great. That's what he said. He doesn't do expletives very much, Ferdy, so when he says *fucking* great by phone this is really a big matter for him. Ferdy can get enthusiasms despite jail. They're very internal. It's one of the sweetest things about him.'

'I can see that. Fucking great, how?' Kerry replied.

'The ... yes ... the *joy* in his voice,' she said.

'Fucking great, how?' Kerry replied.

'He said he loved to learn of healing and gestures of peace.'

'Ferdy said?'

She gave a minor shrug but winced slightly, as though the movement had brought all-over physical pain. Her face was still lovely but perhaps not so full of fight and juice as Kerry remembered it, a little haggard. Was she ill? 'Now and then he speaks like that,' Lydia said, 'Sort of total pulpit arseholes.'

'Most villains do. It's spells of nostalgia for a decent life. But they talk it up too big because they've so much to compensate for. Same with statesmen and brokers.'

'He asked me to pass on to you in his own words that he loves to see healing and gestures of peace. I don't know whether that's from the Bible or if he made it up. Ferd has his own ideas. He said: "Let the sergeant know, or any of the others, about healing and gestures of peace." *Others* meaning police generally. I think he views it as a kind of education for you. Ferdy gets Sunday-school flashbacks. It can be really nice in him. New

Testament elements such as grace and *Cast thy net on the other side?* He'll recite in that flyblown accent, but intelligible.'

'Excellent.'

Lydia tidied a few things, preparing to leave with Mrs Sabat for Scout's. The three of them were in the piano room again, the Angela room. When Kerry had first met her, Lydia Nate's movements under the kimono were elegant and sinuous, but now she appeared musclebound, a bit tottery. Put alongside the discomfort she signalled just now, her symptoms might be those of someone who has taken a good neck-downwards hammering – feet, legs, arms, midriff, chest – one which left her face unmarked, but thorough, all the same. Hearing so much in jail, perhaps Ferdy had also been told about Lydia swooping fast on someone prime at the party the other night. Did he commission a skilled chum to remind her whose she was, even though he could not be around till release date? If she stripped for anyone now she might look like a car crash. Of course, the anyone probably looked worse. *His* face definitely would not be off-limits, nor his pants package. She wore a pale-blue trouser suit which covered almost everything.

'When Ferdy rang he said Christine Sabat would need some support at this sensitive time, so do accompany and befriend. "It could be extremely harrowing for her, Lydia.

This is confrontational. She will need you, dear." That was the word: harrowing.'

'Maybe,' Mrs Sabat said. 'But I need to see him and talk with him if I'm going to start to understand this thing. I need to talk with all of them. I don't mean just for a piece of magazine writing, though that's important. But I want to understand – me, personally, a woman – about the death of my daughter. Yes, it could hurt. It will be good to know I have someone like Lydia to turn to if necessary.'

'I'll be there,' Kerry replied.

Lydia said: 'Ferdy guessed that, but he still wanted me to go as well. This was a do-not-pass-by-on-the-other-side plea to me.'

'It *would* help if she could be with me, too,' Mrs Sabat said. 'She's such a friend.'

'Right. What else did Ferdy say?'

'That this was a case, the Sabat case, like no other case, a case of terrible encircling gloom, and thank God for a little kindly light. That's from Sunday school as well, I think, and wonderful. Sankey and Moody or that Cardinal. This particular gloom reaches Ferdy despite distance and his situation. He says to send him clippings from the local rag of the event at Scout Pethor's place today. It will restore his morale and perhaps even the morale of some fellow inmates, "showing, as it does, such happy reconciliation against all the odds, Lydia". I recall those words exactly.

Yes, there's a crap element to them, but perhaps a layer of genuineness.'

Kerry thought Ferdy probably needed someone trustworthy and knowledgeable and cowed like Lydia to brief him on the layout of Scout's place, the type of locks, alarms if there were any, where people slept, door geography, furniture geography, that kind of thing. For a hit inside a property, door placements were crucial. The gunman had to know exactly where the target would be when the door was shoved open, especially if it was dark. Ferdy would probably want only Scout killed, not Scout's wife, Charlotte, or their children. Ferdy had always been known for restraint. Maybe his Sunday school training included *Sufficient unto the day is the evil thereof.* That would apply to night as well as day, obviously. Ferdy would no doubt personally brief the people he told to do it.

'Has Ferdy heard about the rabbit?' Kerry asked.

'He said, "Fucking unfortunate",' Lydia replied.

'He's badly upset then, if he swore again by phone?'

'Animal welfare's a thing with him,' Lydia replied. 'He wrote to Mr Blair to back him on the anti-hunting bill.'

'It doesn't reach rabbits.'

'All the same.'

Detail of Scout's place would not be something Ferdy could ask Mrs Sabat to note for him. He did not even know Mrs Sabat. In any case, Lydia might have been trained in such work. Ferdy would see the dark business danger for his own outfits if Gain were declared the only offender in the Sabat case and then apparently killed by an avenger, avengers. And Ferdy might have a powerful suspicion that Gain *would* be killed, though not necessarily by avengers. In all meanings, this would most likely be an in-house job. The Pethors could then escape the stink of the case and thrive. At present, the two business complexes, Ferdy's and P.D.'s, had something like equal flaws in their leadership: Ferdy in prison, the Pethors tainted by Angela Sabat's murder. This kept them more or less level. But, if the Pethors emerged from the Sabat blame through nicely piling it all on to Gain, they would be strong again while Ferdy was still locked up. They might steam past Ferdy's outfit, maybe annihilate it. As far as Kerry could recall, Ferdy had at least a couple of celled years to go yet for violence and dealing substances wholesale. Also as far as she could recall, there might have been something about one or other of the Pethors or both helping to put Ferdy there, as a witty trade rivalry gambit. Was Vic in on that? As well as dark news about the rabbit, and about Lydia getting herself comforted, hints of long-term further business trouble would also reach Ferdy, where he was, and he might decide to do something to neutralise competition, and satisfy old enmities. It would not be just kind-heartedness towards his woman's new friend, Mrs Sabat. Would he knock off Scout first of the brothers?

'I expect Ferdy will want to know exactly how Scout manages the feeding of the rabbits now it's been shown as a risk activity,' Kerry said.'

'Poor creatures,' Lydia replied.

'Did he ask you to check on that, so Ferdy can be assured the animals are getting their proper nourishment?'

'It's a problem. The rabbits have done nothing to be victimised this way.'

'Not many rabbits get it easy. Did he ask you to check?'

'Just to be present,' Lydia replied. 'This is Mrs Sabat's occasion, not mine. The possible healing and gestures of peace.'

So, what must Kerry do? Oh, Christ she yearned to consult Vic. He'd see the essentials. Perhaps she saw the essentials herself, but did not want to give them too much clarity.

Lydia Nate said: 'Could you drive us? I think I've turned my ankle. Braking's difficult.'

'Yes, I *thought* you were limping.'

'Did it on the stairs.'

'It happens to all of us,' Kerry replied.

'No, I doubt that.'

When you thought someone was scheming a murder you ought to blow it, stop it, surely, and especially blow it, stop it, if you were a police officer. That category again – accomplice, accomplice, accomplice: the idea scared and sickened her. What if you *knew* the person to be murdered was an unconvicted murderer himself, though, and realised this might be the only way he would ever get done for it? Did that weird and sloppy lecture-room concept, natural justice, start sticking its nose in here? But could you *know* someone was guilty, if the jury said the opposite? Did her certainty in fact come from the foggy realm of gut feelings, instinct, rumour, folk wisdom and hearsay, all of which the law would have nothing to do with, and rightly? Natural justice wool?

The law required evidence, didn't it? *Didn't it, Vic?* Could Vic have answered straight, *if* she asked? *Had there been evidence, Vic?* She would not and could not have put that to him even if Vic were in front of her and ready to take his cigarette out of his mouth and talk. It was like saying, *Are you a crook on P.D.'s salary bill, Vic?* Accomplice, accomplice, accomplice. Who would brand a lover with that? Would you want to wrap your legs around such a man and hold him like a trophy? She was not sure. Love and sex did all kinds of things to people. Perhaps it would be difficult to accept a *husband* who was corrupt. Social virtues mattered in a marriage because marriage was a social contract. But could you expect a partner in adultery to be impeccable? It was absurd, wasn't it? Partners in adultery were by definition *not* impeccable. God, she would have liked to discuss this with Vic. He would be biased, though.

In Scout Pethor's cheerful sitting room with its flower pictures and soothing green velvet curtains he said: 'Mrs Sabat, I certainly don't want to make much of the attempted ambush that took place here when I am talking to someone who has seen real tragedy and is still living with it. But my point is, Mrs Sabat, this shooting showed us that monstrous, unjustified hatred against at least myself, and possibly my family, still exists out there. I greatly hope you do not share it. It's a privilege that I can put this uneasiness to you direct and in my own property. I'm so grateful you've been able to visit here today.'

'I've done a study of racism since it happened, as you'd expect,' Christine Sabat replied.

'Yes, I heard you were a writer looking for themes,' Scout said.

'It needn't be a constant state of mind in

someone, not always readable in the face like, say, Himmler's,' Mrs Sabat said. 'Race feelings can be spasmodic, a matter of mood, of impulse, conditioned by time, the company a person might be in, place. Your face, Mr Pethor—'

'Oh, please call me Scout.'

'I don't see racism there, not even though you're talking to a black, whose companion is also black.'

'Thank you,' Scout replied. 'I prize tolerance. Lydia, as we fondly refer to her, is also welcome here. Ferdy Nate has been a valued colleague in better times, and will be again, I'm sure, eventually.'

Mrs Sabat said: 'I see a childlike sort of face, and did in the street that day, a face not set in one particular cast, and which could take on any look, according to mood, impulse, time, company, place.'

'Night, with a mate, Bale Street?' Kerry said.

'I don't know whether you'd like to look at where the rabbit was killed, Mrs Sabat,' Scout replied. He waved a hand towards the shed, visible through French windows. Kerry thought Lydia Nate had already given some attention to these. She looked intently into the garden now. Kerry looked as well, to see what gripped her. A bulky man in his twenties and wearing a navy tracksuit was strolling down the path, just passing the pond, his back to them. Part of the protection? Scout did not mention him. Lydia kept watching, perhaps trying to work out from the hang of his jacket whether he was carrying anything, perhaps wanting him to turn and show his face, but he disappeared into the shed. 'It's an experience, to look at the actual spot,' Scout said. 'I think Sergeant Lake would agree with that.'

'This is a true rabbit experience,' Kerry said.

Scout was in one of the armchairs and suddenly leaned forward to speak very urgently to Mrs Sabat on the settee: 'You'll be pleased to hear that the reward we've offered is producing remarkable material. I won't elaborate now. I'll leave that to Philip. He'll be here shortly with his lovely friend, Susan Phelps, and a press photographer. Philip thinks it would be best if we restricted it to one photographer only. He doesn't want you over-bothered, and neither, of course, do I.'

'He's your tame picture man, is he?' Mrs Sabat asked. 'And his editor's tame, too?'

They were drinking white wine or fruit juice. There was a table with sandwiches and cakes on. Scout said: 'In some ways the information being gathered by the reward offer is embarrassing to us, I have to concede. But, as I mentioned, it is for Philip to make the disclosures as and when.'

'As and when what?' Kerry asked.

'Oh, after checks, of course,' Scout replied. 'Philip and I know the police are interested only in authenticated information. As it should be.'

'Embarrassing stuff?' Kerry asked.

'Yes, I think I can say that much.'

'How so?' Kerry asked. 'Do you mean the new information is the same as the old information and declares you and Matty Gain did it? Would this *really* be embarrassing? You've been through all that once, haven't you? You must have developed a skin against it by now. And you're always wearing a dab of most aromatic double jeopardy behind your ears.'

'I do hope this is a friendly occasion, Sergeant Lake,' Scout replied.

'Nobody's going to gun a rabbit,' Kerry said.

'I suppose if I have my picture taken with you it will announce to the world we're buddies now,' Mrs Sabat said.

Scout smiled, as if warmed by a fine thought. He seemed to mistake the tone of what she said. Yes, seemed. 'Although it will be only one photographer, he works for an agency and his photographs are sold everywhere. I love that idea – proclaiming to all the progress we've made. Perhaps the pics will be useful when you are doing your own article, Mrs Sabat. I understand you hope to write about the case and its aftermath.

Brilliant! This unsolved crime is indeed one that interests the world. It has what are referred to as overtones, you see – race and the police and so on.'

'That so?' Mrs Sabat said.

'I certainly don't hold it against you, the screaming at us in the street on our way to the Inquiry,' Scout replied. 'You had many frustrations to release, so why not at us?'

'Yea, you two seemed as good as any.'

'We were both nonplussed rather by the rape reference.'

'You two would be prey to a higher degree of delicacy than most, I should think,' Christine Sabat replied.

'And this must be Susan and Philip now, plus snaps man!' Scout cried. There had been a long ring on the doorbell. Scout did not get up from his chair but shortly the three new visitors entered the room with Scout's wife, who had let them in. The newspaperman carried a couple of cameras around his neck and seemed jumpy. Susan Phelps looked as neat and distant and non-bimbo as when Kerry met her at the reward launch party, and still not much like a teacher of slow learners.

'Now, isn't this something?' Mrs Sabat said, beaming, her eyes as hard as shrapnel. 'I'm so glad I came. I get to meet in a happy social setting two out of three people who were involved in the death of my daughter.'

'Well, not *involved*, Mrs Sabat,' P.D. replied gently. 'At least, not as far as we two are concerned. Involved? I mean, what does involved mean?'

'It means she thinks you and Scout either did it or were part of it in some other fashion,' Susan Phelps said. She had a way of talking with terse clarity, perhaps part of her training.

'Mrs Sabat, my brother and I are very aware of your pain and suspicions, believe me,' P.D. said. 'We have often spoken together about you, and especially lately when we knew you would be calling on him. But *involved* – that's not a word we—'

'Oh, God, Phil, all this smarm and now a fart-arseing discussion on words,' Susan said. 'What did you expect if Mrs Sabat is invited to see Scout and you – that she'll behave like Little Goody Two Shoes? This woman is still raw and full of rage. She thinks she's being soft-soaped and used.'

'What I told them,' Charlotte Pethor said.

'Who's the guy in the garden?' Mrs Sabat asked. 'This house like a fortress?'

'Yes. As a matter of fact, I would love to see the site where the mother rabbit was slain,' Lydia Nate said.

'Neighbours leave floral tributes in plastic wraps there,' Kerry said.

P.D. held up two hands, like surrender or like an order to keep silence. 'Sorry, but I'm still hung up on this word *involved*.' His small-featured, cheery face looked resolute.

'Hell!' Susan replied.

'It's the core of things, isn't it – I mean, if I may say, with respect, the misunderstanding revealed by it?'

'I think so,' Scout replied.

'You see, Mrs Sabat, it might be true to say my brother was involved, in the sense that he was accused. But that's a very loose use of the word involved. The acquittal declares categorically, unchallengeably, that he was *not* involved. And, as for myself, I have, of course, never been accused in any fashion of connection with this admittedly vile crime. And yet these terrible, offensive rumours persist. Hence, Mrs Sabat, what you call "the guy in the garden". Yes, we fear another attack on Scout. Wouldn't we be naive if we did not?'

'He's a bodyguard?' Lydia asked.

'It's a necessity,' P.D. replied. 'We hope temporarily. Oh, certainly, only temporarily.'

'It's appalling,' Lydia said. 'He's on continuous duty? He doesn't have to take on the responsibility alone, I hope, poor lad. He lives in? How long do you think it will be wise to keep Scout protected like this?'

'Well, until these disgusting slurs disappear,' P.D. replied.

'This is why it's so good to see Mrs Sabat here today,' Scout said. 'She can certainly help dispel the atmosphere of unfounded animosity that does persist.'

'Ah, the pictures,' Mrs Sabat said.

'I thought down near the rabbit shed,' P.D. replied. 'This would tell the story so completely.'

'Yes,' the photographer said.

'I'll come and watch,' Lydia said. Scout's wife went with them, too.

Susan helped herself to a couple of sandwiches and more wine. She seemed good at buffets. Kerry remembered that from the reward party. Susan Phelps said: 'What's it all add up to?'

'What?'

'The word's around about you and Phil at Old Drovers' Lane.'

'Oh, look, I—'

'And the word's around about you and the veteran cop at Old Drovers' Lane. Othen? And elsewhere. A steadiness between you? The one who starred at the Inquiry. You're a bit flagrant.'

'I—'

'You and Phil – that can't be anything. A business thing. He said a business thing when I asked about the buzz. I believe it. You wouldn't go with offal like him.'

'*You* do.'

'I'm offal, too – for doing it. I don't know how it happened. It did. I'm stuck with it now. He's a ... Well, he's what you know him to be, but I'm still stuck with it, until he decides something else. I sound feeble? Maybe you understand. Yes, maybe. You're stuck with this old cop, aren't you? The one who might be crooked. Marriage doesn't matter, does it? Does corruption? Don't get scared, Phil tells me nothing about that sort of thing. I wouldn't know if they were tied together commercially. I think all you want is to save the ancient, dandy officer, if he *can* be saved. Can he?'

'The Inquiry hasn't—'

'Does saving Othen mean destroying Phil?'

'I can't destroy him.'

'You sound damn regretful.'

'I hope so,' Kerry replied.

'Destroying him or destroying Scout. That would more or less do for Phil – because of the twin bonding. And do for the business.'

Kerry found herself floundering. Susan Phelps' apparent early boredom and detachment had gone. Suddenly, she was agonisingly intent about P.D. Kerry said: 'I can't destroy either of them, especially not Scout. He's deeply and legally pure.'

'I don't mean that kind of destroy – not a law matter.'

'Which kind, then?' Kerry asked, knowing the simple answer.

'Destroy. Like that. Literal.'

Kerry laughed.

'Others can destroy for you. Ferdy, Ferdy's

people. You're linked, aren't you? A closeness with Mrs Sabat through the job and then via her with Mrs Ferdy and via *her* to Ferdy himself. What's his woman here for?'

'A friend of Mrs Sabat, as you say. It's a strain for her. Christine Sabat might *need* a friend.'

'Casing the home and garden, making sure the real execution party doesn't fall in the pond?' Susan replied. 'You go along with it? Naturally. You reason that if the Pethors and Gain are wiped out there'll be no need for any vengeance folk out there to get at Victor Othen for covering up. And what the Inquiry eventually says won't matter much then, either.'

It wasn't a bad assessment. 'Wiped out? That's mad.'

'Ferdy would love it for commercial reasons as much as anything. Oh, I know you'll say the reward only exists to produce made-up tales that will load it all on to Gain.'

'Will I?'

'And that the shooting here was just a blind.'

'Will I?'

Susan stood at the French windows looking down to the photocall. 'I reckon Ferdy's girl would like to run her hand all over that minder, and not for the customary kicks. Why does Mrs Sabat agree to the pictures, agree to come here at all? It ought to be unthinkable – Christ, to hobnob with ... I mean, to come on to this territory.'

'Research.'

'She's lulling them – Scout and Phil?'

'For what?' Kerry replied.

'And you're part of it?

'Of what?'

'This should be unthinkable, too. A cop, for God's sake.'

'What should be unthinkable, too?' Kerry asked.

'This is conniving at murder.'

'What is?'

'You know.' She groaned. 'Christ, she *is* posing with him.'

'I expect she's been told Scout didn't do it,' Kerry replied.

'Of course she's been told it – by the court.'

'She's been told it in a different form today, I should think.'

'And she'll believe it?' Susan asked.

'Shouldn't think so. Do you? She'll show the whole episode as macabre opéra bouffe when she writes it up. She's a journalist. The *New Yorker* likes macabre opéra bouffe.' Kerry had stayed in an armchair. Susan came and sat near her in another chair. She had what people called good bones and they stood out now in her cheeks and under her eye sockets, a small patch of red on each. Kerry supposed it was anger or despair. In anyone they were feelings that often ran each other close. God, if you were locked to P.D. Pethor there must be a lot of both. Susan Phelps said: 'Have you considered what Ferdy might think and do, though, if he heard you were taking from Phil?'

'He won't. I'm not.'

'Bedding someone who took from Phil and now at it yourself.'

'No,' Kerry replied. 'Neither.'

'You're sure about Othen?'

'And about myself.'

'The hundred.'

'What hundred?'

'The hundred for the little girl. She rang again to say thank you and tell Phil you'd taken her to the bank and given her the cash. Some of these kids are so used to deceit they think they need to confirm any act of honesty.'

'Who pinches from kids?'

'OK, noble of you. But do you know what happens if one asks one's bank whether a particular cheque has been paid in? They send a photocopy. Phil could do that. Then the copy might get to Ferdy. Obviously, I wouldn't send it direct. All those nosy prison guards eyeing it in his mail. But I'm sure Phil would know someone else in that jail and could get him to pass it on to Ferd.'

'Ferdy's become so crucial, hasn't he?'

Susan reddened a bit more, perhaps angry that Kerry stayed conversational. Susan's voice crackled with an attempt at hardness, but not much of a one. She didn't have it. This was a woman who gave patience and care to unbright school kids. She couldn't turn fully brutal: 'Look, it's time you got dutiful, Sergeant, and stopped inertia-aiding this little scheme against Phil and Scout, or we ask for the cheque copy and it goes to Ferdy. You'll need to get a minder for *yourself.*' She sat far back in the chair and lowered her head. 'I told you I was offal. I've learned how to pull some dire strokes. There's a standard of living endangered here. I've got to look after it. You understand about that? Why you're still with your hubby despite Othen.'

Kerry leaned over and touched her arm comfortingly for a couple of seconds. 'There's a bit more to learn, Susan. Perhaps you're slow on this stuff and need a teacher. You can't believe I'd let a cheque into my account with P.D.'s signature on it as things are just now. It would be innocent, yes, but, as we all know, innocence is a bit of a variable. It depends where you're looking at it from. One of the first things they taught us on the accelerated promotion course was that if you were going corrupt go very careful as well. It's in all the Home Office manuals: An Officer's Handy Guide To Corruption – seven or eight pages. Well, what you'd expect, I imagine. I'm not corrupt, but it could certainly appear that way, you're so right. P.D. schemed it? He's *such* an opportunist. No wonder he's where he is and has you with him. Irresistible, I should think. Yes, could be I gave the child her hundred by drawing my own cheque, of course. She wouldn't know – a bit of business at the till, her standing behind me, and really interested only in making sure the cash did arrive.'

'Oh, come on. You're saying philanthropy? The police?'

'Who pinches from kids? But no, not philanthropy. Nothing so large-minded. The cheque has a six months' life, you know. It can be paid in when all this is not quite so steamy – after things have sorted themselves out a bit. P.D. will probably still be solvent, if alive. I'll risk some patience. One of the other tips in the Officers' Handy Guide To Corruption explains there are hot times and less hot times, and suggests making dangerous moves only in less hot times. And I kept P.D.'s letter, to explain all, anyway.'

Susan raised her head and turned direct to Kerry, as though to offer her fine, long face in frank shame: 'So, I had a go. Am I a fucking amateur, then?' she asked quietly.

'Well, of course you are,' Kerry replied. 'What else could you be? But not offal. You've left your usual ground for the sake of your bloke, that's all. Save him, save him, save him, whether he's offal or not. It *does* happen, women for men, men for women. They behave untypically, irrationally, disastrously sometimes.'

'You?'

'Here comes the photographic party,' Kerry replied.

'You? It would help me to know I wasn't the only one.'

'I just said it happens to many,' Kerry replied.

'Yes, but I want to know this from someone who's also stuck in it.' Her voice was full of entreaty.

'Here comes the photographic party,' Kerry replied. Mrs Sabat entered first through the French windows with Lydia, then Charlotte, P.D. and Scout. The photographer left.

P.D. said: 'I've been telling Mrs Sabat that, much to our horror, several people responding to the reward offer have named someone really very close to us as the likely murderer of her daughter.'

'Oh, dear, such a shock,' Kerry replied. 'Who would that be? Not Matty Gain?'

'But how did you know?' Mrs Sabat asked.

'This is what I meant when I told you all earlier it was embarrassing,' Scout said.

'Three people saw Matthew with Angela Sabat after he and my brother had left each other, apparently to go home,' P.D. said.

'You knew?' Mrs Sabat asked.

'Hunch,' Kerry replied. 'It seemed a likely.'

'But under your British law I believe nothing can be done about this, because the man Gain has already been found not guilty. Am I right?' Christine Sabat asked. She seemed composed. Perhaps she thought the information did not much change what she already knew. For her it might not be very relevant that Angela was killed by one man, not two, if the courts could not touch him. Didn't she realise there were people about who could give the courts some secret, violent help? Had she just been getting her picture taken with one of them, for her own purposes?

'Nothing could be done about it even if he had not been acquitted,' Kerry said, 'because Mr Pethor is never going to disclose the names of his three witnesses, are you, P.D.?'

'Confidentiality, you see, Mrs Sabat,' P.D. replied. He was standing, his body slightly hunched, as though to suggest diffidence and sensitivity. Everyone else had sat down. 'I had to guarantee this or the information would never have come.'

'You know the names, do you?' Kerry asked.

'First names – or what might be codenames,' P.D. replied.

'So how will they collect their reward?' Kerry asked.

'Secret drops.' He turned tutor and his voice grew apologetic for the slang he had used: 'Leaving money at an agreed spot in this kind of situation is termed a *drop*, Mrs Sabat.'

'You don't say,' Mrs Sabat replied.

'Sergeant Lake will be familiar with this word, won't you?' P.D. asked. 'There was the little girl whom I think you know.'

'Were you embarrassed or distressed by her information, too?' Kerry asked.

He smiled. 'One recognised it immediately as an attempted confidence trick, of course. Probably setting up some hate figure – a teacher? But I felt she deserved encouragement, and so paid out a fraction. My, but there were very detailed, dramatic instructions for the payment!'

'And by traceable cheque,' Kerry said.

'Because she was a child.'

'You knew that?' Kerry asked.

'Her voice.'

'And will you be paying the other three by traceable cheque?' Kerry asked.

'Cash. Certain amounts each,' P.D. said.

'And obviously *not* traceable. No accounting to prove the payments.'

'Confidentiality,' Scout said.

'We could easily set up an operation to identify the people who arrive to collect,' Kerry said.

'I feel that would be in open breach of the original pledge of non-disclosure,' P.D. replied.

'Oh, absolutely,' Scout said.

Mrs Sabat said: 'I do understand about the confidentiality, but if the need is to get witnesses who will testify in a court then surely—'

'But the need is *not* to get witnesses who will testify in court, you see, Mrs Sabat,' Kerry replied. 'There can't be a court because Gain is protected by the best protection in the book, double jeopardy.'

'That sounds almost like a quote from *Catch 22*,' Christine Sabat said.

'It's close,' Kerry replied.

'So, what the hell is the purpose of the reward, the search for witnesses?' Mrs Sabat asked.

'Yes, what the hell *is* the purpose, P.D?' Kerry said.

'Surely in some ways the quest for truth is its own justification,' Scout said.

'Do you believe all this shit, Mrs Sabat?' Kerry replied.

Charlotte Pethor said: 'Oh, now, that's enough. We don't have to put up with talk like that in our own house, and from a police officer. The children will be home from school shortly.'

'Do you believe all this shit, Mrs Sabat?' Kerry repeated.

'Are you saying Mr Pethor has heard no voices with information?' Christine Sabat said.

'I'd swear to one,' Kerry said.

'This is just professional scepticism – perhaps quite proper professional scepticism on Sergeant Lake's part,' P.D. said. 'Plus, possibly, a touch of mischief.'

'Absolutely,' Scout said. 'I don't believe she gives proper weight to the reward and responses any more than she does to the shooting here.'

'To put Gain up for avengers?' Mrs Sabat asked.

'It did move me, the site of the rabbit's death,' Lydia Nate said. 'Yet, I suppose you still have to go down regularly to the shed with feed, Mr Pethor? Quiet courageous. Is that once or twice a day, I wonder? I felt quite relieved the guardian figure was there while we were waiting for the pictures to be taken. He looked very capable. Would someone like that, engaged in very real protection duties, be entitled to carry arms?'

P.D. said: 'Not that in any way at all the death of the rabbit is being compared with the death of your daughter, Mrs Sabat.'

'Absolutely not,' Scout replied.

Susan Phelps stood up abruptly from her armchair and made for the door leading to the hall and front of the house. 'Thanks for the spread,' she said.

'Such a lovely room,' Lydia Nate said. 'Well, altogether a charming house. Such lovely proportions. And four bedrooms?

305

You'll need them, won't you, with children growing up and demanding their space and somewhere for chums stopping over?'

Twenty-Four

In the early evening, while Kerry was preparing a meal for her and Mark, she had another call from Gain. Mark answered first, grabbed at the receiver as soon as the bell went. It was his way these days and nights. He had always been quick to the phone, but now he was frantic. Perhaps he expected to get fired that way, instead of face-to-face at the office. Or even get forgiven over the phone.

She felt certain Stephen Comble would not end things like that. Stephen was a gent. He could be a right narrow, prim, blind twit, too, but gentlemanly with it. If he were going to do anything dickheaded about Mark's job he would do it properly, across a desk, most likely with a terrific *no-hard-feelings* handshake to conclude. Stephen was from the old school, the old school for slow learners in worldliness, and possibly Susan Phelps could give him some help.

Kerry herself must try to get at him soon.

Very soon. But it would have to be a seemingly accidental meeting, and this was not easy to fix. She would look absurd if she scurried down to Stephen's office simply and obviously to plead for Mark's job. On the other hand, she hated to see Mark squeezed so roughly by his worries, and she did not want to be married to a desperately deflated ex company director. Christ, Mark had been right about the damn reward launch, hadn't he? Didn't that garrison him? Or was there now no unambiguous right, just as there was no unambiguous innocence and guilt?

Mark passed the receiver to her: 'One of your no-names,' he said, handing over the mouthpiece. He put on a weak, slimily deferential tone. She had heard him imitate her callers before. It was almost forgivable. He felt he was excluded. He was. He mimicked: ' "Could I speak to Sergeant Lake, please? This is a matter of urgency." They all are, aren't they, Kerry? But this time it doesn't sound like a kid grass.' In his present state, Mark did not really believe anyone else could have urgent trouble, not comparable with his. 'This won't mess up the night, will it?'

She took the phone. 'Lake.'

'Can you get to me? Now,' Gain replied.

She recognised the gentle voice, even gentler this evening, from stress or the determination not to be overheard. She liked it little better, and found a *no* almost in her mouth. 'At home?' she asked.

'You'll need a pencil and paper.'

'Right.'

He spoke an address, not his own and not local. It was in Hackney, London, and she wrote it on her wrist. 'I had to get out,' he said.

'How?'

'The minders, you mean?'

'Yes, are you sure they weren't behind you, aren't close?' Did she mean she hoped they were?

'Those bloody pictures in the press – Scout and Mrs Sabat. Pals! Has she fucking gone mad, to allow that?'

'Yes, I know,' Kerry said.

'And P.D.'s been putting it around, like I thought – that I was the only one.'

'Yes, he will. Are you sure nobody knows where you are?'

'You do.'

'Well, I've got an address you gave me.'

'It's where I am.'

'You say,' she replied.

'What point in lying?'

'You've got the habit,' she said.

'Once those pictures were in the press, plus the rumour about me – well, the pictures said that, anyway, didn't they? So, a siege at our house – reporters, more photographers, TV, radio.'

'Yes, I heard. And there was a crowd after

Mrs Sabat and Scout.'

'Pethor's two heavies had to try and deal with them at my place, forgot about me for five minutes. My mother gave me all the cash in the house and then joined them outside, to help keep it going. They were all busy with one another, screaming, trying to do deals. I climbed over the dividing wall into the next garden, then into the next and the next, and out into the street behind ours. I walked it to the station. I was going to pick up a cab, but there are a lot of blacks driving, and I can be recognised.'

'A star.'

'I've always had a place up here. For business.'

'It's known?'

'Only to my mother.'

'Are you sure?'

'Pretty sure.'

She said: 'Why do you want me?'

'Yes, fucking why?' Mark muttered.

Kerry told Gain: 'You're in a different police area now. I can't protect you there, you know.' She would not want to protect him anywhere. That's what her brain told her. Instincts might be different, though. If someone telephoned and seemed to want help, there was a ridiculous, mawkish element that ordered her to offer it, even when Matty Gain was the someone.

Gain said: 'I told you, I don't need protect-

309

ing. I'm clear.'

'Yes?'

'What do you care, anyway? Are you part of it?' he asked.

It was a question that seemed to come her way often lately. She answered the same. 'Of what?'

'The scenario. *Get rid of Matt.*'

'It's an idea.'

'Bring a recorder,' he said.

'Why?'

But Gain had rung off. She tried to get the number through ringback, of course, but, of course, got nothing. Mark watched. He said: 'More shadiness?'

'Routine stuff. You're right, these people do like a bit of melodrama.'

'Meaning you have to go out.'

'I must do some listening.'

He hunched down in his chair like a sulking kid. 'God, Kerry, *I* wanted some listening here. I need to talk about—'

'I'm certain things will be all right, Mark.'

'Of course you're not certain things will be all right,' he snarled. 'Things are worse.'

'I can't believe that someone like Stephen Comble—'

'You've spoken to him?' He hardly waited for her to answer. 'No. What could you say, for God's sake?'

'I'd say—'

'It would be preposterous, wouldn't it, to

argue with him?' Mark replied. 'He's correct about the launch party, isn't he?'

'Of course he's not correct. He gets more and more wrong. Look, I must go. It might not be just melodrama. Someone could be very exposed.'

Oh, God, don't let him ask which someone. She would not have told him, but she did not even want to be asked. 'I might be very late.'

'Right. Great.' He stood up, angry, and paced a bit. 'You said, out of this police area, didn't you?' She should have done the call on the extension. 'How can you operate on another force's ground?'

The distance seemed to depress him as well as what he called the shadiness. Always the shadiness of some of her work unnerved him. He felt he was losing her. Kerry would drive to London. She wanted to be mobile, not tied to Gain, and there were no overnight trains to bring her home. She would have liked to say this to Mark – that she wished to get back to him immediately it was possible. Of course she did. She would say it because it was true and because it might console him. But she thought that when she said it she should be standing a bit closer to him, touching him, and she crossed the room, put an arm around his waist and her head on his chest. 'Mark, I'll come home the minute I—'

'Today, Stephen seemed even more convinced he had it all totally spot-on. Perhaps to you it looks like a minor difference between colleagues, something quite trivial, daftly expanded. But Stephen doesn't like what he calls *thematic* differences with board members. He's always said so. By thematic he means a disagreement which to him is symbolic of something far more than itself – a sign of something deeply alien.'

'To him.'

'Of course to him.'

'But *his* view is deeply alien to you.'

'Perhaps. Stephen is very wise. Anyway, what I'm saying is that this clash over the Pethor catering is thematic,' he replied. 'And harmful.'

She took her arm from his waist and drew away.

Mark said: 'Those pictures in the papers – the girl's mother and one of the Pethors, the acquitted one. Doesn't publicity like that say the court was right? It supports Stephen's attitude.'

'Stephen can go fuck himself,' Kerry replied.

She did not find the Hackney address until after eleven p.m. It was the kind of street where you would not want to leave your car overnight as a regular thing, but she might get away with it this once. There were not many spaces, anyway. It was actually called The Avenue and had large multi-flatted

Victorian houses on both sides of a grass island where beech and oak grew: a lot of living units, a lot of vehicles. The properties had once been imposing, even grand, and Kerry climbed a flight of wide stone steps to ring for 4A in a panel of bells. New-looking voice boxes had been fixed alongside but nobody answered. God, had someone else found him? Gain might have made it easier for them by coming to a far-off, anonymous bolthole like this. It angered her a little to discover she could still not help worrying about him. But this anger was brain again, not instinct: if someone asked you in that kind of voice to get to him quickly he became your responsibility, didn't he, even someone like Gain?

The door opened and he was there in the dark hall. She could make out the squat body and plump, round face. 'So, are you all right?' she asked.

'I'll confess,' he said.

Twenty-Five

I, Matthew Hone Gain, in the presence of Detective Sergeant Kerry Lake do hereby confess to the murder of Angela Sabat, carried out jointly with Peter Vincent Pethor, known as Scout. This statement is given voluntarily by me at a London address which, for safety reasons, must remain utterly confidential.

Kerry switched off and said: 'Keep the *hereby* if you have to, but not *utterly*. It sounds purple. And it's best to leave me out of it. This is going to be an anonymous tape, otherwise they'll want to know how I was in touch with you and where you are.'

'But to authenticate – to identify me. I'm just a voice. People can imitate voices. I'll do it as I want.'

'Put in plenty of things known only to you and your mother. *She'll* authenticate.'

'That won't be enough,' Gain replied. 'I know about courts. They don't like anonymous stuff or doubtful stuff.'

Always this explanation needed, even to him: 'It's *not* for a court.' Kerry replied.

314

'There can't be a court. The court has been and gone. It fucked up. Remember? If it hadn't, you wouldn't be confessing. As it is, you can confess and still be safe – from the law, that is. And the tape is not anonymous. It's you, Matty Gain, all through. It will be enough for what we want. What we want is to knock sick the Pethors and the Inquiry.' She could have said as well, to knock sick Stephen Comble and his ludicrous, stunted theory that innocence was innocence, that courts could confer it, and that if Mark couldn't accept this he was out of sympathy with the firm and Great Britain and really ought to consider his position. Gain did not know Comble, though, and the name would be meaningless to him. 'I'm running from the start again,' Kerry said.

I, Matthew Hone Gain, in the presence of Detective Sergeant Kerry Lake, do hereby confess to the murder of Angela Sabat, carried out jointly with Peter Vincent Pethor, known as Scout. This statement is given voluntarily by me at a London address which, for safety reasons, must remain utterly confidential. When I refer to safety reasons, I mean that I might become a target for people, possibly black, who feel Angela Sabat should be avenged privately, because the courts have failed to avenge her. I would understand such feelings. I mean also that I might become a target for those mentioned herein with myself,

315

white. I have feared them for a long time and this fear is the main reason for my confession now. I believe that by bringing the Pethor twins to renewed public attention in this way, I will make it impossible for them to conspire in secret to make me the sole culprit in the Sabat case, and possibly to kill me or have me killed, as if by black people seeking to punish an unpunished racial crime, but really by their own white plotting – and even possibly their own hands. I wish it to be on record that if I am mysteriously injured or killed the most probable assailants are P.D. Pethor and his brother Peter (Scout). In order to prove my identity, I wish to say that when I was a small child living with my parents and sisters in Warrington, we had for a short time a black and white cat called Prince Albert. I would also state that at this time my mother used to go to a hairdresser called Francine's in Date Crescent.

He waved a hand to tell her to switch off again and, when she did, said: 'I could sell all this to the tabloids, you know.'

'Not the stuff about Prince Albert.'

'The tale I'm going to tell,' Gain said. 'The correction of evidence Scout and I gave at the trial.'

'Well, you *might* find a paper willing to take the libel risk.'

'Libel the Pethors? How the hell could that happen?'

'Scout's so clean in law. Like you.'

'Nobody believes it.'

'Yes, some do. My husband's boss.'

'Ah, that piss you off?' he asked.

'Of course.'

'He might have been right,' Gain said.

'Yes, he might have been. He isn't,' Kerry replied.

'The one who did the buffet?'

'Yes.'

'And I suppose your husband was against because you'd told him to be.'

'He was against because he knew it was right to be against.'

'He's got trouble because of it?'

'He *had* trouble,' Kerry replied.

'OK. But, anyway, P.D.'s different. We couldn't libel him. He hasn't been acquitted of anything.'

'He hasn't been charged,' Kerry said. 'You'll see from what I'm going to say that he could be done as accessory.'

'How could we prove P.D. accessory to a murder when the people he allegedly helped are innocent?'

'Not just allegedly. I'm going to—'

'He's innocent, too. Legally. You've heard of guilt by association? This is innocence by association. Papers would have to be very wary. But, of course, the stink of the Sabat death will stay. More so. That's what we want, plenty of destructive ill repute to cripple P.D.'s businesses, maybe get the twins battling among themselves, doing each other bad damage. These will be limited achievements, but limited achievements is all we can manage now. It's generally all the police *can* manage.'

'Is Ferdy Nate paying you? You'll take out the competition for him?' He clenched his chubby face in concentration. 'Or do you go two ways, like some? Have you got a passion running with his girl, Lydia? Or Mrs Sabat? Are you doing it all for Lydia, or Mrs Sabat?'

Kerry moved a hand towards the recorder switch. 'You ready for more?'

'Wait. I wouldn't want to deal with the press. Too dangerous – there might be tracing, publicity.'

'Publicity is what it would be about.'

'No, I mean publicity saying where I was, maybe bringing my mother in. That's no good.' Again the sudden tightening up of his features: 'Listen, could *you* sell it for me, say split the takings, three quarters to me, a quarter to you. We're talking six figures here.'

'And then the tabloid that fails to get the tapes does some spoilsport digging and comes up with a headline, "Girl cop flogs race killer's confession." '

'They can't call me a race killer, the bastards. I was cleared.'

'You're saying on the tape you're a race killer.'

'But that's different.'

'Is it?' Kerry said. 'Anyway, I'm not going to hawk it.'

'What *will* you do with it? I want it heard. It's got to be heard by the right people, or it won't help me.'

'Let's see how it all sounds.'

He leaned across and might have taken her wrist for emphasis, but she saw it coming and backed in time. 'You *know* what you'll do with it, don't you?' he said. The normally gentle voice went suddenly bitter and harsh.

Of course she knew what she would do with it. First thing, she would shove a copy down Bert Nipp's forensic throat and possibly the lawyer, Geddage's. Then another down Stephen Comble's. She might get yet another to Mrs Sabat. Kerry felt the fine certainty she could save both her men. She considered it the sort of role that suited her. She was made for it. That dog-eared, wrinkle-eyed Julie could never bring off anything like this for Vic, and he would realise it, be radiantly, everlastingly grateful. And Mark could never do it for himself, and he would realise it, be radiantly, everlastingly grateful. There might be some other uses for the tape afterwards, too. She nodded towards the recorder: 'Right?'

'Fucking slippery cops,' he said. 'My uncle Alf always told me never to give anything to a—'

'Which maximum security college did *he*

graduate from?' Kerry asked.

Gain was sitting opposite her, the recorder on a coffee table between them. He still did not begin talking for the tape again but looked up and gazed fondly around the flat. 'You thought this would be some sort of shit heap, didn't you?' he said.

'It's bijou,' Kerry replied. And it was, once you were into the flat. The front door to number 4A had been reinforced on both sides with steel sheets. All the other doors giving on to the bare first-floor landing were also steel-covered, at least on the outside. The landing was lit by a weak bulb high up under reinforced glass and metal bars. The flat itself, though, was clean, neat, even luxurious. Perhaps Gain was right and she had expected a pit. Foolish. After all, he had been brought up in a big, nicely furnished house in a prestige district. Gain had inherited standards. The flat was wall-to-walled in what looked like four-to-five-star-hotel-quality dark-blue carpet, and there were modern leather-covered easy chairs, the glass-topped coffee table, what could be a rosewood dining table and a half-full rosewood book case. She could see some Wodehouse there and *For Whom The Bell Tolls* and an antiques guide. The books looked used. This could be a rounded murderer with a sense of humour. She hated the dopiness of Wodehouse herself but many said he was brilliant with comic metaphor, so perhaps Matty was into metaphor. They drank Coke.

'I know some good people in this area,' Gain said.

'Good how?'

'People who look after themselves.'

'Diet? Lots of fresh air?'

'They look after themselves. They'll look after me. Some of them owe me. If the Pethors or any of them come hunting I can pick up a phone.'

'London's getting a lot of street gunfights,' Kerry said.

'Yes, I heard. It would suit you, maybe.'

'What?'

'Me and some friends blasting away at the Pethors and vice versa. Annihilating one another.'

'You do guns?' Kerry replied. 'Be careful. The Met have armed response cars, quite quick-arriving if the traffic's right, and heavy stuff in the boot. Bang-bang-bang from all directions.'

'That *would* suit you, wouldn't it?' Gain said. 'Simplifies things.'

Oh, yes. She switched on.

It was unusual, Scout and myself to be waiting at a bus stop. I mean, Scout is forty-one. This is not an age to be still riding on buses unless you don't make any money. But my car was in dock and his wife, Charlotte, is fussy about the breathalyser

– goes on at him. He's been done once. She didn't really like him being out on the town with me – ladding, she called it – so he has to behave a bit. We were going to the Panache club on the bus and then a taxi home or to a girl's on the way, see what happened. But I think Scout felt ashamed to be in a bus queue when the 31 came in with the black girl on it. He didn't want to be seen like that. Degrading, especially in front of a smart black girl. He was from the Pethor family and wearing one of his great suits but you might have thought he did not have a car. She might have thought it. I believe this is really why he said to follow her. It was not just to follow her, it was to pretend we had not been waiting for the bus at all but happened to be passing the spot when the bus came in and we were really on our way up Bale Street to Lakin Street where the local action was, which we were both dressed for.

Well, so we walked behind her up Bale Street, towards Lakin, and we gave her some jollying – a bit, that's all.

Kerry switched off: 'What's that, jollying?'

'Oh, you know.'

'No. Shouting? Like the woman witness in the car heard?'

'Yes, shouting. More like chanting.'

'Chanting what?'

'Oh, you know.'

'No, what?' Kerry said.

'Jollying her.'

'Race stuff?'

'Well, she was black, wasn't she? You can't go around pretending she's not black. She was. This was only telling the obvious, not abusive. Just a fact. Rhymes and so on. I mean, some of that political correctness stuff is too much, isn't it? She had that way of walking some of them have. You know.'

'Who?'

'Like owning the place. We didn't know then she was American but if we had known that and she walked like coming over here and owning the place we would have jollied her even more, I expect.'

'When you were jollying her, it was enough to make the woman witness in the car worried for Angela Sabat.'

'In a way I blame her,' Gain replied.

'Who?'

'That silly lady in the car. P.D. could never find her, you know. We told him what car make, but we didn't have all the number. We'd had some vodkas and a smoke, of course, before all this, and it was hard to remember numbers.'

'P.D. tried to get to her?'

'He's very good with witnesses, I must admit. He'll talk to people who might be witnesses and convert them like a gospel preacher so they decide they'd really rather not after all, and they'll discover they didn't actually see anything anyway. Or he'll show them how to get it wrong at an ID parade – mess it up. Those bus stop people. It could have been difficult, but P.D. found them, don't ask me how, and had a conversation. This is a real skill. It was because of identification – *no* identification – that we got off, wasn't it? No reliable identification. But the woman in the car – no, P.D. never reached her in time, and so she appears at the trial.'

'But not very helpful with identification,' Kerry said.

'This wasn't because P.D. had advised her, just that she didn't get a proper sight. That's why I said I blame her – well, in part. We knew she had seen us – gawping out of the window of the car, looking so … so fucking *involved* and *worthy*. You know how women can seem when they're looking out of a car window.'

'No, how?'

'Sorry, but it's true. So, I thought, she'll be around again on the one-way system for another gawp. This is a busybody. Best get off the street now. *Now.* Maybe otherwise we would have talked to the girl in the street for a while. Perhaps that would have been all.'

Kerry said, 'I'm switching on again. Go over that bit, will you?'

'Which?'

'The woman in the car.'

Kerry started the recorder.

Gain began. 'While walking behind the girl

and occasionally calling out to her in a cheerful but maybe slightly provocative way, I will now admit, we noticed a woman in a Fiat Punto SX who was driving down Bale Street staring at us through the passenger window. She did not stop but we thought she might go around the block and return, perhaps to pull up and interfere this time. So we decided in a hurry it was best to get off the street. That is, get off the street and take the girl with us. There was nobody else about in Bale Street at the time. We had to run a few steps to catch up with the girl and when she heard us running she looked back and then she started running, too. She should not have done that. This turned it into a kind of chase or a hunt. It was exciting and it also made us a bit angry, her trying to get away.

'If we had not had some drinks and the smokes it might not have made us angry, because, really, we would have realised that if a girl in an empty street at night hears two men running behind her when they have been shouting at her she would think this was a dangerous situation and try to get away, especially if she is black and the men are white. I don't think there was anything sexual, not for Scout or me, although she had a figure, definitely, like many of them do, all present but not burly. Her mother was definitely wrong when she shouted in the street the slur that we did not even notice she was shaggable, only black. This was terribly sad and so unfair. I know I thought the girl was quite a piece and I think Scout did, too. But it was not about things like that at the time, it was just the hunt. The fun of it and the pressure. We had to get her off the street and into the building site before she reached Lakin Street, because once she was there she could lose herself in one of the caffs or cinemas, plus there were always many people around in Lakin Street even late, including blacks – they might try to protect her, you know what they're like. They would think of her as a sister. Although we said in evidence at the trial that we lost her in Lakin Street, this is not true, of course. I fear we both lied about this, as suggested by P.D. Pethor. She did not reach Lakin Street.

'So we caught up with her because she was in heels and could not really run and we were one on each side. Scout said: "Madam, we would like to show you around a site of some attractive new properties which might interest you." It was a joke, naturally. He was like acting a role, like an estate agent, and pretending the girl was an important client. She did not want to come. Of course not; but we were holding one arm each. She tried to stay cool and she answered like it was a serious idea, this invitation to see the properties, but she said, "I can't now owing to other commitments, but I'll take a rain check." I thought this was really brave of the girl, her voice all right, nothing panicky, not that I could see, and the politeness. She was not struggling yet. When she talked we knew for the first time she was American. It was her accent but also when she said take a rain check, which is American, meaning I'll pick up the chance some other time when it is more suitable. So Scout said, "Are you from the deep South, my little cotton picker?" But she said, "Detroit." And Scout said that being from a mighty city she would probably want a grand property when she settled in this country and that luckily this building site had many executive-standard houses and it would be a good idea to look at them at night like this before the crowds arrived to view.

'She did start to get in a bit of panic then and she was tugging, trying to get her arms free and she began to scream. We were becoming anxious and more angry because we thought that the Punto woman could show again and if she saw this going on and heard she would stop and try to do something civic or get to a phonebox or use her mobile – if women are driving by themselves they usually have a mobile. We start pulling the girl hard towards the building site and she is still struggling and kicking out and yelling and screaming. There was a gate to the site, locked with a chain at night and we had to get her over this, it was not easy. Scout climbed over first and I had to hold her by myself while she's fighting and then lift her so Scout could get a hold of her and drag her over. This girl had plenty of strength and body. Then I had to get over after her fast to help him control her. But because she was fighting like that and not just fighting to get away but fighting to keep her clothes down he could not keep a grip on her as she was going over the gate, and she didn't have any balance because of the struggling and she fell, she fell pretty hard against the gate on the other side. She did not move. Her skirt was up and showing a lot but she did not move and because she did not try to put her clothes right again now we both thought she had hit her head and was knocked out and couldn't care any more about where her skirt was. She was cut on one leg. I climbed over and we stood there looking down at her, and a bit scared.

'But she was only acting. It was brave again, really. She rolled away from us suddenly and sort of growled and then got up and started running further into the site. I thought this girl definitely had something, some true spirit and guts, and she made a hunt worthwhile, like news reports of hunting a stag which would not give in. We went after her, but not running fast because we did not want the chase to end too quickly or everything would be too easy. We were shouting a bit again, not jollying shouts like the ones in the street but more like huntsmen's horns, high, musical sounds, no words, because of the excitement and fun. It was a bit dicey in there, foundations and holes in the ground, you had to be careful and do some leaping, like in a proper hunt, not hedges, of course, but sewer trenches and so on.

'Because we let her run ahead a good way we lost her for a little while and Scout got really ratty, said we had been a pair of twats. We had to start searching some of the houses that were half built or less and luckily we did find her eventually, crouched right down against the start of a dividing wall between two rooms in what they called the blue house at the trial. Scout found her and he started to laugh then, he was relieved. But she jumped up – she had found a masonry chisel, a heavy thing, a foot long, and she came at Scout with it. You could have guessed she lived in Detroit. He was still laughing and he dodged about, keeping out of reach of it. He is forty-one and he looks heavy and awkward but he's still pretty good on his feet.

'I had been searching another house but when I heard him laughing I came fast to the blue house and saw him jumping about while she tried to hit him. Although it was dark, of course, there was enough light from the moon to see that. I thought again of the way some stags can turn and fight at the end. So, I picked up a brick from a stack and went to join Scout, so she would have two to deal with and get confused. She was gasping and tired, her hair down over her face and there was spit hanging from her mouth. The next time she went for Scout I was able to get in close quickly on her left hand side and give her a true crack with the brick on her head. She did not go down straight away, she was strong even now, but she was dazed and her legs went weak like a boxer after a hiding. Scout jumped in and grabbed her arm at the wrist and twisted it so she dropped the chisel. He bent down fast and picked it up. She had bent towards it as well and I was able to give her two more cracks with the brick, this time on the back of her head. I thought I felt something in her skull break at the first blow. Then Scout stood up and as the girl began to topple hit her twice on the head with the chisel and then twice more when she was on the floor. You see, this is what I mean when I say it was not from disrespect or anything like that that we did not fuck her. We did not have time, that's all.'

Kerry changed the tape. In the telling, Gain had gone from the fervour of the recollected thrill to a sort of offhand flatness, as if the death of the girl had finally turned into something workaday, inevitable. She restarted the machine. Gain continued.

'Almost as soon as it was over we realised how bad things were. I wanted to get off the site immediately and away. We both had some blood on us, but nothing too obvious. We could have walked home without anyone noticing. It was nearly one a.m. by now and, as long as we didn't go into Lakin Street, there were unlikely to be many people about. I thought we should separate, avoid cabs and get out of sight. It seemed crazy now that the idea of a hunt could have made us act like that, not decent or intelligent.

'But Scout called P.D. on his mobile. These two, twins, they depend on each other a lot, especially Scout on P.D., although Scout is the older one. You know how twins are, often. P.D. arrived in his car straight away and said we were total and outright cunts. He came in the red Laguna, not his usual Saab with the personalised plate, because it would be too easy to identify, I expect. He had a flashlight and did a real squint at the spot where the girl lay. He took the housebrick and the chisel and put them into the boot of his car for losing somewhere later on. Then he took us to his place. He's got a girl but she doesn't live in, so it was all right there. He made us tell him everything from the very beginning at the bus stop, describing all the people we had seen, including the woman in the Fiat, of course. He said he would do a trawl. We stripped. He gave us both some of his

clothes. They were all right for Scout, naturally, because he and P.D. are about the same
build, being twins. They were big on me, but
it was just to get me home. I knew my mother
would be asleep, and Scout thought
Charlotte would be as well, so nobody was
going to notice we'd come back in different
clothes from the ones we left in. He said he
could burn our original clothes on a garden
bonfire next day. He gave Scout some shoes
as well but P.D.'s would not fit me and I
promised to bring my trainers in the morning
so he could burn them with the clothes. I did
that. There could have been footprints in the
site mud and specks of blood on the trainers.
Then he drove us both back to near our
homes. I walked the last few hundred yards,
so there would be no noise of a car approach-
ing our house, and I expect Scout did the
same.'

Gain sat back in his chair. 'And this
concludes the confession of Matthew Hone
Gain, certified as true.'

Kerry switched off. 'What time was it when
you'd finished everything and went home?'

'About four a.m. It took a long while to tell
P.D. everything. He was making notes and
was very fussy about getting every detail of
what happened. Thoroughness is a big thing
with P.D.'

'Right. So, from the time he turned up at
the building site until four a.m. you were

with him continuously and he did not get in touch with Vic Othen?'

'Couldn't have.'

'I suppose he might have called him immediately he heard from Scout – before driving down to meet you at the site.'

'No. P.D. was worried later when he heard Othen had been there at three a.m. He said it meant someone else knew about the killing – some *voice* as he called it, meaning informant – and had rung Othen. This could be another witness.'

'And never found?' Kerry asked.

'Othen wouldn't disclose where the tip came from, would he?'

'It's a bit of ancient gallantry. Detectives of Vic Othen's vintage don't name their tipsters, even if not naming them lands the detective in shit.'

'Yes, I suppose he *is* gallant, isn't he, or you wouldn't be fucking him.'

'Can you put this last bit on the tape?' she said.

'You want something to set him right with the Inquiry, do you?'

'Of course I want something to set him right with the Inquiry,' she replied, 'and to piss on that virtuous lawyer, Geddage.' And to make sure Harry Bell in his deviousness could not make a burnt offering of Vic.

Matthew Gain did that tortured rearranging of his face. 'Do I care what they say about your lover boy?'

'Vic Othen and I could try to see your mother stays all right,' she replied. 'There might be trouble by association for her if people hear this tape.'

He gave a short, almost silent whistle. 'Tough bitch, aren't you? Who taught you how to lean, Ferdy Nate? You're sure you could look after her?'

'We'll try,' she said.

'Can you speak for Othen, then?

'Most likely.'

'He's only on the side, isn't he?'

'We're colleagues who understand each other.'

'Yes, I heard.'

'He sticks by any undertaking. That's why he kept quiet about his source at the trial.'

'He sticks by you? Isn't he with someone else?'

'He'll stick by me on this,' she replied.

He stared at her. 'Oh, sorry, you're hurt. Shouldn't I have mentioned he's with someone else?'

'He'll stick by me on this,' she replied.

He enjoyed a couple of deep, thoughtful breaths. 'All right. Switch on. From Scout's call to P.D. on the mobile, yes?'

'Exactly there. And make sure you put in the bit showing there was no call from P.D. to Othen throughout and that P.D. said there must have been another voice.'

'Is this what the whole thing is about for you – putting Othen right?'

'We're rolling,' she replied.

Twenty-Six

Kerry typed out a script for Josie Cosse to read and then listened in on the extension. Josie would have to ad lib a little, too. She could manage that. Josie had already done something like this once when phoning P.D., a mixture of script and off-the-cuff. She was a bonny actress, a gifted liar. There was a future for her somewhere, perhaps as a police detective, if she could make do with the money. But possibly she would find ways to augment that.

They were at home in Kerry's place. Mark was at work. He had said yesterday that things had changed there, and suddenly Stephen seemed to have come round to thinking Mark might have been right about the launch buffet after all. 'Strange,' Kerry had said.

'He doesn't talk about *dangerously fundamental thematic differences* between us any longer,' Mark replied.

'Oh, good.'

'He feels he has been narrow and hidebound in assuming that a court's word on innocence or guilt is necessarily always the right word.'

'I thought he would grow up,' Kerry said. 'You didn't speak to him, did you?'

'No. I got the impression you didn't want that. Humiliating – a husband getting his wife to crawl to the boss.'

'So he must have thought his way to a changed view on his own.'

'Must have,' Kerry said.

'Perhaps the enlightenment is more valuable, stronger, coming like that.'

'Yes, a kind of lone intellectual journey, with the prize of truth at the end.' A lone intellectual journey but guided by a tape or two.

Josie dialled 141 to hide her number and then rang the reward offer number again. She had on jeans and a T-shirt with *YOU WHAT????* written on it in green. When P.D. answered, Josie said: 'Mr Pethor, it's the mysterious observer once more. You know? The hundred quid girl?'

'Ah, yes. This is nice.'

'Yes, well a hundred quid is all right but it's not going to change my life, is it?'

'I'm glad we were able to help,' Pethor replied.

'I've got something more for you.'

'Yes?'

'You didn't find that man I mentioned to you, did you?'

'Not yet. But, of course, we are still searching.'

'It doesn't matter. I found him myself.'

Pethor said: 'Really?' He had sounded bored until now but his voice grew tense suddenly and alert. He suspected, didn't he, that someone else had been around Bale Street and the site and must have contacted Vic. But how could the child know this? Pethor would be sceptical, of course, but baffled and scared as well. Baffled above all. Fine.

'Yes, I found him and I spoke to him,' Josie said.

'Oh?'

'He's not the one.'

'Not the one?'

'Not the one who did it – did the girl. But he saw everything. He was there, watching.'

'He told you this?'

'Yes,' she said.

'I've never understood how you yourself knew he was present. You couldn't have been in the vicinity as well, could you?'

'Could I?' she replied. Josie began on the script: 'I read about the trial, and I think what he says happened is totally different from what was in the newspaper court reports.'

'Oh?'

'Two men, one about forty, one thirtyish, both in smart suits, fighting with the girl in Bale Street and dragging her towards a gate leading to the building site. These men, neither very tall and quite hefty. One of them was a bit like you, really, I suppose, and about the same age. Dark hair. That is, the older one. This was just after the woman drove past in a Punto SX. He said she came back again, which is right, isn't it – that was in the trial? But by the time she came back the three who were in Bale Street had gone. They were over the gate and into the building site, although the girl fell when they were forcing her over.'

'Fell? I don't recall anything like this at the trial.'

Josie left the script for a while. 'No, of course not, because in the trial the three did not go over the gate, did they? The girl ran to Lakin Street and the men lost her. That was the story.'

'Story?' Pethor said. 'I prefer the word *evidence*.'

'Yes, I wouldn't be surprised. After a while this witness decided to go after the three and he climbed over the gate, also.'

'Really?

'Yes, really. The girl had managed to get away from these two men in suits and they were looking for her – playing at hunting her, making sounds like the horn they have for fox hunts. She couldn't run very fast because she was in heels, and there were all sorts of obstacles on the site. They did not rush, anyway. They were enjoying it, a game. After a while they found her. She was crouched down and hiding in one of the uncompleted houses, in fact the house that they called the blue house in the trial. She had picked up a big masonry chisel to defend herself and she tried to attack one of the men, the one who looked a bit like you, Mr Pethor.'

For a while he stayed quiet. Then he said: 'Are you reading this? *Masonry chisel.* How do you know words like that? Has someone written this for—?'

'But the other man came and he had a housebrick and when the girl was concentrating on the other man, that is, the man who looked like you, Mr Pethor, the younger one hit her with the housebrick on the head and she staggered. Then the one who looked like you jumped in and made her drop the chisel. He bent down to pick it up. And the girl tried to pick it up, too. I expect she knew that if she didn't have a weapon she would be no good against these two at a spot where nobody could help her.'

'This *witness* could have helped her, if what he says is true. If there's any such person.'

Josie stayed with the script. 'When she was bending like this, the younger man hit her twice more on the head with the housebrick and, as she was falling, the older man, the one who looks like you, Mr Pethor, hit her twice with the big chisel, also on the head. And when she was lying on the ground he hit her twice more. The thing about a masonry chisel is it's heavy, a real weapon. She looked as if she was dead then.'

'Where *was* this witness? He wasn't seen?'

'The older one, the one who looks like you, Mr Pethor, went outside and was talking into a mobile. Not long afterwards another man came in a red Renault Laguna. He looked a bit like the older man, the one who looks like you, Mr Pethor. So, obviously, the one who came in the Laguna also looked like you. Do you get it? Sorry it's complicated. The Laguna man called the other two something not very polite, really – he called them *cunts*. Then he took the housebrick and the chisel and he put them into the boot of the car.'

'Where was the Laguna? How could the witness see the car if he was near the house? The car could not get on to the site. It must have been in the road.' Pethor probably believed no part of how the girl said she had come by this account – well, of course he believed no part of it – but at the same time seemed compelled to treat the call as if it made sense. And, also of course, he *did* have to treat it as sense, because he knew from debriefing his brother and Gain on the night that what she said *was* sense. Was fact.

'After this, the Laguna man looked around where the body of the girl was, like checking. He had a flashlight. When he was satisfied, the three of them drove away.'

The line went silent again for a few moments. Then Pethor said: 'It's rubbish.'

'This is information worth a fat reward, don't you think, Mr Pethor?' Josie read. 'More than a hundred. Much. The press might pay a lot for this information, but I would rather it was private, for you only.'

'It *isn't* private, is it? There's the "witness".'

Josie did not answer at once. There was nothing in the script to deal with this. Then she said: 'He won't talk to anyone, except to me. I give him my body. Wednesdays. Do you understand what I mean when I say *give him my body*?'

'It *is* all rubbish, isn't it?'

'Is it?'

'Blackmail.'

'Is it? Do you know anyone with a red Laguna who calls men *cunts*?'

'Who's behind you – Lake? Has she talked to Gain?'

Josie read again: 'Would you like to bring something really plump to the cave tomorrow? That's about five o'clock in the afternoon, nearly high tide. And cash, not a cheque.' She put the phone down.

Kerry did, too, and joined her in the living room. 'Nice, Josie,' she said.

341

'I thought Wednesdays would be the right sort of day if I was offering a man my body. It would give him something to look forward to about halfway between weekends.'

'I've heard men say Wednesdays are a desert without a girl's body about.'

'Most of them are after it all the time, not just Wednesdays,' Josie replied. 'I don't know if you've noticed.'

'Well, yes.'

'You're pleased? Will he bring loot? Was he right, Kerry, *is* it blackmail?' She sounded gleeful. 'Blackmail on a white male for the death of a black female. Words can be so funny. But I thought I'd better not say that to him. It sounds smartarse.'

'You *are* a smartarse.'

'I expect I'll be due for something.'

'Oh, yes, something. But *I'll* go to the cave.'

'That safe?'

'I'll *make* it safe.' It should be safe and probably it would be private. She still kept a watch for Groves and Shewring, or any other tails, but continued to see nothing. That was over.

'I'd always trust you about money, even when it's cash.'

'Thanks, Josie.'

Twenty-Seven

It was another harsh day in the little bay, with high, noisy breakers driven in by a wind off the sea and heavy, swirling squalls of cold rain. Kerry arrived at the cave before five o'clock and found nothing. She sat down again and watched the waves while she waited. P.D. came at about ten past five. He wore a trenchcoat, flat hat and wellington boots and carried a black briefcase. She thought he looked good, still full of sex and challenge, despite the hat. He walked into the cave with true vigour and confidence. It could have been his office suite.

'I knew it would be you,' he said. 'That sick thing, Gain, talked, wherever he is, did he? He could be made sicker, wherever he is. And worse than sicker. He wants to poison Scout and me.'

'Why not? Listen, the girl knows I'm here. There are five copies of the tape, one with Bert Nipp, one with Geddage, one with Stephen Comble, one with Mrs Sabat, the other ... the other, safe but accessible if I disappeared.'

343

'I'd expect all that,' he said. 'Did you think I might try to throttle you and let the sea take the body? Am I nuts?'

'You're a twin, and twins do mad things for twins. What's in the bag?' she replied.

'Thirty grand. That's the mad thing the twin does for the twin.'

'The *latest* mad thing,' Kerry said.

'It's as much as I could get together.'

'Most of it donated to the reward funds by terrified firms.'

'Some of it mine,' he replied.

'You'll never get better material than this. It should be the full fifty thousand. Oh, less a hundred. You won't have to pay more reward to others. Nothing else to say.'

'Can't be done.' He opened the briefcase and brought out a couple of packets of fifties and twenties in a big transparent envelope. When he gave this to her their hands touched. She thought he felt good, his skin dry, the fingers strong. She momentarily prolonged the contact.

'It's short,' she said. 'So you'll need to offer me something else to make up.'

'Yes?' He gazed at her in the half-light of the cave. 'Oh, yes.' He sounded suddenly hearty. Perhaps the idiot was thinking of the back of her hand in the Mercedes.

'Yes. You and Scout get out of this city,' she said, standing. 'For keeps. Shut the businesses. Go.'

344

'Christ!'

'I give you a week,' she said, 'or the tapes are available to the press and everyone else. Scout and you and the businesses become real vengeance targets then. And Gain, of course, but what do you care about him? Although the law still couldn't touch him or Scout, you'd get done for obstructing the course of justice. That's a big offence, lovely big sentence. Mind you, the tapes might be published, anyway. Perhaps Bertie Nipp will decide to issue them. The Inquiry is probably privileged – no libel danger. Conceivably, Mrs Sabat will get a magazine piece printed on the whole situation here. Transatlantic scoop! It's a sad worry for you, but I can put up with it.'

'Christ, you'd have said the same whatever money I'd brought.'

'Of course. The courts are a bit lame. They need special help. I'm their fast-track wheelchair.'

'But what kind of policing is this, for God's sake – by even the roughest standards? You take a pay-off and still want—'

'Best-of-a-bad-job policing,' she said. 'The only kind around. OK, P.D., so you might open up somewhere else, build another business. I doubt it. Takes too long. If you do … well, that's obviously damn grim for wherever it is, and I'm sorry, but at least it's off my patch. I sound egocentric, narrow?

Police victories are usually small ones, not very clear ones. I've learned that much.'

'If we go, Ferdy Nate takes the whole local trade. You're donating a monopoly. Thought of that?'

Yes, she had. Kerry recalled party night at the blue house, where what looked like Ferdy's little army was present in suits, and where Neville, the reporter friend of Mrs Sabat, asked what the occasion was *for*. Nev's journo nose had sensed dangerous power. Ferdy's army was still dangerous and could be worse if nobody like P.D. balanced him. But that was not the problem for now. And, anyway, it looked too weighty for her rank – her rank at present. She said: 'Ferdy Nate might beat up a black woman or get her beaten up. He hasn't killed one. This won't seem much of a distinction to you, but it will do. We'll cope with him and his.' She was not sure P.D. got all this because wind roared and whistled around the cave and rain hammered on the wall.

'Excuse me,' he said, 'but are you taking from Ferdy?'

'I've been asked already.'

'And?'

'It didn't seem worth answering.'

'Or a passion with Lydia? Or Mrs Sabat?'

'I've been asked already.'

'And?' Pethor made a sudden all-out lunge for the money envelope. She felt the cold, strong fingers on her wrist, heard a tiny, uncertain sound in his throat, like a dark prayer. Breakers pushed close to the mouth of the cave. Kerry thought there was something superb and ridiculous about being manhandled here by a brilliantly attractive man in wellingtons who'd once conferred the tribute of a spontaneous hard-on. The situation now seemed to recall Wagner, though she could be wrong. She struggled to keep hold of the cash, but might have had to release it if there'd been no interruption.

Josie, standing just inside the cave, screamed: 'Get off her, you cunt! Some of that's mine.' Today, she wore yellow oilskins and a sou'wester, like a Bugsy Malone trawlerman. Pethor let go of the money and stood back. Under the flat hat he looked ashamed. Josie said: 'I *do* trust you about money, Kerry – even cash – but it was a bit of a worry because of the weather, so I came. I didn't want any of it blown away. Or you blown away.'

Kerry took a piece of paper from her pocket and held it out to P.D. 'What is it?' he said.

'Gain's London address.'

He took it. 'You want us to wipe one another out.'

'He said the same.'

'And?'

'It's off this ground,' Kerry replied. 'What

can I do?'

P.D. turned and at once left the cave, walking with that same vigour and confidence. So, keep going and keep going and keep going, P.D., with all the vigour and confidence you can hang on to.

'I expect you'll give the money to Mrs Sabat,' Josie said. 'Something soft like that.'

'Yes, something soft like that. If she'll take it.'

'She used to be a journalist, didn't she? That's what it said in the papers. She'll take it. But my share first.'

'Absolutely.' Before they went out into the wind Kerry counted ten twenties from the package and gave them to Josie.

'I thought I really read it all right on the phone and did the bits in between quite well,' Josie said. 'Plus making myself sound like a slag.'

Kerry gave her another fifty. They walked back across the beach. 'Save it, Josie,' she said. 'You'll need an education fund one day.'

'Oh, God, Kerry, you sound like somebody's mother.'

'Now and then I do rehearse.'

'What do you mean? You're not having a—?'

'I'm rehearsing in good time.'

'Don't,' Josie said. 'You wouldn't like it. You're not a milktit, you're somebody who takes big money off men with briefcases in caves.'

At headquarters Kerry worked it so she could bump into Vic in a corridor. 'I hear a buzz from the Inquiry that things will be totally OK for you,' she said.

'Of course. So they should be.'

'Yes, so they should be. They've got some new information.'

'Really?'

'Yes,' Kerry said. 'It's not all immaculately verified and maybe not publishable, but it's powerful, and good enough for an Inquiry.'

'New information?'

Kerry said: 'It really wasn't P.D. who told you about the *incident* that night?'

'Of course it wasn't. I hear many voices.'

'Couldn't you have said that off the record?'

'Some things I don't talk about. Dangerous names are dangerous names on or off the record.'

'Sometimes you don't talk at all. What the hell was the matter with you at the rabbitry? That everlasting silence?'

'I know. I was stunned by the cleverness of what they'd devised – the imitation attack. Magnificently choreographed. I decided we'd never beat them. For a while, I'd forgotten about *your* cleverness. I thought policing might be just people like me and Harry Bell. Unforgivable.'

'Don't compare yourself to Bell.'

'Why not?'

'Who knows what he really is?' Kerry replied. 'I've tried to sort him out.'

'Hopeless.'

'Well, there you are then.'

'How do you mean, there I am then?' Vic said.

'You can't compare yourself to him because we don't know what he really is.'

'Do we know who anyone really is?' Vic said.

'God, don't go cracker-barrel philosopher on me now.'

'Sorry. I'm not Oxbridge trained.'

'Stuff the false humility, Vic.'

'But *do* we know who anyone really is?'

'You?' she asked.

'You?'

'We all vary a bit. Harry does nothing but vary.' Kerry kept chatting, almost shy about saying what she wanted to say. 'If Christine Sabat ever gets a piece printed on all this it should be nice to you, and me.'

'Naturally.'

'She doesn't know it, but she might have to wait a while for a convincing end for the article to show up. The climax.'

'Oh?'

'Possibly in London.'

'That right?'

'Hackney,' she said.

'Oh, really?'

Had the sod discovered it all for himself? He heard more voices than Joan of fucking Arc. 'Listen, do you know what I feel like?' she said.

'I expect so. The Coronet?'

'Not to celebrate, because there's nothing to celebrate, is there? It was always going to be all right for you, wasn't it?'

'True.'

'But just because I feel like it. My treat. I've got a hundred-pound cheque it's probably OK for me to pay in to the bank now.'

'What hundred-pound cheque?'

'Can you make it to The Coronet?' she replied. 'Or have you got to scuttle back home to Julie? That *is* her name, isn't it?'